The View

The View

Untamed

www.urbanbooks.net

Urban Books, LLC
300 Farmingdale Road, NY-Route 109
Farmingdale, NY 11735

ISBN 13: 978-1-60162-915-9
ISBN 10: 1-60162-915-X

First Trade Paperback Printing July 2019
Printed in the United States of America

10 9 8 7 6 5 4 3 2 1

Distributed by Kensington Publishing Corp.
Submit Orders to:
Customer Service
400 Hahn Road
Westminster, MD 21157-4627
Phone: 1-800-733-3000
Fax: 1-800-659-2436

The View

by

Untamed

Dedication

To finding lasting love and true happiness

Acknowledgments

As always, I am forever thankful to my Lord and Savior Jesus Christ. All that I am is because of you. There will never be a day that I am unappreciative for this gift you've given to me. #MyShepherd #HisFlock

To my hubby, Chris, thank you for being everything to me and supporting my dreams. It all comes down to love, and our love is never unsure. I love you. To my kiddos, you push me to go harder for my dreams, and I do so, so that you'll have an example to push harder for yours. I love you.

To Black of BlackEncryption Designs, your talent is heaven sent! You always bring your A-game and deliver above and beyond what's asked. Thank you for encrypting this novel with your stroke of genius.

To poets Kiana Donae and Tammie T. Bell Davis, thank you ladies for allowing me to share your gift of writing with mine. I absolutely admire your scribes, and it's my honor to share them with the world.

To Diane Rembert, I know that God sent you into my life for a whole lifetime. I can't ever thank you enough for everything from the initial phone calls to the late night emails and the hours-long conversations, lol! You are the best.

To N'Tyse, when predestined moments meets prayer and mixes with preparation, it's a win! You are anointed, appointed, and assigned to do this, and I am blessed that you have been assigned to me! I am forever thankful to you, and I look forward to our climb together.

Acknowledgments

To Carl Weber and the Urban Books/Kensington family, thank you for the opportunity to allow readers across all platforms to read and fall in love with *The View*. I saw this moment in my head for years before it actually happened, and believe me, I am savoring the moment.

To the readers, thank you for supporting me, and I have one question: Are you #TeamMichael or #TeamHudson? Ha! Let's get into it after you read *The View*.

See

With me it begins with a feeling, a simple thought of how it should be
It sparks in my mind and travels through my veins
Then back to my eyes, where the vision is plain
I see clearly what I want from it; my gaze draws it near
My willingness to accept it also holds me back with fear
I know that when I touch it, electricity plays a part
Jump-start the blood with fire, a passion, putting the beat in my heart
The skin of my hand, a cool shade of brown, soft like satin upon contact with yours
The touch alone has me wired, feeling sexy, wanting to explore
Now it's time our lips should meet, entwine, with the purpose to please
Tenderly providing a promise of what's to come is worth the release
Now contact to the point of no return
Feeling all I have to offer, taking all you have to give
I'm getting lost in you, and I love it; this is how souls should blend
It's like I'm dreaming yet wide awake
The pleasure of you has me feigning way more than I can take
You could be like my morning and night with a lazy Sunday afternoon
And I'll embrace you with a sweetness you'll never want to leave soon
Caught up in the ecstasy of all I ever dreamed of
Happy with the illusion that I'll always know as love

Prologue

Four years ago . . .

Karli examined herself in the mirror. The bustier and thigh-high panty hose she wore, which she had received at her bachelorette party, were a nice compliment to her curvaceous figure. She turned slightly, glimpsed her rotund backside, which she had tried to hide for years as a teen, then had finally accepted and embraced as an adult. Old feelings of embarrassment resurfaced at the realization that for the first time, someone other than her mother and her best friend, Catrina, would see her naked truth. She placed her hands on the bathroom sink and swallowed the lump in her throat. As she slowly raised her head, her hazel-brown eyes showed a fear that she was finally coming face-to- face with.

"You can do this, girl. Pull yourself together," she coaxed herself just before picking up her champagne flute and downing another glass of liquid courage.

After placing the flute down, she stared at her three-carat diamond wedding band and smiled. What was she afraid of? The man who'd chosen her and given his all to her was waiting on the other side of that door. If anyone deserved all of her, it was him. She bit her lip and squared up. It was time.

She opened the door and sexily waltzed out into the plush honeymoon suite, her eyes fixed on her new husband, Michael. Inside she trembled, but she managed to display a confident exterior. As she crossed the room, Michael turned around on the bed. Instantly, his eyes bulged. Karli slowed her stride, afraid that he might not like what he was seeing.

"Oh. My. Dear. God," Michael gasped, eyeing his beautiful bride. He stood, and instantly his manhood began to rise to the occasion.

He'd dutifully and diligently waited for this moment with his new wife. Since he had turned his life over to God a year before he met her, the struggle to remain celibate had been real for him, especially after meeting Karli. It was love at first sight, and he had known deep down that one day she'd be his wife. He was so happy that she'd agreed to marry him after only six months of dating. While he had desperately wanted to make her his wife as soon as possible, he'd be lying if he said the only reason had been love. No, some of it had definitely been lust. Before their marriage, his wife's caramel complexion, smooth skin, hazel eyes, thin waist, and extremely rotund derriere had had him ready to plead to God for forgiveness and go ahead and jump into that pool of sinful delight. However, once he'd found out she was a virgin, Michael had known this was God's test for him, and His way of letting him know He'd saved the best just for him. He hadn't even touched her, and he'd known without a doubt that she'd be the best lover he'd ever had.

Michael slowly glided over to his wife and stood in front of her, admiring her sexy ensemble.

She stared at him with a lost and somewhat confused look on her face, hoping she didn't turn off her new husband. "Is something wrong, baby?" Karli asked.

Michael flashed his gorgeous smile at her and caressed her face between the palms of his hands. "Absolutely not. Everything is perfect. You . . . are perfect. You are gorgeous, beautiful, magnificent, and glorious. The most beautiful sight I've ever seen in my life." He took her hand and slowly twirled her around. "I love you. Every little bit of you. And I can't wait to make love to you . . . my wife."

She lovingly wrapped her arms around his neck as he wrapped his arms around her waist and pulled her against him. The attraction and intensity ignited between them.

"I love you, Michael," Karli whispered with bated breaths between passionate kisses.

Soft and sensual music by Miguel played in the background as Michael led her to the bed and sat her down. After he took a seat next to her, slowly he unhooked the clasps holding up her thigh highs and eased them off her legs. Then he unbuttoned her bustier, revealing all her glory. What a sight she was to behold. Her shyness caused her to cover herself. Michael recognized this was new to her, and rather than rush her, he kissed her hands and allowed her to remove them herself. He wanted her to be completely comfortable in their first moment, her first time.

With one arm around her back, he gave her the softest, sweetest kiss and lay her down on the bed. With their eyes locked, he stood and removed his pajama pants and boxer briefs, revealing a hard-on unlike any Karli had ever seen—which was really none. She'd actually seen a man's package only once, and that was in the one porn movie she'd forced herself to watch with Catrina in college, cringing the entire time. The apprehension must've shown on her face as Michael slid in bed beside her, because he held her and caressed her in his arms.

"Don't worry, baby," he whispered. "We'll go as slow as needed. We'll take our time—"

"Do it right," she sang, repeating the words to a song, and giggled nervously.

Michael laughed. "Yep, just like that. I'd wait an eternity to be with you." He turned her face to his and gently kissed her pouty lips.

"Aw, baby," she cooed, interlocking his hand with hers. "I thought I'd be ready, you know? I don't want to disappoint you. I want to make love to you. I'm just so nervous."

Gliding his finger along her jaw, he smiled at her. She was so delicate, so precious. He knew then he'd protect her and love her with all his might for all the days of his life. Indeed, she was the greatest gift God had ever given to him. Nothing could compare to the gift of her love.

"You're not a disappointment to me, Karli. I admire you. I admire your strength and courage to hold on to your precious flower, and I thank you for wanting me to be the one to allow it to bloom. I will always cherish you and our love. I will always take care of your needs first. I will always be here for you. Whenever you're ready, come to me. This moment may be ours, but this is all about you. From this day forward, it is all about you."

Karli gazed at him, and for the first time, she felt completely free. She knew he loved her, and even the vows he had spoken at their wedding paled in comparison to his willingness to put her first and foremost. After leaning forward, she planted the most passionate kiss on his lips. The fire in her eyes was evident. With a slight nod, Karli gave Michael the permission that he'd been waiting on.

Michael eased on top of her and planted slow kisses against the nape of her neck, then trailed his tongue along her earlobes. The softness of his touch began to send her body into a frenzy. His massive hands found her voluptuous breasts, and he gently rolled her nipples between his thumb and forefinger, creating just the right amount of pleasant pressure she could stand. Her breathing increased as he took his time enjoying every inch of her body, trailing kisses from her breasts down her stomach, making love with his tongue from her belly button all the way down to her thighs.

"Michael," she moaned breathlessly.

After parting her thighs, Michael admired the nicely shaven treasure that lay between. His mouth watered as he prepared for his feast. Anticipation surged through him as he relished the fact that he would be the first to pleasure his wife in this manner and the first to taste her honeysuckle. His head game had always been on point. Although he hadn't used it in nearly two years, it was just like riding a bike. Once you learned how, you didn't forget.

After easing his face down to her crevice, he parted her already moistening folds until he saw the throbbing flower bud. His tongue encircled it slowly as he licked her sweetness in delight.

"Oh . . . my . . . oh my God," Karli moaned as her body betrayed her attempts to keep calm. The amount of ecstasy surging through her was nearly unbearable. "Baby. Oh, baby!"

"Yes, baby. You taste so good." He continued his feast.

Tremors rumbled from the base of Karli's stomach through her legs as she clenched her thighs around Michael's neck and held his head, screaming out in sheer delight, "Oh, Michael! Oh, Michael! Yes, Christ! Jesus! God Almighty!"

She showered his mouth and lips with her essence, and he didn't stop until he had retrieved every drip drop. Peering up at Karli, he saw that she was lost in a euphoric high, tears streaming from the corners of her eyes. He was ready for her. Panting and at full staff, he sat up, positioned himself between her legs, and stared down into her beautiful eyes.

"Trust me," he whispered to her.

She nodded, too lost in the wonderful feelings he'd given her to turn back now.

As he gently positioned her legs and pushed, he noticed her tense slightly and wince from the discomfort. Lovingly, he caressed her face and whispered, "I love you," to her as he continued to push against her, and a few moments later, they both felt her hymen give way. He paused briefly to allow them both to cherish the moment of her deflowering. Then, gently he guided himself inside her, and they began to rock together easily as he took them both to unimaginable heights. When he released, she released with him again, and then he lay there for a moment, pulsating and trying to calm his beastly urges.

"How was it for you?" she asked, rubbing her hand across his head.

"It was everything I've ever wanted."

Karli's eyes clouded with tears, and she kissed him. "This is the most beautiful memory of my life. It was better than I ever dreamed it would be. You are more than I ever dreamed. I love you, Michael."

"Mrs. Karli Fitzgerald-Sanders, I love you too."

She smiled at him. "Just Sanders, baby. I changed my mind, and Daddy will just have to get over it and understand. He gave me away to the best hands ever. I am forever and always Mrs. Karli Sanders."

Chapter 1

"Come on. Come on. Pick up!" Karli urged quietly yet frantically as she held her cell phone to her ear.

"What's up, girl?" said Catrina, her best friend, when she answered.

"Ahhh!" Karli screamed as she sat inside her Jaguar F-Type R.

Catrina laughed heartily. "I take it that means you got the promotion."

"Girl, yes! I'm so freakin' excited. It's so awesome!" Karli fanned herself, trying to regain her composure.

"I hope you're not in your office, screaming like that, though. Your bosses and coworkers will think you've gone mad, Miss *Senior* Executive Marketing Director!"

Laughing at her friend, Karli quipped, "Absolutely not. I pretended that I was taking an early lunch so I could come to my car, scream, and call you. Besides, no one knows yet. They will make the official announcement at the upcoming gala."

"Well, I am absolutely ecstatic for you, and I will definitely be in attendance. Have you told Michael yet? And you know Mama Pat and Papa Chris are going to want to know immediately."

"No, I've only called you, but that's because I want to surprise them. I'm thinking we can plan a family dinner to surprise them with the good news."

"You know I'm down with it, and I know the perfect place. Jean-Georges on Central Park West."

Karli smiled. "You were reading my mind, sis! Yes, please set it up for this Saturday night for us. I will make sure everyone is in place."

"You got it, hon." Catrina paused. "Hey, since you're taking an early lunch, anyway, meet me for lunch and we'll have some celebratory drinks on me."

Karli pressed the button to start her car. "On you? Shoot. I'm already pulling out of my spot. I'll be there in a bit."

Catrina howled. "I figured that would make you leave early. Just don't tell Deacon Sanders I had his wife out drinking. You ain't getting me in trouble."

Karli rolled her eyes. "We drink socially sometimes."

"Yeah, okay. You just hurry up so we can plan this surprise dinner for this weekend. And congratulations again, sis. No one deserves this more than you."

Karli smiled brightly while saying her temporary good-bye to her friend. Inside, she beamed. She'd been working for McCallan and Associates, the largest marketing firm in the Northeast, ever since grad school. She had interned there during her senior year and then had landed a junior executive position straight out of undergrad. For four years, she had toiled and proved herself time and time again, all the while climbing the ranks. Now not only was she the firm's youngest senior executive ever, but she was the youngest female and the first black woman to achieve that rank. Yes, she was doing the damn thing.

All the effort it had taken to do well in private school, graduate from high school at sixteen, to double major as an undergrad, and then to finish grad school at only twenty-three years of age was surely paying off. Add to that her wonderful husband, Michael, who owned his own sports entertainment law firm; her beautiful lifetime best friend, Catrina, who was an elite model talent scout in New York; and her awesome parents, Chris and Patricia Fitzgerald, and she had everything she ever could've dreamed of and more. Yes, she was riding high, and she didn't ever want to come down.

Chapter 2

Michael sat at his desk, overlooking the hustle and bustle of the Financial District in New York, and reviewed the final contract for a high-profile client that played for the Buffalo Bills. He loved his job, and even though he had three partners and a team of lawyers on staff, he still took personal care of his elite clientele. To this day, it was the reason he felt he was so successful in the business.

As soon as he closed the file, his cell lit up. After glancing at the number, he lit up as well. It was his wife, Karli. After four years of marriage, he still loved her every bit as much as he had the day he took her hand in marriage.

He couldn't imagine what his life would be like without her. Most young men had their vices, some more detrimental than others, and for him, it had been women. Unlike his father, he hadn't seen the benefit of settling down with just one woman when there were so many flavors to choose from. His dad always used to tell him that no matter what he accomplished, until he could truly love and be loved by the right woman, he'd never truly feel complete. He had shunned love and had used sex as his temporary shield, until those empty days began to get the best of him. Then he'd changed his focus, changed his ways, and changed his beliefs, and then along came his Karli. Now he was complete.

"And to what do I owe this pleasure of speaking with the most beautiful woman in the world?"

"Baby, you are so sweet. I hope you stay this way when I'm flabby and wrinkled." She laughed.

"Baby, I'll be this way with you for all eternity."

He was sure she was blushing on the phone, as she always did. His mind floated back to their morning round of lovemaking, and he began getting aroused. He shook himself. He had to stop before he got too worked up. Both of them had high-powered careers, and he knew she wouldn't be able to meet him for a quick round. Besides, Karli wasn't into that. She was very image cautious, and the last thing she would want was to smell like sex among her colleagues.

"I love it when you say that," she cooed, snapping him back to reality. "Before I get too caught up in flirting, the reason for my call is to check your schedule for this Saturday. I wanted to be sure you're free and clear of any business."

He leaned forward, opened both his work and personal calendars on his computer, and quickly scanned them. "Looks like I'm good, baby. So what's going on Saturday?"

"Well, we have reservations at seven p.m. at Jean-Georges, and I wanted to be sure we could keep them."

"Jean-Georges? What's the occasion?" he asked, puzzled and hoping he hadn't forgotten something special. "Or are you just trying to get me drunk and take advantage of me?"

She giggled. "I'd love to do that, but it's actually a surprise. Sorry, though, it's not a romantic surprise. Catrina will be there and, hopefully, my parents. I only wish your parents could be there too."

"Wow. The whole crew. This must be one hell of a surprise," he said excitedly. "Do I need to try to see if my parents can fly in from Chicago?"

"No, we can tell them over the phone. There will be plenty of time to fly out and see them face-to-face when we take vacation. Let them continue enjoying their retirement."

Michael's wheels began turning. Normally, he was the one surprising her with trips and gifts. He wondered what the excitement could be about.

"No, I'm not telling you anything until Saturday," she announced, interrupting his thoughts.

"You know me. A man can wish, right?"

"Wish all you want, Mr. Sanders. It won't come true until Saturday, after seven p.m. I know I have to be specific with you."

"I'm a lawyer, so you better," he joked.

She laughed. "Bye, nut. I have to go. I'll see you tonight. If you beat me home, please reheat dinner."

"Anything else, Queen Sanders?"

"Ha-ha. funny! I love you, baby."

"I love you more, baby. See you tonight," he said, and then he hung up.

I wonder what in the world this surprise is about, he thought. Thank God it was Wednesday. At least that meant he had only two painstaking days to suffer through not knowing.

"Everything all right, man?" asked Bryson, his friend and partner, snapping him out of his thoughts. He stood in the doorway.

"Huh? Oh yeah. Come in. I was lost in my thoughts, man."

Bryson entered the office and sat down in the plush chair on the other side of Michael's desk. "I see. I called your name twice, and you didn't hear me. You sure you're good?"

Michael smiled. "Oh yeah, man. Karli has a surprise for the family, and she wants us all to meet up at Jean-Georges for the big reveal. I'm just wondering what it could be about."

"Hmm, interesting. Do you think—"

Michael's cell lit up again before Bryson could finish. "It's my mother-in-law . . . What were you going to say, Bryson?" he said as he was picking up his phone.

"Maybe she's—"

"Is she pregnant, Michael Brian Sanders?" his mother-in-law asked at the very same time that the words came out of Bryson's mouth.

"Huh?" Michael asked her and Bryson at the same time.

"Don't you 'huh' me, Michael. If she's pregnant and you two are making me wait until Saturday, I swear to God—"

"Whoa! Wait a minute, Mom. I don't know anything, either. Karli just called me a few minutes ago, saying she had a surprise and wanted to reveal it during dinner at Jean-Georges." He paused for a moment and got excited. The smile on his face was a mile wide. "Do you really think that's it, Mom? Do you think my baby is having my baby?"

"God, I hope so!" she yelled happily. "I've been trying to get you to knock her up since you married her!"

"From your lips to God's ears!" he said ecstatically, thinking this had to be it. "Mom, look, we can't let on that we know, but when Saturday evening gets here, I might just get escorted out of Jean-Georges for an exuberant celebration!"

Mama Pat laughed hysterically. "Honey, that makes two of us!"

"Look, Mom, I have to go. Let's be cool, though. We don't want to upset the mommy to be."

"Aw, I won't. Oh goodness, Michael, I'm so happy. You and my daughter are going to make such great parents. I can't wait to be a glam-ma!"

Michael shook his head. "Thank you, Mom, and stop watching reality TV. Love you."

After he hung up, he looked at Bryson, and Bryson shook his head. "Damn! My boy is about to be a pops!"

"I'm so excited, man. I hope it's a boy, but I don't care. I'm going to love my seed unconditionally! Man, I can't believe my baby is having my baby!"

Bryson tucked the files he was holding under his arm. "Well, this can wait until tomorrow. You're way too amped to focus on this. How about we get out of here and grab a beer to celebrate?"

Michael shook his head. "I must decline. I need to go gift shopping for Saturday, and besides, Karli would have my head if she knew I was out drinking. You know the good deacon can't do all that."

"We drink socially all the time."

"Yeah, after work or on trips. Every now and again, Karli and I have a drink at a restaurant or relax with a glass of merlot at home. I can't be coming home, smelling like a brewery. Besides, she's carrying my seed, and it might upset her stomach."

Bryson laughed. "Man, you are already overboard. You do know Karli is grown, right, Michael? You have a habit of being overly protective of her. She's a strong woman, far from fragile."

Michael shrugged as he stood, and then he grabbed his suit jacket and put it on. "Karli may be a strong businesswoman, but I know the inner Karli. And protecting her will always be my job. I promised her that on our wedding night."

Bryson held his hands up. "You know your wife. Who am I to second-guess it? So where are you going?"

"To Tiffany or Jared or somewhere, to get her a gift to commemorate being a new mommy and to look at gifts for our baby."

Bryson nodded. "This child will be just as spoiled as his mother," he joked. "Fine. Go. I'll make sure everything is taken care of for today."

"Thanks, man." Michael patted his shoulder. "Next week, beers on me!"

Still seated, Bryson pointed at him. "And I'ma hold you to that!"

Michael was so happy, he nearly ran out of his office. He'd wanted to have kids since they first married, and he couldn't wait to welcome Baby Sanders into their family. Six years ago, he hadn't thought he ever wanted to be married. It was funny how life could change so drastically, especially when the right woman came along.

Chapter 3

Karli stood in her cotton yoga pants and tank top, stirring her famous spaghetti sauce. She wasn't the queen of cooking, like her grandma used to be, but she'd learned to dazzle a little bit before her granny passed. Her parents had had her so focused on school that they'd forgotten key elements of life, like cooking. Italian food was her specialty. Thank God that for the most part, her athletic husband was a clean-eating fanatic, so she hadn't had to tell him that she wasn't a Southern cuisine type of chick. It made her life so much easier to make simple meals, like grilled chicken Caesar salad or baked salmon, instead of making a disaster of fried chicken and macaroni and cheese.

Michael's biggest culinary indulgence was sweets. He was a cake, pie, and cookie-eating man. She hated sweets and she wasn't a baker, so she used that as an excuse for not indulging his sweet tooth. To him, she was a whiz in the kitchen. Even though she knew better, this worked in her favor, because he was content with the meals she prepared.

"Damn! I forgot to get more merlot," she huffed, inspecting the wine cooler. She grabbed a bottle of pinot gris. "At least Michael will drink this."

She set their plates on the dinner table, then poured his wine and grabbed a bottle of Voss water out of the refrigerator for herself. As soon as she was finished, she heard the door opening and went to greet her husband.

"Hey, you," she cooed as Michael placed his briefcase on the floor and his keys in the key dish.

He reached for her, brought her to him, and engaged her in a deep kiss. "Hmm, hello to you too. It smells delicious. What did you make?"

"My famous spaghetti. Go get washed up. I just set the table for dinner, and it will be served by the time you return."

Michael winked at her and patted her behind before barreling upstairs. He returned in less than five minutes in a white T-shirt, sweatpants, and Adidas slides.

"Looks and smells good," Michael said, rubbing his hands together as he sat down at the table.

"Not as good as you," she replied, flirting. She leaned over to kiss him.

Michael closed his eyes and inhaled her sweet scent. Biting his lip, he murmured, "You better stop before I have to skip this meal."

Karli giggled and moved to the side to toss the salad. Michael stared lovingly at his wife. *My God, she is an effortless beauty*, he thought. Her messy bob and the way those yoga pants clung to that never-ending mountain of lusciousness were calling out to his loins. He sipped his wine and tried to keep his excitement at bay. He noticed that she had chosen water for herself instead of wine, and smiled to himself.

Karli tasted a bit of the salad. "Hmm, this is good."

She licked the vinaigrette from her lips as she served the salad, and out of the corner of her eye, she noticed Michael's lustful stare. *Lawd, this man of mine is so fine*, she thought.

As she looked over at his chiseled chest in that T-shirt, she spotted his slight erection and decided dinner could wait. She was high on life, and everything in her world was finally perfect. The excitement of her impending announcement, mixed with Michael's good looks and erection, turned her on completely. She didn't know if it was the fact that she felt completely accomplished or what, but a different type of friskiness had overcome her, and she needed her man. She was down for celebrating in every way possible. Looking over at him once more, she decided that, oh yes, dinner could definitely wait.

She turned and stepped over to his chair. Shocking him, she straddled his lap and kissed him passionately.

"Wh-what?" Michael asked huskily.

"Let's make love right here. Right now." She captured his lips again. "I need to feel you inside me," she whispered sexily, surprised at the words that slipped out of her own mouth. She began kissing him all over his neck and ears and felt him growing underneath her.

"Mmm, Karli," he moaned. She was literally making him lose control. "Baby, wait."

With lust-filled eyes, she removed her tank top. "Wait for what?" she asked, then moved back to his neck.

Michael composed himself long enough to get the words out. "We really need to eat."

She looked at him with confusion. "We can eat anytime." She turned and pushed his plate back. "In fact, I have something much better than this spaghetti that you can eat." She paused and looked at him longingly. "Let me . . . let me feed you." The words came out weakly, as she'd never been the risqué type.

Nevertheless, tonight was the night for new beginnings, and for her, that also meant new adventures. Why not? They were young and married, free to do any and everything they pleased; and at the forefront of her mind was pleasing her husband, while also satisfying her own primal urges.

That caught Michael off guard. This pregnancy was doing something to his wife. She'd never been frisky like this. As much as he wanted it—hell, liked it—he knew she was eating for two, and he didn't want her to miss meals.

"Whoa! Wait, baby. Let's just eat, and then I can take you upstairs, draw you a warm bath, and make sweet, sweet love to you," he said between kisses on her neck.

Karli was baffled. She didn't want any spaghetti or a damn warm bath. To be frank, what she wanted was her husband's face between her legs, followed by some out-of-this-world, backbreaking sex. She was riding the wave of her emotional high to the fullest and was hoping that, since he was obviously ready, they could get it in until they were too exhausted to move.

"Michael," she said coyly, snaking her hands around his neck.

"Karli, come on, baby. Let's eat." He patted her rear end, signaling for her to get up.

She shook her head. "Okay," she said as she slowly stood. Then she walked over to her seat and plopped in it.

Michael said a quick prayer and dove right in. "Man, this salad and the spaghetti are awesome, baby."

"Uh-huh," she said, slightly upset, as she drank her water from the wineglass.

"You're not eating," Michael said, looking up at her. Karli sighed and sat up before picking up her fork and digging into her salad. Michael smiled. "Good. So how was your day?"

Karli gave him the one-word response "Good," and then he went on about his day and his clients, not even noticing that she was pissed. *Who turns down sex for food?* she thought as he droned on.

Once they finished dinner, he began clearing their dishes. "You barely ate anything."

"No appetite, I guess." She shrugged.

Worry lines creased Michael's forehead.

"It's nothing, Michael. I'm fine. I just wasn't that hungry."

He nodded. "Okay, baby. I'll grab the rest of the dishes and load the dishwasher. You head upstairs and get ready for your bath."

"Sure, baby." She rolled her eyes behind his back and dashed upstairs.

Sometimes, he aggravated her with his babying routine. She knew he meant well, but he didn't know how to turn it off at times and recognize she was a grown woman. She loved it and hated it at the same time. Ever since they'd met, he'd treated her like this prized jewel that he couldn't scratch, scrape, or damage. She loved that he wanted to place her on this pedestal. But she hated that he acted as if she could never come down, like she had to be in some sort of glass case for all eternity. In the comfort of their own home, she should be able to let her hair down, and he should let her. Hell, he should want that for himself. Shouldn't he?

Deciding to shrug it off, she disrobed, found his favorite lingerie set, then sat on the side of the bed and pulled out her poetry journal. Writing poetry had always been her personal release, so she began to jot down a piece.

Fahrenheit on high, steamy vapors cause a sexy scene
Your eyes look up, down, and all around, but my cottony thighs want you in between
Candlelight foreplay, shadows picturesque on the walls
You grab my neck and cover my mouth so our sex sounds don't reach down the hall. . . .

Instantly, the words began to dispel her anger. She decided to appreciate the pampering instead of resenting it. At least she had a man who catered to her, instead of an imbecile who ran the streets with every loose woman there was. While that may have been his modus vivendi in the past, he'd brought the best part of himself to their marriage, so she chose to focus on that.

"What a beautiful sight," Michael mused, breaking her reverie as she replaced her journal and stood up, revealing her total nakedness. She picked up the lingerie, which she'd set on the bed, and awaited her bath. "You won't need that lingerie."

She smiled. "I'm ready whenever you are." She walked up close to him.

He bent down and kissed her softly. "What were you writing?"

Shrugging, she shook her head. "Oh nothing. Just jotting down plans for tomorrow," she fibbed.

Michael nodded and gently kissed her again.

Her insides cringed at the lie. Her poetry had always contained her personal thoughts and had always been her way of coping with her day-to-day life. Lately, she'd been writing more erotic pieces, to make up for the lackluster passion in her own bedroom. Any other time she would have told him what she was jotting in her journal, but she refused to tell him about her poetry. He was already put off by her attempts to make love on the dining room table. There was no way he could bear to hear the tantalizing thoughts in her journal.

Michael went into their bathroom, lit the tea-light candles, and turned on the faucet in the tub. Once the water had filled the tub, he went back into the bedroom, took her hand, led her to the tub, and helped her immerse herself in the warm water. His powerful hands kneaded every kink in her shoulders and neck from the day, and the sponge bath that followed had both of them on fire. Michael eased into the water with her, and she took the sponge and gently lathered and washed his manhood.

His eyes rolled in the back of his head. "Hmm, you don't know what you're doing to me."

Karli slowly straddled her husband. "Let me please you," she whispered seductively in his ear.

Groaning, Michael stood, lifting her up with him. Karli giggled, her legs still wrapped around his waist and her arms wrapped around his neck.

"Ooh, you're bringing out the freak, huh?" Karli panted, kissing his neck.

"I got your freak."

He put her down and stepped out of the tub. Not exactly what she had in mind, but she was too hot to argue the point. After reaching for her hand, he helped her out of the tub and dried them both off. Then he scooped her up and carried her to their bed.

"I love you, Karli," he whispered as he laid her on her back and spread her legs.

"Uh, baby, let me—"

Before she could finish, he slid into home and began to work her skillfully. "You were saying?" he asked huskily, gliding in and out of her honey pot.

"Michael," she moaned.

He hoisted her legs up higher on his waist, and her back arched. He moved his nine-inch missile deeper inside her love nest, causing her oasis to cream and pulsate.

"That's it, baby. Cum for Daddy."

Karli gazed into Michael's sensual bedroom eyes and rubbed his strong jawline. Caressing every inch of his six-foot-two, chiseled, dark chocolate frame with her body, she allowed the orgasm to overtake her and wailed out his name. Her cries sent him into overdrive, and he gripped her rotund mound tighter, dove as deep as he could, and released fiercely, with a deep growl.

"Baby," she moaned in ecstasy.

"I'm so sorry, Karli. I don't know what came over me. I was just so into it. I didn't hurt you, did I?"

Baffled, Karli shook her head. "No, baby." She caressed his face. "Baby, it was amazing."

He smiled demurely and kissed her forehead, then looked at the place where his hand was. "Shoot. I left a little print."

"Who's going to know? I know I'm light skinned and everything, but no one will see anything in that region," she joked.

Michael playfully messed with her hair and lay beside her. "I know that's right. Nobody better not try it," he joked. "I just don't want to manhandle you."

Karli hit him playfully. "And how do you know I can't take it?" she said flirtatiously, although she was serious.

Michael laughed, pulling her close. "You are such a little tease tonight, you know that?"

"But you like it, right?"

Michael smiled at her. "Yes, I like it, and I love you," he said, then kissed her lightly.

They continued to hold each other until they drifted off to sleep.

Chapter 4

"And you have everything set up with the maître d' and the servers?" Karli quizzed as she laid her ensemble across the bed.

"Yes and yes!" Catrina yelled. Karli had her on speakerphone. "I wish you would concentrate on getting dressed, so we can make it to the restaurant on time. Everything is under control."

"And I agree." Michael waltzed into the bedroom. "Hey, Catrina."

"Hey, my third favorite man in the entire world!"

"Oh, so now I'm third?" Michael said before kissing Karli on her cheek.

"Yes, right after my dad and Papa Chris." Catrina laughed. "Get your wife. Apparently, she bumped her head or something and forgot who her best friend is."

They all laughed, and Michael nodded, though Catrina couldn't see him. "Yes, if anyone has their stuff together, it's you."

Karli threw her hands up. "Okay, you two can stop ganging up on me. I got it. You got it under control, and you want me to get dressed, so we can leave on time to beat the traffic. I'm listening. Bye, girl. See you in a bit."

"Ooh, Michael, I will have to remember to call on you all the time," Catrina joked. "See you guys in a little while." With that, she disconnected the line.

"I see you're almost dressed," Karli said.

Michael nodded. "Yes, and you need to be as well. You know how you get about outfits."

She huffed. "Smart-mouth. At least my make-up and my hair are done. I'm just going to oil my legs, put on my dress and shoes, and I should be ready to go," Karli said, admiring the one-shoulder red lace dress lying across the bed.

"Do you think that it will be a little too cold to wear that?" Michael asked. "I love it, but I'm just saying."

There goes Father Michael again, she thought. "I have a mink wrap that I'm wearing. I'll be fine. The car service will drop us off at the door. Surely, I won't catch cold in five minutes."

Michael waved his hands in surrender. "Let's just make it in time for these dinner reservations."

Thankful for his concession, Karli gathered her outfit, ran off to the bathroom, got dressed, and slipped on her beautiful wedding ring and diamond tennis bracelet. Then she stepped into her gold Louboutin shoes to complete her look. She spritzed on her favorite perfume, Euphoria, and waltzed out of the bathroom and down the stairs.

"Can you get any more radiant?" Michael asked as she descended.

Blushing, she kissed his cheek when she reached the bottom of the staircase, and then she turned so that he could put the mink wrap over her shoulders. Unable to resist, Michael leaned down and kissed the side of her neck.

"And you're looking very debonair, baby. Now, you better stop with your sexy self before we miss these dinner reservations," Karli purred seductively.

Biting his lip, he twirled her around to face him. "Is that such a bad idea?"

Just as soon as his words came out, the doorbell rang. They laughed while softly embracing each other.

"Saved by the bell," Karli said with a giggle.

Michael opened the door, exchanged a word with the chauffeur, and then allowed his beautiful wife to lead the way. Once they were outside, the chauffeur escorted them to their waiting town car. The entire way to Jean-Georges, they held hands and giggled, both ecstatic about the impending reveal.

They were the last to arrive at the restaurant, and once they spotted their dinner party milling around, they rushed over to hug everyone.

"Bryson? You and Jess are here?" Michael said, surprised, before he one-arm hugged Bryson and politely kissed the back of Bryson's wife, Jessica's hand.

"You know I wouldn't allow them to be left out," Karli said, playfully tapping Michael's arm before hugging Bryson and Jessica.

"I just thought I'd surprise you, man." Bryson laughed and winked at Michael.

"Well, I, for one, am almost over the moon to find out about this news," Karli's dad said as he hugged his daughter. "You look radiant, baby girl." He then turned to Michael. "As always, son, you're keeping a smile on my daughter's face."

The two men pulled each other into a one-arm hug. When Michael pulled back, he smiled over at Karli. "That's the plan, Pop. That's the plan."

"I just love you two," Karli's mom cooed before hugging Michael and her daughter. "Now let's go sit, so we can hear the news."

Catrina shook her head. "Our table is ready, but per Karli's orders, the reveal won't happen until dessert. And before you two lawyers chime in, dessert will be the last course of the evening."

Everyone laughed as Michael and Bryson smirked and gave each other knowing looks. They could loophole any situation, so everything had to be airtight when you spoke to them. They were the best of the best in the business, and they didn't mind using those great lawyering skills to their own benefit in any situation.

Once they were all seated at their private table, they began choosing their wines and courses. Michael almost spoiled the surprise when he began to question Karli about choosing wine over water. Thank goodness he caught himself and thought better of ruining her moment. Though Michael was a little worried about his wife drinking alcohol while pregnant, he decided that a couple of glasses to celebrate the announcement wouldn't hurt.

Everyone talked, joked, and laughed for over an hour, enjoying the great food and the great company. When the waiter came to the table to ask about dessert, Karli nodded to him. He smiled, returned her nod, and left the table. A few moments later, he was back at the table, this time with a domed silver tray in his hands, which he placed in front of Michael. Michael, Bryson, Jessica, and Karli's mom all gave each other knowing looks as Karli stood, with her wineglass in hand.

"I know you all have been wondering for half of the week why I called this dinner. Well, I could lie and say it's only because I love and adore all of you and enjoy your company, but that's not the only reason," she joked. Laughter erupted from the entire group. "I won't keep you waiting any longer. I've made you guys suffer long enough." She turned slightly to Michael. "Baby, I love you. You have stood by my side and supported me since the day we became a couple, and that support has only gotten stronger since you made me your wife. It is my honor and pleasure to share this moment with you, the man that I love. Will you remove the silver lid on the tray and do the honors?"

Michael stood, proudly rubbing his hands together. "Absolutely!" he exclaimed as everyone watched in anticipation.

He lifted the silver dome and found an envelope underneath it. Laughing, he picked up the envelope. "The mystery continues," he joked, and everyone laughed. After opening the envelope and retrieving the paper inside it, he cleared his throat and began to read.

"We would like to extend our warmest and sincerest congratulations . . ." He paused as his heart began to race and his face brightened, as did Karli's mom's and Jessica's. "To Mrs. Karli F. Sanders, who has been selected as our official candidate and will . . . will . . . become our senior executive marketing director. McCallan and Associates thanks you for your services."

"Yay!" Catrina clapped.

Karli's father jumped up excitedly and hugged Karli. "I'm so proud of you, baby girl. Extremely!"

Michael dropped the paper and plopped down in his seat. The wind had literally been taken out of him. A promotion. She wasn't pregnant. All of this was about a stupid promotion. He took deep, slow, and deliberate breaths to try to keep his emotions at bay. He had been so sure she was pregnant, and in an instant, his hopes and dreams had just deflated. He felt so foolish. He had been all excited over a promotion, which assuredly would keep him from becoming a father anytime soon.

"Michael, Mama, Jess, Bry, you all aren't happy for me? What's going on?" Karli asked, completely taken aback by their sudden somber moods.

Michael wiped his hand down his face. "Karli . . . I . . . Yes, I'm happy. We're happy . . . ," he stammered, looking at the others who wore sad expressions as they all nodded in agreement.

Suddenly, the waiter appeared with another silver tray and placed it in front of Karli before Michael could signal him to stop.

Karli blushed and placed her hands on Michael's shoulders. "A surprise for me! Michael, I should've known you were trying to get me back."

"Um . . ." Michael attempted to intervene, but before he could, Karli lifted the dome on her silver tray. Staring at her was a pair of baby booties, one pink and one blue, which were encircled by a diamond tennis bracelet with charms that spelled out the word *Mommy*.

The wind left Karli's chest as she slowly slumped back into her seat and gazed at Michael, then at her mom, Bryson, and Jessica.

Covering her mouth, she gasped. "Is that what you thought this announcement was about? You all thought I was pregnant?"

Quickly, Karli's mom jumped to Michael's defense. "It's probably my fault. I called Michael and put the idea in his head—"

"And I told him it was probably the same thing," Bryson confessed as Jessica nodded.

"We all thought . . . I thought you were having my baby," Michael said somberly. "I mean, it made sense. The other night at dinner, you didn't drink any wine, so I just thought . . ."

Karli placed her hand against her forehead. "Michael, it was white wine. You know I really don't care to drink it. I just cook with it, but you like it."

Michael raised his hand. "I'm sorry. Forgive me for being too forward. It's my fault. Who would be thinking about a baby, right?" he said sadly.

It was a nice attempt, but it was of no use. The air in the room was so stale that it had altered everyone's mood. What was supposed to be a joyous occasion was now one huge misunderstanding wrapped up in a ball of disappointment. Nothing could salvage the occasion.

Karli's father decided to save face. "You know what? I'm sure that will be our next celebration. I think that I will go get the waiter and take care of the tab, so that we can go." He stood, kissed Karli's cheek, and gave his wife the eye before leaving.

Karli gently picked up the bracelet and the booties, feeling awful. "I really screwed this up."

Michael retrieved the Tiffany box from his pocket and slid the bracelet out of her hand. "I have the receipt. I will take it back—"

"Nonsense. Just keep it for our next celebratory dinner. Ain't that right, sis?" Catrina said nervously before taking a huge gulp of her wine.

Karli nodded slightly. "Yeah, just keep it."

Michael placed the box back inside his inner jacket pocket and stood. "Pardon me. I'm going to use the restroom."

Karli's mom looked over at her daughter and touched her hand. "Honey, I'm so sorry—"

"Just let it go, Mama," Karli said, placing her hand on her forehead.

Just then, her dad came up and told them that he'd taken care of the tab. They all hugged Karli, congratulated her, and apologized. She bid them all good night, and by the time Michael resurfaced, the car service was waiting for them.

The entire ride home, they were silent. Michael tipped the driver once they arrived, and then they walked inside their home. Michael haphazardly threw his jacket across the living-room sofa and went into the kitchen for something to drink. Karli slid out of her Louboutins and followed.

"So are you going to say anything to me?" Karli asked as Michael closed the refrigerator and opened a bottled water.

He took a long swig from the bottle. "What's there to talk about? You got a great promotion. That's awesome news for you. I'm happy for you."

Karli sighed. "It's awesome news for *us*."

"Right . . . *us*." He placed the bottle on the counter and walked out of the kitchen.

Karli followed right behind him. "Michael, what is your problem with this? It's not like you didn't know that I was a candidate for the position. Granted, it's been six months—"

Michael spun around. "I don't have a problem, Karli. I remember. You got it. Good!"

Karli was fuming now. She knew what the real conversation was about: Michael wanted children. That conversation was one she'd been avoiding like the plague, but with this turn of events, she knew it was time to talk about it.

"Why don't you just say what's really on your mind? You're mad because I'm not pregnant."

Michael threw up his hands in exasperation. "Yes! Yes! Karli, that's it. What the hell is so wrong with wanting to have a baby? Every time I bring it up, you never say a word. I mean, my God. We've been married for *four years*. I'm not getting any younger. Now you have a new position, and I'm happy for you, I really am, but when will you have time for a family, huh? Tell me *that*."

Karli swallowed the lump in her throat. "Michael, you've always known my goal was to move up the ranks. That's not fair to me. I worked my ass off for this promotion. I deserve this."

"And we deserve a family. Damn it!" Michael yelled, placing one hand on his waist and rubbing his forehead with the other.

Karli jumped at his outburst. She had never seen him so upset in the four and a half years she'd known him. "Listen. We are not old. I'm twenty-eight. You're thirty-five. We have time to discuss things and plan for our child—"

"Why don't you say what's really on *your* mind, Karli? Huh? Let's not tiptoe around this subject anymore. Let's put it all out there. The real truth of the matter is you don't want children."

Instantly, the air turned stale again. He'd said it. Karli was afraid of his reaction, but she was also happy at the same time that those words had never come out of her mouth. It was true. Karli didn't want to have children. She would never say never, but she just couldn't envision it now. She'd worked so hard to achieve her dreams, and she just wanted to accomplish all she'd set out to do, and having a kid right now was not in her plans.

"Admit it," Michael hollered angrily. "Just admit it. I mean, with as much as we get it in, we should have at least two kids by now. We don't even know if something is wrong—"

Karli put her hand up. "Okay, Michael, let's just drop this. We don't see eye to eye right now, and cooler heads will not prevail if we continue this discussion." She turned to leave.

"Karli, you wanted to talk about this." He caught up with her and spun her around by her arm. "Why are you dropping it now?"

"Just drop it, Michael."

"No, we need to—"

She threw her hands up. "I said drop it," she yelled, tears falling, and then she ran upstairs.

Michael followed her. Something wasn't right. He thought over what he'd said, and then it dawned on him. "Karli, why in the world have you not gotten pregnant? It has been four years."

"Nothing . . . nothing," she struggled to say in a teary voice.

Growing concerned, Michael allowed his anger to dissipate and focused on comforting his wife. "Baby, please, what's going on?" he asked, moving to her side quickly and then holding her before she could shrug away. "You know I love you. You know you can tell me anything. Please tell me what it is. Is there . . . is there something wrong medically?"

Karli's lip quivered uncontrollably, and he held her tightly.

"Oh, baby. What's wrong?" he pleaded, holding her face between the palms of his hands. Staring into her wet hazel-brown eyes, he lovingly stroked her hair with one hand. "Whatever it is, we'll get through it together."

"Michael, please stop it," she pleaded tearfully.

"I will spare no expense in getting you the medical—"

"I'm on birth control," she hollered, snatching away from his embrace. "I haven't gotten pregnant, because I'm on birth control."

Michael stumbled back, looking at her with confusion. "But, but you were a virgin when we married. You weren't on birth control when we met, because you had no reason to be."

Ashamed, Karli wiped her eyes and turned to face him. "I got on birth control a month before our wedding, and I've been on it ever since." Karli broke down and fell on their bed.

Suddenly, Michael felt as if he couldn't breathe. Hot tears flowed from his eyes, and he turned slowly and walked out of their bedroom in a daze.

"Michael," Karli cried.

Her cries fell on deaf ears as he aimlessly walked down the stairs, unsure of where he was headed, the pain of the spoken truth gripping his body. His wife had been lying to him, and even worse, she didn't want kids with him.

Chapter 5

"Michael . . . what? What are you doing here?" Bryson asked after opening his door due to the incessant ringing of the doorbell. "It's almost midnight."

Sloshed out of his mind, Michael leaned on the doorframe. "I'm shorry to bother you, but umm . . . I need a place to, umm . . ." Michael paused to take a breath, trying to fight back his emotions. "Shit. Karli don't want to have my kids, man." Covering his face, he fell back against the door. "Why the fuck she don't want my kids, man?"

He was so tipsy, he almost fell over. Bryson grabbed him and held him to keep him from falling, then ushered him inside. "Come on, man. Come inside. Let's get you some coffee and a blanket."

Bryson helped Michael into his living room and sat him on the sofa. His wife, Jessica, came down the stairs just then, and when she saw Michael, she closed her robe and looked at Bryson with confusion.

"Stay right here, Michael. I'll be right back," Bryson told him as Jessica stepped into the living room.

"Sure. It's not like I have a home." He fell back against the sofa, with his hand over his face.

Bryson nodded to Jessica, and they eased out of the room into the hallway.

"What the hell is going on, Bry? Why is Michael in our house, still in his dinner clothes, at midnight? What the hell happened between him and Karli?" Jessica quizzed.

"I don't know, babe. I'm still trying to piece it together. All I know is he just slurred some jumbled-up notions about not having a home and Karli not wanting his kids."

Jessica gasped. "Oh no! They probably had a huge fight after the dinner party. I would call Karli, but I'm not sure if I should."

"Just hold off. Let me find out exactly what is going on. Go upstairs, and I'll be up shortly." They kissed each other, and then Jessica went back upstairs as Bryson headed back into the living room to check on Michael.

"You got something to drink?" Michael slurred.

"The only drink you're getting is coffee after we talk." Bryson sat on the coffee table in front of Michael. "Bro, what happened tonight?"

Michael leaned back, in deep contemplation. He wanted the comfort of his friend and partner, but he didn't want to relive the hell that he'd just experienced. Most men would think he was being a bitch. That didn't matter to him. He was a married man who actually loved and cared for his wife. Men like that were built differently. They were wired differently than the Average Joe. What seemed petty to average guys meant the world to men like Michael.

Michael trusted Bryson and knew he was cut from the same cloth, so it wasn't that he couldn't confide him. It was simply that it hurt too bad to think that the woman he had pledged and devoted his life to had been keeping such a deep secret from him. And to add insult to injury, she didn't want a family. Sure, she had never admitted it, but she didn't have to. The mere fact that she'd gone behind his back to protect her eggs from being invaded by his sperm was enough proof. He didn't need to hear her say the actual words to know that the writing was on the wall. He read gray very well.

"Let's not relive it."

Bryson scoffed. "It's early ass in the morning, and you're at my house, drunk out of your mind. You gotta tell me something."

"Can I just sleep on your sofa tonight? I promise to talk to you in the morning. Tonight I just need to clear my mind."

Bryson threw up his hands. "You know I don't mind, but clear your mind of what, man? At least tell me what's going on."

"What's going on is that I will never have a child with my wife when she has been on birth control behind my back for four fucking years!" he hollered, his voice cracking. After swallowing hard and taking a deep breath, he lowered his voice and said, "Now, is that enough information for you? Can I rest now? Can I not think about my messed-up life just for tonight? Is that okay with you?"

Bryson was so stunned by what Michael had revealed, he could only nod his head, get up, grab a pillow and blanket from the hallway closet, and hand them to Michael. "We'll talk in the morning. Get some rest, man."

Michael grabbed his arm. "Please don't tell Karli I'm here. I'm not ready to deal with her yet. I can't face her. Please."

Bryson assured him. "We won't tell Karli. That's my word."

Bryson stood in the doorway until he saw Michael lie down on the sofa and cover himself with the blanket. He knew that his friend was in a bad place, and as much as he wanted to be a friend to Karli and call her, he couldn't. He knew she must be worried sick and going out of her mind, but he wouldn't betray Michael. From the sounds of it, he'd already experienced enough betrayal for one night.

"And?" Jessica asked as soon as he came into their bedroom.

Bryson shrugged. "I don't know the whole story. We're going to talk in the morning. All I do know is that Karli has been on birth control their entire marriage and didn't tell Michael about it. That's all I know."

Jessica was shocked. "I can't believe Karli would do something like that, especially to Michael." She shook her head and picked up her cell phone. "I'm calling—"

Bryson stopped her attempt to contact Karli. "No, you're not. Michael doesn't want Karli to know he's here, and if you call her, she's going to know he's here and show up. I promised him."

Jessica put it down. "Bry, she needs to know where her husband is. I'm sure she is going crazy right now. Besides, we know only a little bit of the story. There has to be more to it than what he blurted out in a drunken haze."

"I'm sure there is, but that's not our business—"

"He made it our business when he rang that doorbell."

"So if it's our business, then it's our business to do as he requested and leave it alone," Bryson countered defensively. Grabbing his wife's hands, he continued his plea. "I'm not protecting him, but he's the one who showed up to our house. For now, our loyalty is all he feels he has. Don't take that away from him. He's depending on us."

She groaned. "Ugh. All right. I won't say a word. He's welcome to stay as long as he needs us."

The next morning Jessica made them all breakfast. While she cooked, Bryson gave Michael fresh clothes and allowed him to shower in the guest bathroom. While they ate, Michael confided in his friends everything that had happened from the time Karli and he got home last night until the time he staggered onto their doorstep.

Jessica shook her head. "Michael, are you sure she never told you?"

"Not to be mean, but I would've remembered something like that." Michael let out a deep sigh. "Besides, if she had told me, she would've said something at that time. She was too remorseful." As he rubbed his hand across his head, his jaw tightened. "What kind of woman does some shit like that?"

Jessica put up her hand. "Whoa. I know you're upset, but don't go down that path. You said yourself you haven't spoken to her about it."

"I think she said all she needed to say, don't you?" Michael replied, fuming.

"Okay, let's take a break," Bryson interjected. He eyed his wife. He didn't like the fact that she was poking the bear, even if what she said made sense. He loved Michael and Karli like a brother and sister, but he didn't want to have to check Michael about his wife, either. Now was not the time to go into battle.

Bryson went on. "Look, we understand what you're saying, Michael, but I think Jess is only trying to say that at some point, you and Karli need to talk about what happened and figure out what you're going to do about it. However, you're welcome to stay with us as long as you need to in order to sort it out."

Michael held his head down in surrender. "You're both right, and I'm sorry, Jess. It's hard for me right now to deal. What else could she lie to me about?"

Jessica stood and patted Michael's hand. "And that is why you need to talk to your wife, whenever you're ready." She hugged him and then kissed her husband. "I'm going grocery shopping. I'll leave you two boys here to chill out for a while."

Five minutes later, Jessica was behind the wheel of her car. As soon as she was down the street, she grabbed her cell phone and pressed the button to instantly activate Siri. "Call Karli mobile," she said into the phone.

Chapter 6

Michael had left the house on Saturday night and still wasn't home three days later. He had refused to answer Karli's calls, and if it hadn't been for Jessica sneaking in a call to her on Sunday and telling her that he was staying at her house, Karli wouldn't have known whether he was dead or alive.

After three days of missing her husband and being in turmoil over her marriage, she broke down and confided in Catrina. She had to before she lost her mind. She'd called Catrina immediately after work that day, and as soon as Catrina got home, Karli had gone over in baggy sweats, hauling a box of tissues. She had been a red, puffy-eyed mess of tears for the past hour, as she'd described the events after the botched surprise dinner.

"Tell me again why you didn't tell the man you were on birth control," Catrina said insistently as Karli wiped her eyes and clutched her friend's throw pillow as they sat on the sofa.

Karli sighed. "Stop trying to make sense of it. Of course, now it doesn't seem logical. At the time, I wasn't thinking."

"Honey, it was logical when you made the decision, but that decision was made four years ago, Karli. Jesus. Why haven't you told him in four years? I would be upset too. We all know your mama and him have been waiting on the edge of their seats to hear the word *pregnant*. Hell, I thought you were off birth control my damn self."

Karli jumped up. "I don't need you to judge me. Damn! I came here for comfort. I know what I did was messed up," she hollered before collapsing back down on the sofa. "Honestly, I never meant to not tell him, but then once he started going on and on about kids, I became scared, because so much time had lapsed, and then I started avoiding the conversation altogether."

Catrina rubbed Karli's back and wrapped an arm around her shoulder. "That's understandable. Did you try to explain that to him?"

Karli nodded. "Yes, but he left before I could, and I haven't talked to him or seen him since." She cried harder, leaning into her friend. "My husband hates me."

"Aww, honey. He doesn't hate you. He's just upset. He'll come around. You just have to give him time to digest this so you all can talk."

"I'm trying. I just don't know how to pull myself together. I just got this promotion, the gala is Saturday, and I begin my position next week. I can't deal with the job while my marriage is in shambles." Karli continued to cry. "I don't want to lose my husband."

Catrina eyed her sympathetically. "Don't worry about the gala. If Michael is not back, we'll just say he had to go out of town on business. In the meantime, take Monday off to give yourself a day. You don't want to lose Michael, so don't. You are a strong woman. You've fought for everything in your life, and you won't stop now. So on Monday you make your husband's favorite lunch, put on one of those bad-ass outfits that highlight your voluptuous behind, go to his job, and get your man."

"I don't even know his schedule for Monday, and again, he's not answering my calls."

Catrina held up her finger. "Watch me work," she said, dialing a number on her cell phone. "Hey, you. How are you? Good. I wish I could say this is a pleasure call, but

I need a huge favor. Can you please look at Attorney Sanders's schedule for Monday and email it to me? Nothing like that. I'm just trying to set up a surprise for him and Karli. Thank you, sweetie. We'll do dinner next week. Bye, cutie," she cooed. Then she hung up the phone and rolled her eyes.

Karli couldn't help but laugh. Catrina always had a man in her back pocket, and her fierce model looks surely helped. Karli didn't even have to ask who had supplied Catrina with all the information. She knew it was Jamal Timms, one of her husband's junior associates. He had it bad for Catrina. She'd never give him the time of day, but she'd never let him know it. She had a habit of collecting men in business, mostly to do what she'd just done—get the inside scoop.

"Michael is going to have Jamal's head one day for entertaining your foolery. While you're lecturing me, you do know that whenever you and Harris get serious, you're going to have to cut that out."

Catrina waved her off. "Harris and I are good just the way we are. Great friends with excellent benefits," she joked.

Karli couldn't do anything but shake her head and laugh with her friend. Catrina and her antics were the perfect temporary distraction from her personal hell. Soon Jamal sent the email with Michael's schedule, and Catrina opened it on her phone. It showed that Michael had nothing scheduled from one o'clock until two-thirty on Monday afternoon.

Karli checked herself out in the mirror once more before she left to surprise her husband. There was no way Michael could resist her in her fishtail pencil skirt, her deep V-cut buttoned-down blouse, and her sexy Zanotti pumps. Her hair was on point, make-up was flawless, and she smelled scrumptious.

She ran to the kitchen and double-checked her picnic basket, which was filled with Michael's favorites: homemade turkey and ham club sandwiches, veggies with ranch, and Voss water. She'd even gotten him one of his favorite sweets, chocolate cheesecake cupcakes from Brooklyn Cupcake.

Karli drove to his office and said a small prayer as she exited the car and made her way into the building. She got on the elevator, and when it dinged and opened on Michael's floor, she took a deep breath, exited, and then approached Stephanie, his receptionist.

"Mrs. Sanders, how are you?" Stephanie greeted her.

"Hey, Steph! Is Michael in his office?"

"He sure is. He doesn't have any clients or phone calls, so you can go on in."

Smiling, Karli thanked her, then walked to Michael's office and lightly tapped on his door.

"Come in," Michael called out.

Karli entered his office and closed the door behind her. He never even looked up from the paperwork he was completing.

"Hello, Michael."

He paused instantly and took a moment before he placed his pen down and looked up at Karli. Slowly, he sat back in his plush leather chair and wiped his hand down his stress-ridden face.

"What are you doing here, Karli?"

After walking up to his desk, she placed the small picnic basket on top of it and stood back. "I . . . um . . . well . . . You didn't get to come to the gala, and I didn't see you at church yesterday, so I decided to make you some lunch and bring it to you. Have you eaten?"

"No, and thanks," he said dryly as he picked up his pen and began tapping it on a notepad. "Is there anything else?"

This was harder than she'd anticipated. In all the years she known him, he'd never been so cold and short with her. Karli swallowed the lump in her throat. His demeanor alone told her that she needed to make her plea quickly.

"Michael, I miss you. I miss us. I haven't seen you in a week, and I miss you at the house. Aren't we going to talk about this?" She began getting choked up.

Michael let out an exaggerated chortle. "Talk? Oh, so now you want to talk? Clarify this for me, Karli. Do you want me to talk to you just like you talked to me when you chose to get on birth control? Or do you want me to talk to you the same way you talked to me when you didn't tell me for the past four years how you were on birth control? Better yet, do you want to talk to me about how you don't want children and how you never intended to talk to me about that? If that's what you want, then I think we've said all there is to say, which is nothing." Michael's nose flared, and he was absolutely brimming with anger.

Karli raised her hands in defeat. "You're right. I was wrong for that, and I own up to it. I want to talk about us. I'm not ready to give up on us."

Michael stood and walked around to the front of his desk, leaned on it, and folded his arms. "Well, I don't. I'm not ready to talk to you. I'm not even ready to see you."

Karli had expected many things, but not this brash treatment, which instantly overwhelmed her and filled her with emotion. Couldn't he see how truly sorry she was? Didn't he care about their marriage anymore? The tears that welled in her eyes began seeping out of the corners as she stared at him. He looked away from her.

"Please, Michael. What are we supposed to do? Live separately? You're my husband. I love you, and I need you at our home."

"I can't come home right now."

"If not now, when?"

"I don't know," he stressed impatiently, trying to keep his composure. "To answer your question, I skipped church because I didn't feel up to it. Pastor Monroe knew I wasn't going to be there. And what did you tell your boss and colleagues about me not being at the gala? Let me guess. You lied to them too?"

Karli put her hands up again. "That's not fair. I couldn't very well tell them the truth."

Michael looked away, because he knew he was being petty. He was just still so angry. "Look, Karli. I will come home. I'm just not sure when. I need my space and time to get through this."

She slowly approached him to test the waters and placed her hands on his chest. "Michael, we're married. We're supposed to get through our tough times together. We can't do that if you're in one place and I'm in another."

He swallowed the lump in his throat. He loved his wife, and everything in him wanted to pick her up and make love to her on his desk right then and there. Her scent was intoxicating him, and she had on an outfit that just wouldn't quit, with some of the sexiest pumps that had ever graced her dainty feet.

Closing his eyes, he gently grabbed her hands. "I may come home this week, Karli. I don't know. Even if I do, it's only out of respect for our marriage. I'm not ready to discuss things with you or to pretend we're the couple we were a week ago. I can't even say I'll move back into our bedroom."

Karli gasped. "Michael," she said in exasperation. "What are we going to do when you're back at home?

Live like roommates? We're practically roommates now. I can't deal with this turmoil in my life with this new promotion—"

"Oh, so it all comes back to you and this damn promotion, huh?" Instantly, Michael became infuriated. "You can't function at your job, so that's why you want me home. I can't believe you," he snarled. He glared at her. "Get out," he demanded as he dropped her hands and gently pushed her away from him.

"Baby, you know that's not what I meant—"

"It's always about you and what you want and don't want. Just like that selfish move to get on birth control. I can't deal with this now. Get out," he barked, interrupting her again.

She attempted to reach for him. "Surely, you don't mean—"

"Get out now! *Go*," he demanded forcefully.

Karli jumped, taken aback by his harshness and fearful of his anger toward her. She placed her hands up in surrender. "Okay, okay. Your lunch is in the basket."

She turned slowly to leave, trying to hold back her tears, but her body began to tremble slightly, and her throat was thick with emotion. She knew she wouldn't make it to the elevator before she was a heap of tears. But Karli did manage to make it to the restroom, and she rushed through the door and locked it behind her before she silently cried her eyes out. When she was finished, her face was red and her eyes were puffy. There was no way she could ease past Michael's receptionist or anybody else in the office while she was looking this way. At the sight of her, someone would surely call Michael, and then all their business would be out in the street. She had to get ahold of some modicum of dignity. Checking her purse, she was relieved when she found that she had some essentials inside it to work with.

After easing up to the sink, she stared at her reflection in the mirror. This should have been one of the happiest times of her life. Now, it was one of the worst, all because of a simple error in judgment and a dream position at work. Was her mistake worth all this hurt and pain? she wondered. Could they simply not find a way to move past it? Coming out of her thoughts, she decided to hurry and get herself together before someone came knocking on the door. She washed her face, put on her Shade Dolls aviators, and retouched her Poetic Designs lip gloss in an effort to mask her emotions. Luckily, she made it out of the office without anyone becoming alarmed and to her car before breaking down again.

Chapter 7

Michael plopped down in his chair after Karli left. He hated the internal struggle he was having with himself. He had a million reasons not to go home, but the one reason he did have to return home ate away at him like a flesh-eating parasite. Love. He loved her so much, but her actions had truly hurt him.

It didn't help that she had come into his office, looking like the definition of *seduction*. He was a man, and her body called him something awful, but it was the principle of the matter. If he allowed himself to get caught up in his emotions at the expense of his principles, he'd forget how to be the man he'd fought to become.

Karli had taught him that attraction wasn't everything. He'd been smitten with her from the moment he'd laid eyes on her, but her intellect, her drive, the manner in which she carried herself—she was such a woman of class and distinction—were the qualities that had made him fall head over heels in love with her. Those qualities had given him a taste of what having a real woman could do for him, and Karli had given him that "it" feeling, which he'd only ever seen before in his father's eyes when he gazed at his mother.

Her love had been a cure and a reward from God. Nothing in the world had felt better to him than loving Karli and having that love returned. Therefore, when he committed himself to Karli, he vowed to give everything to her: his heart, his emotions, his love, his future kids—his life. Above all, it hurt to know that the woman to whom he'd given everything wasn't willing to give him every part of herself in return. So yes, he stuck to his guns, even when it hurt like hell.

Principles or not, he was about to partake of this basket of goodies. He was enjoying the last remnants of his turkey and ham sandwiches when Bryson entered his office.

"Michael . . . Wait a minute . . ." He paused. "Where the hell did you get that from?" he asked, peeking inside the basket.

Michael wiped his mouth with a napkin. "Karli brought it."

Bryson smiled brightly, taking a seat. "So you two are talking again."

Michael shook his head. "She dropped this off, trying to spark a conversation, but I'm not ready. I can't do this with her right now."

Bryson sat back in his seat, shaking his head. Michael already knew he was pro Karli, so he allowed Bryson to get whatever thought he had about the situation off his chest.

"So you mean to tell me that your wife sacrificed her work schedule to bring you lunch and come and talk and you denied her?" Bryson said, exasperated. "What did she want to talk about? I can't wait to hear this."

Michael sucked his teeth. "What else? Us. She wants me to come home."

"And she's right," Bryson said. Despite the menacing look Michael was giving him, he continued. "Look, man, you two are married. Your problems should be worked out in the comfort of your own home. I'm not kicking you out or nothing, and Jessica and I enjoy having you, but the truth of the matter is that she's right, Michael. The longer you allow this to fester, the greater the divide you'll have in your marriage."

"So I'm just supposed to roll over and take whatever she does? I'm supposed to just accept it because we're married? Miss me with that."

Bryson shook his head. "No, you're not. You're supposed to go home and try to work through it, because you're married. You took the vows. Both of you. If you love her, and I know you do, you have to be willing to try. Otherwise, why stay married?"

"You sound like her." He groaned.

Bryson shrugged. "It's your call. No pressure. My guest room stays open to you." He stood and placed a file on Michael's desk. "This needs your final approval," he said before swiping a celery stick from the basket and walking toward the door. "She made a mistake, Michael. And the good deacon should learn to practice forgiveness." With that, he walked out of the office, leaving Michael flabbergasted.

Chapter 8

Since Karli had called in sick on her first official day in her new position, she spent her second day moving into her new office and setting up her new accounts. She did everything she could to avoid all work that required coherent thinking. Not even writing could relieve the stressors in her life today. She felt mentally frustrated and physically drained, and at the end of the "workday," she couldn't wait to get into her bathtub to relax.

After Karli entered the house, she threw her keys in the key dish, kicked off her heels, and rubbed her forehead as she walked to the kitchen. She had a headache that wouldn't quit. She searched her purse for the ibuprofen she'd purchased at lunch, popped the top, and downed two tablets with a glass of water. She hung her suit jacket on a chair at the breakfast table and walked into her family room, rubbing her neck.

"Long day, huh?"

Karli nearly jumped out of her skin. She snapped her head up and saw Michael sitting on the sofa in some sweats and a T-shirt. Tears of joy filled her eyes, and she ran to him and nearly knocked him over. She kissed him all about his face.

"Michael! Oh my God! You're home!" she yelled happily. "I didn't see your car."

"It's in the back. I thought I'd surprise you. Surprise." He smiled demurely.

She clasped her hands behind his neck and looked him over as if he were a figment of her imagination. She studied his baby-smooth chocolate skin; his neat goatee; his low-cut waves; his deep, sensual brown eyes; and those pearly white teeth.

"Baby, thank you for coming home. I'm so sorry. I love you so much." Without giving him a chance to respond, she kissed him fervently on the lips and began unbuttoning her blouse. "I'm going to make love to you so fiercely," she murmured against his lips.

"Karli, wait," he said with bated breaths.

She pulled back and looked at him, pushing her hair behind her ears.

"As much as I want to do this, I can't."

Karli shook her head. "Can't? Can't what?" she asked, confused.

Michael nudged her off him, stood up, and began pacing the floor. "Honestly, Karli, I came home because I can't run from this. I'm just not beat for the BS. I'm still high-strung, emotional, and until I can calm down about this situation, I'm just not ready to deal. I'm staying in our guest bedroom until I'm ready. I just need time."

Karli stood, upset at his revelation. "So basically, it's the same as it was when you weren't here, except you can see my suffering instead."

"How in the world did this turn into me hurting you or wanting to hurt you? All I've done is cater to you! Now that I want space, it's too much. You created this problem, or did you forget that in all your attempts to justify your wrongdoings?"

Karli's nose flared. "I never tried to justify anything. I just wanted to explain what happened and why. I own my mistakes. All I want to do is move on with our lives."

"Well, you owe me time and space so that we can eventually do that, because the entire reason for this is your mistakes."

Karli threw her head in her hands, trying to hide her frustration and her tears. Smoothing her hands over her hair, she conceded. "Fine. Michael. Do whatever you want to do. Deal with it how you choose. I can't fight like this anymore. I just can't. Just let me know what I'm allowed and not allowed to do concerning you."

Michael only nodded in return, then watched as she ascended the stairs. Once upstairs, Karli ran a bath and cried silent tears as she sat soaking in the tub until the water ran cold. After her ritual of moisturizing her body and face, she put on her short black satin negligee and black satin slippers. At least she could give him something to make him wish he'd changed his mind.

She left the bedroom, fully intending to sashay around in front of his office, but as she approached the room, she found the door closed and heard him working. *So much for giving him a tease*, she thought. She changed her course and headed to the kitchen, where she saw dishes in the sink from the dinner he'd apparently made for himself. Shaking her head, she rinsed the dishes off and loaded them in the dishwasher.

Not feeling very hungry, she opted for a banana, some veggie sticks, and water for her dinner, then grabbed her laptop bag and headed to her office to get some work done as well. She couldn't allow her personal life to keep her in limbo, so she took a page out of her husband's book and worked through her pain. By the time she glanced up at the clock four hours later, it was close to midnight. She rubbed her eyes and yawned before she saved her work and closed her laptop.

Out of a new habit, she got up to check the house and set the alarm. When she came back up the stairs, she and Michael ended up meeting in the hallway.

"I was just checking the locks," they said simultaneously.

Michael exhaled, and Karli could tell he was turned on. The longing in his eyes betrayed his calm demeanor. Karli raked her fingers through her hair.

"Well, I loaded the dishes. If you want me to cook tomorrow, just leave me a note or something in the morning, before you leave, please," she said.

Michael nodded and folded his arms. "I can do that."

The uneasiness between them began to bother Karli, so she cut the meeting in the hallway short. "Well, good night." She turned and walked into their bedroom without giving him a chance to respond.

Karli said a prayer, then slipped into bed. She made sure her cell was charging and set her alarm clock. Sighing, she pulled up the covers, and soon sleep easily found its way into her tired eyes.

Though sleep came easily, it was turbulent. Karli's emotions were running rampant, making her extremely restless. Namely, it'd been more than a couple of weeks since she'd felt her husband's touch, and thoughts of him consumed her. Running her fingertips down her thighs, she began moaning, as the sensation sent tingles through her body. She bit her lip as her hands slowly moved up her thighs to her stomach and finally landed on her breasts. She gasped at the feeling of another set of hands on her body. The hem of her negligee moved upward as feathery kisses trailed from her inner thighs up to the edge of her thong.

"Michael," she moaned with bated breaths as her back arched from the pleasure.

Strong fingertips glided over her nipples, and she clasped the hands, held them in place. Her body craved him, as if she were an addict suffering from withdrawals. As the kisses continued, her heart filled with love. Her mind drifted over all the memories they had made: the day they met, their first date, the proposal, their wedding. Michael was everything to her. She'd never had a true relationship until Michael. Before him, every guy had been a temporary companion to go to prom with in high school or to catch a movie with in college. Her levelheaded and career-driven ways had made her different from other young women. Though guys had been attracted to her, they'd quickly bored of her; and honestly, she of them and their mannish ways. Until Michael. He had come along and had been a breath of fresh air, and she was still taken with him—the love of her life—to this day.

As the pleasure mounted, she gave in to it, allowing him total access. Suddenly, her eyes fluttered open, and lost between a dream state and reality, she thought she saw Michael on top of her. She quickly wiped her eyes to see if she was indeed dreaming. She wasn't. Michael was actually in the bed—their bed.

"Michael?" she asked, sleepily turning her head briefly to see the clock. It read 2:25 a.m.

"I'm sorry. You just looked so fine tonight and yesterday, and I've been tossing all night. I need some so bad."

She smiled, caressing his face. "Oh, baby—"

Michael shook his head. "I'm not here to make love to you."

Cocking her head back out of confusion, she looked at him. Her eyes focused in the dark. He was clearly naked and on top of her, with his hands stuck inside her thong.

"Aren't you here to make love? Weren't you just kissing on me?" she asked.

"Kissing on you, yes. Here to make love, no. Karli, what I need right now is just to have some unemotional and unfeeling sex. A release."

Karli paused and took in what he had said. "Are you . . . are you trying to treat me like a ho? Are you trying to do a 'hit it and quit it' on me?"

Michael put his head down. "I'm not treating you like a ho. You're my wife. This is one of your duties. I just can't make love to you. I can't be all lovey dovey and emotional. I just want to get some from you and go back to my room. That's it. At least I'm not trying to go in the streets for it."

Karli covered her mouth and shook her head. "Absolutely not! You will not treat me like I'm just here to be your cum catcher. I'm your wife."

Michael sat back on his knees and looked at her apologetically but sternly. "I'm sorry. That's all I can offer you. But I need some bad. So honestly, what are we going to do around here?"

"Use your fucking left hand!"

"Been doing that all week." He moved to get up. "You asked what you can do, and this is it. If not, I can just go back to the guest room. I'm not going to make love to you, because I can't. Sex is what I need right now. Sex is all I want right now. That's it."

It was one thing to be kinky and freaky together in love, but this, this was unfathomable. Karli had never seen this side of Michael. Truly, he was reverting to the man he had told her he used to be before they met. She couldn't believe that this same man who had vowed to love, honor, and protect her was being so cold and uncaring of her emotions, her heart, and her body. A feeling of betrayal welled up inside her, and she slapped him before she realized what was happening.

"How dare you!" she seethed. "How dare you treat me like this? What I did may have been wrong, but it doesn't warrant this type of caveman behavior from you. Get out!" she yelled.

Michael's anger rose. "It's not caveman. Slapping me like that, *that's* caveman behavior. The hell is wrong with you? You care nothing about my feelings for four years, and then you want to complain because I'm choosing to attempt to get sex from my wife? Fine. If I leave, I'm leaving the house, and you better pray to God that Vaseline continues to do the trick."

He jumped up from the bed and began to put his pajamas back on, and Karli grew frantic. Though she was pissed, she didn't want to lose the opportunity to make it work. She felt so low and cheap, but if using her would keep him here, then she'd allow it. Well, she prayed that instead he would change his mind or at least simply make love to her. She had faith that he wouldn't actually go through with this madness. It had to be a test.

That's it. Just a test to see if I'm willing to do anything to keep him.

She was going to prove him wrong, and in turn, he'd forget this stupid "ho sex" plan and treat her like his wife.

"Okay, Michael." She swallowed hard and lay back on the bed. Her voice and her hands trembled as she nodded. "Do what you need to do."

He nodded his head and took a deep breath. After slowly easing back in the bed, he hovered on top of her and quickly removed her thong. He leaned over and took the K-Y Jelly out of the nightstand drawer, then slicked his manhood, opened her legs, and slid inside. He lay pressed tightly against her as he barbarically pumped and grunted, with his face almost buried in the pillows. Karli held in her cries as hot tears slid out of her eyes while her husband had his way with her without any regard to her pain. She couldn't believe that he was actually going through with this. In that moment, her heart shattered.

Panting, he sat up and, without warning, flipped her onto her stomach, stretched her out, and entered her kitty from behind. Karli just lay there as he rammed her and then, with the roar of a lion, released deep inside her. She continued to lie there as he got out of the bed and went into their bathroom to clean himself. When he returned, Karli was lying in a fetal position. He didn't even bother to clean her up or check on her. She heard him slip on his pajamas before he leaned over, kissed the top of her head, and nonchalantly said, "Thanks. Good night." The next thing she heard was the bedroom door closing.

Karli lay there, feeling sore, violated, used, cheap, unwanted, and completely unloved. She'd suffered severely from her mistake. Now, thinking over her marriage, all she felt was numbness. She was so tired that her eyes eventually closed, but nothing could shut out the pain that racked her heart.

Chapter 9

For the past two weeks, Karli had hardly said two words to Michael. She had spoken only if he had spoken first. She'd moved throughout the house as if he was truly an unwanted houseguest. Michael knew it was his fault. He never should've demanded sex from Karli as if she were some ho, like the ones he used to indulge in.

Though what she had done was wrong, so was what he had done. At least she hadn't intentionally tried to hurt him. However, he'd definitely wanted her to hurt like he hurt, but now he was left wondering at what cost. She was his wife, and every day it ate away at him that he'd treated her so harshly. That fact humbled him. It made him see how she felt when he placed himself on the taking end. He was ashamed of himself and deeply concerned about the state of his marriage. In one month, they'd gone from a loving and doting couple that everyone envied to exes without the official paperwork. He shuddered to think about a divorce. He'd never let it get to that—he loved her way too much for that—but he wondered if his actions had pushed her to consider it. He knew what he needed to do, and it was what he should've done from the start.

"Aren't you going to church today?" Michael asked after he walked into the kitchen and found Karli barefoot and in sweatpants and a tank top. He was dressed and would have to leave in fifteen minutes to arrive on time.

She shook her head. "No."

"You didn't go last Sunday."

"I won't be going this Sunday, either."

"Karli, I think we should plan to go to church together. We—"

She looked up from her cell phone and blew out a breath in frustration. "I can't go now. It's too late to get dressed. Why do you care if I go or not? You'd want us to go in separate cars."

He jiggled the keys in his hand. "No, I wouldn't. I want us to go together."

She waved him off. "Go to church, Michael. I'm good. Maybe next week."

He walked up to her and placed his fingers under her chin. Slowly, he turned her face toward his. "I know you're mad at me. You have every right to be, and I'm sorry. I love you, Karli, and if you want to talk when I get home, we can." With that, he placed a soft kiss on her lips and left for church.

Karli shook her head after Michael left. It'd taken him two weeks to apologize for something he never should've done. She was beyond disgusted at his behavior and couldn't believe that now that he had something to be sorry for, he wanted to talk and be forgiven. Sadly, she struggled, because the selfish side of her wanted to say to hell with him, but her heart beat slowly when she thought of life without him, at least the "him" that she had grown to love and had married. Old Michael had resurfaced, however, and his brief storm had left irreparable damage.

Luckily, her job had been keeping her so busy that she really didn't have time to focus on her personal issues. Honestly, she wasn't speaking to Michael, because she was upset, but her avoidance of him wasn't due solely to that. Her absences and her unwillingness to engage in conversation with him were also due to the fact that she'd been tasked to land a new account, and it had entailed hard work so far. Lewis Investments, one of the largest investment firms in the city, was looking to move their marketing and research to a new firm, and Lewis higher-ups had scouted McCallan and Associates and one other marketing firm. Karli had been hard at work devising a marketing campaign that would reel Lewis Investments in. Talk about throwing her to the wolves. She hadn't even been in her new position a good month, and already she had to prove herself, but she was up for the challenge. Tomorrow she would be presenting her new campaign, and she had to make sure it was on point, which was the real reason she had missed church last week and was missing it today.

As soon as she finished her fruit and oatmeal for breakfast, she sat in the living room and put the finishing touches on her PowerPoint and Excel spreadsheets with the help of her assistant and her junior executive. Her team had been instrumental in helping her pull everything together. By the time she was finishing up, Michael was walking into the house after church.

"I know that's right, Stacy. Look, girl, you and Edgar have done an excellent job. I thank you all so much," Karli said to her team on speaker.

"Please. You make it easy," Stacy replied. "You're the best boss in the world to work for."

"Aw, thanks, Stacy. You have a good rest of your Sunday, and I'll see you tomorrow." They said their goodbyes and hung up.

Karli stood and turned to see Michael loosening his tie. Then she turned back to gather her things on the coffee table. "I'll be out of your way in a moment. I know you want to watch television," she said as she put her paperwork in the appropriate files. Then she shut down her laptop.

"So work's going good?"

She nodded. "Yeah, it's good," she answered, continuing to clean up her mess. She didn't acknowledge him further.

As soon as she had gathered everything, she turned around, only to find Michael standing directly in front of her. He took her briefcase and laptop bag out of her hands and sat them down on the sofa, then pulled her to him by her waist.

"Actually, I wanted to treat you to dinner so we can spend some real time together," he said. "Would you like that?"

"Michael, I look like a certified mess. I've been in these sweatpants and tank all day, working, and I'm tired. Besides, the restaurants are standing room only by four p.m. on Sundays, and it's already three thirty. There are leftovers in the refrigerator from last night. I can eat that. If you want something else, you'll have to order it. I'm too tired to cook."

Michael leaned down and placed his head on her shoulder. "How do we get back to us?"

She shrugged. "I'm not sure, and right now I'm not up to discussing us."

He looked at her sadly. "Okay. I'll respect that. Whenever you're ready."

Chapter 10

Karli glanced at herself in the bedroom mirror. Her formfitting classic skirt suit with the bustier top gave her the high-profile professional look she was seeking, and her sky-high Louboutins added just the right touch. She looked like she'd been in the game for years.

"You look . . . wow," Michael said after Karli walked into the kitchen with her laptop bag on her shoulder and her briefcase in her hand.

"Thank you," she said, grabbing a banana and a bottle of water. She checked to make sure her purse was in her laptop bag and then grabbed her car keys.

"Big day at work?" he asked, putting his paper down and looking her up and down from his seat at the kitchen table.

"Yes. Major account to close."

Michael wiped his hand down his face. Karli's aloofness had turned them into a couple he didn't even recognize. At moments like this in the past, she would have shared all the details of her work with him. "I didn't know. That's great. Do you think that you'll—"

"Sorry Michael. I have to go. Have a good day at work." She patted his hand and headed out, leaving him stuck on stupid.

On the ride to work, Karli tried not to think about Michael's feeble attempts at conversation. She knew he was itching to "talk," but it bothered her that he expected her to get over what he'd done to her, forgive him, and eagerly engage in conversation with him, even though he had shown no willingness to extend to her the same olive branch. God knows she was trying to will herself past her ill feelings, her resentment, but it was so hard. Every time she looked at him, she was torn between the love she had for him and the anger she harbored. The only way she could process everything with her marriage and make it through the presentation she was about to give was to keep up her old stern, no-nonsense business demeanor.

After she pulled into her parking spot, she took a deep breath and closed her eyes to push back the emotional thoughts threatening to consume her mind. Once she closed this account, she'd have to shift her focus to her marriage. They couldn't continue this way. She couldn't continue this way.

"Okay, Karli. It's showtime," she said aloud.

She pushed herself and finally got out of the car and walked into the building. Karli's team had everything set up. Her boss, Jack Caruthers, had already greeted the executives from Lewis Investments, and Karli's assistant had already led the team of four into the conference room for the preliminary presentation. Karli met up with her boss outside the conference room, and then they entered the room together.

"Carl, Jan, Sue, Paul, this is Karli, the one I was telling you about," Jack announced, addressing the Lewis Investments executives, who were milling about. "I'm sure you'll find her work exceedingly impressive. She's a dynamite wiz, and I completely trust her to show you how McCallan and Associates can benefit you." He turned to Karli and gave her the floor.

"Why, thank you, Jack," Karli said to him, then turned to the Lewis Investments executives. "It's a pleasure to meet all of you. We've prepared a preliminary marketing campaign for you that I'm positive you'll be impressed with. Shall we get started?"

They all agreed to commence. They took their seats, and Karli and her assistant began. Jack quietly left the conference room. About five minutes into her presentation, Karli could tell by the expressions on the executives' faces that she had won them over already. Then, about ten minutes into her presentation, the door opened, and Jack walked back in the room.

"I'm so sorry to interrupt, but we have a special guest," he announced.

Karli smiled. "Not a problem, Jack. Please show them in."

A man walked into the conference room, wearing a sharp Tom Ford suit and a gleaming Rolex. He reeked of money. Karli walked over to meet him, and he met her halfway. His eyes landed on Karli, and he smiled as he drank in her features. Karli's breath caught in her throat at the sight of his piercing ocean-blue eyes.

"It's a pleasure to meet you. I am Hudson Lewis," he said, introducing himself, and extended his hand.

Karli reached out her hand and gave him a firm handshake. "The pleasure is mine, Mr. Lewis. I am Karli—"

"Fitzgerald," he interrupted. "I've followed your work for some time. You helped with a partner company of mine, and their sales skyrocketed. When I heard you were in charge of the presentation for our campaign, I had to clear my schedule."

Suddenly, it dawned on Karli. He was *the* Lewis, as in the CEO and the owner of Lewis Investments. "Mr. Lewis, thank you so much for making time for our presentation, and I hope you'll be impressed with what I've put together."

"I'm sure I will."

"My apologies. I've already begun—"

He waved off her apology. "No need for apologies. I'm the tardy one. I'm a fast study, so I'm sure I can catch on. Please continue from where you left off."

He took a seat at the head of the table, next to his team. Jack decided to sit in on the meeting, to observe Karli's wit and professionalism. For the next hour, she explained her vision for fulfilling Lewis Investments' marketing and research needs and answered all the questions they had with ease.

"Karli, I want to thank you for such a dynamic presentation. It was clear, concise, and highly thought out. You and your team did an excellent job. I'm extremely impressed," Hudson stated at the end of her presentation.

Carl, the lead executive, spoke up. "Yes, I couldn't agree with Mr. Lewis more. I'm sure that we will discuss our decision and get back—"

"We're going with McCallan and Associates," Hudson said, intervening.

Everyone turned to face Hudson, shocked out of their minds that he'd agreed on the spot.

Carl cleared his throat as the others looked at Hudson in confusion. "Sir, I don't mean to overstep my boundaries here, but we haven't agreed on the terms or seen the contract. Wouldn't it be best to gather that information first?"

Hudson waved him off. "Those things are formalities . . . bullshit, really. I go with my gut. It's the reason there is a Lewis Investments today. It's the reason we're successful," he said, patting his stomach lightly. "Gut instincts." He stood and faced Jack. "Get your facts and figures together, and we can settle the particulars later, but you're the company I want behind my company, and I want Karli on my team."

Jack smiled and shook Hudson's hand. "We'll get the paperwork drawn up and have it to you by tomorrow evening, once legal has reviewed it. How's that sound?"

Hudson winked. "Like a winner."

Everyone milled around, shaking hands and exchanging pleasantries, until Jack invited them to his office for a celebratory drink.

"You guys go ahead. I'd like to speak to Karli for a second," Hudson told his team. Then he turned his head so that his blue eyes met Karli's as she packed up her laptop and presentation materials.

Karli instantly froze. His eyes seemed to pierce through her, and she felt her legs begin to tremble. Once everyone had cleared out, Hudson turned and walked a few steps closer to Karli.

"I trust that I can expect more of this from you as part of the team, right?" he said.

Karli smiled and nodded. "Of course. As soon as you admit that you were going to go with us all along." She eyed him suspiciously yet confidently, daring him to deny it.

He laughed and smiled at her. "You caught me. Karli, I didn't lie when I said I'd followed your work. McCallan is good, but when I heard you were the lead, I was sold. You were the selling point. The rest of the meeting was just a formality."

Karli waved him off, trying to hide her blushing. "You are too much. I hope I live up to such great expectations."

"I have no doubt that you will." He extended his hand toward her laptop bag. "Allow me." His intense blue eyes bore deeper into her.

Jesus, the man could stop traffic with those eyes, she thought.

His blond hair, thin beard, and Clinique cologne added to his mystique. By his appearance, she surmised that he was someone with money and a streak of "bad boy."

He stood hovering over her with his chiseled six-foot frame, waiting for her to hand over the bag. "Allow me to be a gentleman," he insisted. "Those shoes are far too nice to try to walk with full hands."

He and Karli shared a laugh, and she handed him the bag. On the way out and down the hall, Karli discussed their next plan of action, once the contracts were signed. They joined the rest of the team in Jack's office for a drink, and then Hudson followed her to her office to obtain her business card.

"Darn. Looks like I'm fresh out of new business cards," she said as Hudson sat her laptop bag on her desk. She opened her desk drawer, retrieved an old card, and wrote her new office number on it. "It's not the latest one, but it'll serve the purpose."

Hudson took it and placed it in his card holder before retrieving his own business card. "Anytime you need me for the campaign, call."

He handed his card to Karli, and their hands touched briefly. Hudson found himself gazing at Karli as the touch sent electricity through him.

Christ. She is beautiful beyond belief, he thought.

"Well, Mr. Lewis—"

"Hudson. Please call me Hudson."

Karli nodded. "Okay, Hudson. I really hate to cut this short, but I do have other work to do. It was a pleasure to meet you, and I look forward to the new venture with your company."

"Likewise." He shook her hand and allowed his fingers to linger a tad too long on hers. He let go of her hand before it became uncomfortable. "Good day, Karli."

"Good day to you, Hudson."

Chapter 11

"So is everything in order and arranged according to your liking?" Jack asked Hudson. Carl and Sue had already signed off on the new contract with Lewis Investments, and now they were just waiting on the final stamp of approval from Hudson.

Hudson didn't answer but sat quietly reviewing the last few remaining pages. Once he finished, he looked up at Jack and Karli. "Only one adjustment is needed. I want a dedicated person for my account. I do not want to be shuffled among McCallan associates. I'm hiring your company, but I trust only one person, and that is Karli. I need that added to the contract."

Jack looked a little baffled, because having Karli in the contract meant that if Karli left the firm—or, heaven forbid, they had to let her go—Lewis Investments would go with her. "Mr. Lewis, I understand that you admire Karli's work, as we do, but I can—"

"If you can't or don't trust your own employees, how can I trust your company?" Hudson said, cutting him off, with a serious expression on his face.

"Hudson, if I may," Karli interjected, shooting a glare at Jack that was an unspoken order for him to be quiet. "How about this? What if I add myself on a contingency basis as the lead for your account for one year? If I do not satisfy the requirements of the contract in that year, McCallan and Associates can assign a new lead, with whom I will work closely. That way, your needs are met, it gives McCallan some leeway, since you are bound for another year, and it allows me to honor my employee requirements with McCallan in case of separation. Would that be fair?"

Hudson's mouth creased into a small smile. "Works for me, if it works for Jack and you."

Jack smiled at Karli and gratefully patted her back for her quick thinking. "It definitely works for me."

Karli grabbed a pen and made a note of the adjustment for legal on the paperwork. "We'll get that added in and have the final copy to you by the close of business today," she said, confidently placing the pen in Hudson's hand.

He signed; then Jack and Karli did the same. Hudson reached across the table to shake Jack's hand.

"I do believe we have a deal," he said.

Everyone cheered and stood. Hudson came around the table and took Karli's hand. "Thank you, Karli," he said, covering their joined hands with his free hand. "You are truly a gem."

"My pleasure, Hudson."

Hudson dismissed his team and stayed behind to converse with Jack and Karli. In the middle of Jack gushing about Karli and getting excited about their impending deal, he received an important phone call and excused himself.

"Karli, I can't wait to get started with the new campaign for Lewis Investments," Hudson said.

Karli folded her arms. "Hudson, you do realize that you hired a team to take care of these things, don't you? Carl and Sue are very capable and are willing to work with me."

Hudson looked at her in both shock and admiration. "I knew there was something I liked about you." He laughed.

"What is that?" She couldn't help but laugh with him.

"Your boldness," he answered. "I'm fully aware that they are capable, but I'm a hands-on kind of man. This firm doesn't run by my allowing others to report back to me. It runs on firsthand knowledge. Sure, there are things I can't handle, but I always know what's going on. Besides, to take the competitive edge, I will have to. That damn E-Trade baby is killing the game."

He and Karli shared a gut-wrenching laugh.

"You don't like the E-Trade baby, whhhat?" she joked, mimicking one of the commercials on TV.

Hudson chuckled. "On the contrary, I love the E-Trade baby. I wish it were my idea, which is why I was determined to have you on my team. I know you were on that development team," he said, looking at Karli's shocked face. "Mmm-hmm, whhhat?" he added, mimicking her. "Didn't think I knew, huh?"

Shaking her head and giggling, she admitted, "You definitely did your research. Now *I'm* impressed."

Hudson looked at his Rolex and then back at Karli. "I'm afraid the only thing I had for breakfast this morning is a cup of hot tea. My stomach is making me aware that it's time to replenish. Have lunch with me?"

A doubtful look spread across Karli's face, but before she could decline, Hudson reminded her that it was lunchtime and surmised that she'd have to eat sometime as well. So she agreed.

As they sat at a table covered with a white linen tablecloth, Hudson ordered a vintage bottle of Barolo Monfortino Riserva to go along with their lunch. Once the waiter brought the bottle and poured the wine, Karli took in the aroma of the wine, swirled it in her glass, and enjoyed the taste.

"This is good." She nodded, in agreement with his choice.

He raised his hand to his chin as he watched her enjoy the wine and smiled slyly. "It is. I told you to trust me." She smiled, tilting her glass in agreement.

After their entrées were served, Hudson said, "I'm intrigued, Karli. Tell me a little about yourself."

Waving her finger in defiance, Karli swallowed her bite of food before replying. "No, sir. You seem to know a lot about my background. Tell me more about you, and I don't want to hear the typical stuff, like where you went to school," she joked.

He couldn't help but chuckle. "What? You don't want to hear about my high school?" he said, ribbing her. A thought came to mind, and he stated, "Okay, well, I started my business—"

"No, nothing like that, either," Karli quickly interrupted, extending her palm. "If I can find it on your company bio, I don't want to hear it."

Charmed, Hudson sat back, in deep contemplation. He was truly stumped, which was rare. No one ever really wanted to hear about him. About his accolades, his credentials, his advice, yes. About *him*, no.

He placed his fingertips on his chin, in awe of Karli. "Wow. I really don't know what to say here." He gazed upward as he grasped for straws, debating what to reveal about himself that was unrelated to his firm. "I like long walks in the park," he said and then paused. "Wait, I sound like a dating service ad."

Karli wiped her hands on her napkin, sat back, and crossed her legs. "And that's what I want to hear. If you like long walks in the park, then tell me that. Hudson, Lewis Investments isn't just a company to you. You *are* Lewis Investments. Tell me what makes Hudson tick."

Hudson was simply amazed. Her intellect was one that he hadn't seen in a long time in his field, and that was saying a lot. He knew several really smart people, but that special intellectual was a rare find. The sunlight shone in the window near their table and danced playfully on her hazel eyes, and he had to look away to keep from getting lost in them. Those beautiful brown pools left so much to be explored.

He cleared his throat and stared at her intently again. "I actually do like long walks in the park. I love hot cups of tea, to get my creative juices flowing, and relaxing glasses of wine, to rest my mental. My mind works continually. I sit idly sometimes for hours at a time, thinking, strategizing. This business makes you click, makes you learn more, makes you shift from idea to idea in search of the next best deal, product, and service. Learning what works and what doesn't, trying new things, revamping old things.

"I'm a contemplative man. I'm an admirer. I search for the beauty in a thing, which is why I love photography and scenic views, but not just what we all can see. I see what most refuse to see, what goes beyond their matrix of thought processes. The inner workings and inner beauty of the thing are what I care about. That is why Lewis Investments stands out, why I stand out."

Entranced, Karli hung on his every word, and it wasn't until he picked up his glass of wine that she focused on the here and now.

"*Salud*," he said.

Karli raised her glass, and he touched it with his own. "*Salud*," she said. They sipped together.

"So tell me about Karli."

Giggling, she swept her hair behind her ear. "Oh, well, I graduated from high school at sixteen—"

Laughing, Hudson put his hand up. "So you're going to give me the bio now?"

"You weren't specific," she said and cackled.

Holding up two fingers, he agreed. "Touché! But I am intrigued by that. Graduating from high school at sixteen? Wow. That is why you are the intellectual that you are."

She nodded in agreement. "My parents were extremely driven about my education, as was I. I was the high school valedictorian, I graduated summa cum laude, with dual bachelor's degrees, at twenty, and I got my MBA degree at twenty-three."

Hudson clapped at her accomplishments. He didn't think he could be any more impressed with her, and yet she kept surprising him. He looked down at her left hand and finally addressed the elephant in the room. "And the ring on your finger says you're married."

Karli looked down at her bands. Honestly, she had almost forgotten she was wearing them. Her face reddened slightly, and she suddenly felt a bit ashamed and, to be honest, alarmed by the thought that she was enjoying the company of a man who wasn't her husband. Hudson was the type of man that you could get lost in. Literally, time seemed to stand still, and the outside world had nearly disappeared, as she sat with him, until he mentioned her marriage.

She nodded and cleared her throat. "Yes, I am. I've been married for four years," she said. "No children," she added meekly, diverting her eyes from him.

Gliding his finger along his lips, Hudson leaned forward to make an assessment. "Pardon me for my forwardness, and forgive me for speaking out of turn, but I would guess from the manner in which you just spoke that your husband wants children and you do not." He sat back and awaited her response.

Her frustration mixed with defensiveness, and worry lines creased her forehead. "I really can't discuss this with you."

Without thinking, Hudson leaned forward again and covered the top of her hand with his. Their attention immediately turned to their hands and to the fact that he was now caressing hers, in what was almost a loving gesture. Strangely, she didn't protest, and he didn't pull his hand away.

"I'm sorry. I wasn't trying to make you discuss your personal life, Karli. It was inappropriate. Forgive me."

She patted the top of his hand with her free one and then removed both of her hands from the table. Hudson leaned back, and for the next few minutes, they ate in silence. It was apparent that Karli was deep in her personal thoughts, and Hudson had already overstepped his boundaries, so he dared not interfere in her contemplative moments.

Something about Hudson made him easy to talk to, and even though Karli barely knew him, she felt that he was open and honest. Normally, she wouldn't talk to a mere stranger about anything in her personal life, but she longed for an unbiased opinion and possible advice. Without warning, Karli looked up at him and asked, "Hypothetically speaking, do you think it would be wrong not to want children? I mean, at least not now."

Hudson wiped the remnants of his steak from his lips with his linen napkin, then wiped his hands. Taking a sip of his wine, he sat back, in contemplation. After placing the wineglass down moments later, he pointed at her. "Can I be frank?"

"I asked, so sure."

"No," he said, so quickly and assuredly, she almost thought he was playing. Hudson noticed her perplexed expression and explained further. "Personally, I feel like this. Even if you're married, if one person wants kids and the other doesn't, the answer is simple. You shouldn't have children. Let's face the facts. Unless you're ready to be God Himself, you shouldn't bring another life into this world. Why do I say God? I know you're wondering." He paused, and Karli nodded, fascinated by his viewpoint.

Then he continued. "Having children is the ultimate sacrifice, the coup de grâce of your existence, because they become the single most important aspect of your life. Your relationship with your child is much like the relationship that God has with us. It is unapologetic, unconditional, and unselfish. It is loving, nurturing, caring, and it entails placing anything and everything to the side and nothing above your child, not your career, your marriage, or even yourself. It is the most blessed and sacred sacrifice that you can make in this world. So if you're not ready for that, then no, you shouldn't bring another life into the equation."

He paused for a moment. "The problem with the world today is that too many people are having children they don't want or love, and because these children don't know love, they don't love themselves and, therefore, can't possibly love and respect others. That's the reason why crimes, violence, and hatred are at an all-time high. So I say that acknowledging—hypothetically speaking, of course—that you do not want children, and that you aren't willing to bring a child into this world to appease someone, is virtually the most respectful and selfless thing that you can do."

Karli was literally stunned speechless. There was nothing to say after his assessment. Hell, his argument was better than one she could've devised, and yet it fit her mind-set and situation perfectly. He'd given her something for her arsenal, even though she was undecided if she should use it.

"Are you all right?" Hudson asked.

Clearing away her thoughts, Karli answered, "Yes, I'm fine. I was just lost in thought." She looked at her watch. "I should be getting back to work."

"Of course."

Hudson called the waiter over to get the tab. He paid the bill with his AmEx Black Card, and then they stopped by the coat check to collect their things before heading out. The attendant checked their tickets and came back with their coats and gloves. Hudson threw his coat over one arm and instinctively held out Karli's coat so that she could slip it on. Once her arms were in, Hudson pulled the coat up on her shoulders and then lightly rubbed them.

Karli tried not to let the feel of his powerful hands and his tantalizingly clean smell intoxicate her. And Hudson's heart raced at the feel of her beneath his hands. He took a couple of slow, labored breaths before stepping back. Karli exhaled. Neither of them spoke as they walked out of the restaurant together and into the brisk New York air.

As they stood outside, Karli turned to him. "I will hail a taxi, since we're going in opposite directions."

"What kind of gentleman do you take me for, Karli? Nonsense. My driver will drop you off at work, and then I can head to my destination. I'm the CEO and owner. They'll wait for me."

Karli giggled. "Arrogant much?"

He held up his index finger and thumb and squeezed them together. "*Un poquito*," he joked.

When his car pulled around, he opened the rear door for Karli, watched her get in, and then climbed in after her. During the ride, they discussed some minor strategies for the marketing plan, and before they knew it, they'd arrived at McCallan and Associates.

"We're here," she said, looking out the window at the building.

"Well, it's been a pleasure, Karli. I will have my assistant call and schedule a time for us to meet next week to expand on the ideas we discussed."

"Sounds like a plan to me."

Hudson opened his door since he was closest to the curb, and then he stepped out onto the sidewalk. Karli scooted over the seat to get out on his side. He held out his hand to help her out, and she took it. After covering her hand with his other hand, he lightly caressed it and smiled devilishly at her, peering at her with those oceanic gems.

"Thank you for having lunch with me. I truly enjoyed your company," he told her.

Blushing, she grinned. "Thank you for inviting me. The food and the wine were great, and the company was exquisite."

Smiling shyly, he fought back a groan. Everything about this woman was perfect. From her silky hair, which blew softly in the wind, her impeccably aligned and brilliantly white teeth, and her sunlit hazel eyes to her shapely figure and sexy dainty feet in her Louboutins. Her sexiness and her intellect were a lethal combination.

"Have a good day, Hudson."

"Good day to you, Karli."

Chapter 12

"Earth to Michael," Bryson said, waving his hands in front of Michael's face, as they ate lunch together.

Shaking himself out of his funk, he looked apologetically at his friend. "I'm sorry, man. I'm just a million miles away. What were you saying?"

Bryson sat his beer down and shook his head. "Okay, let's talk about Karli. You called me to get your mind off her, and yet your wings are cold, your beer bottle is half empty, you've referred to the Eagles as the Jets four times, and I've been talking for the past ten minutes to Jesus and the air. She's on your mind, so talk about her."

Chuckling softly, Michael conceded, "Yeah, I am pretty bad." He heaved a sigh and looked over at Bryson. "I don't know what to do to get my wife back."

Bryson looked confused. "Wait. Did she leave you? I thought you went back home to her. It's been, like, two weeks."

Waving his hand, Michael grunted. "No, she didn't leave me. In fact, she ran to me with open arms when I went back home."

Bryson folded his arms across his chest, and his nose flared. "What the hell did you do to that woman, Michael? She loves you like a drug addict loves crack, so I know you did something stupid."

Michael contemplated whether to explain the actual story to his friend, but then he saw Bryson's growing impatience, and he knew better than to try to lie to him.

Besides, he wasn't a good liar, anyway. He wore his emotions on his sleeve.

Michael sucked it up and began explaining all the happenings of late. Beginning with pushing Karli away when he got home and treating her like a ho for hire, and ending with their nonexistent communication and quality time, he let it all out to his friend. Once he was finished, he felt a sense of relief, but he knew that relief was just from being able to talk to someone, since he couldn't talk to his wife.

Bryson stared at him in disbelief. "I can't believe you. And you're seriously wondering why you can't get your wife back! You treated her like some broad from the hood. She's your wife, Michael. Damn it."

"Don't you think I realize that?"

"I honestly don't know what to tell you. If I treated Jessica like that, not only would I have a well-whipped ass, but I'd be sitting in divorce proceedings, feeling just as messed up as I would look. You're lucky she didn't go postal on you."

"I've tried everything that Pastor Monroe has asked me to do, and she's turned a blind eye and an uncaring ear to me. She's flippant and cold. I don't know this Karli. I just want my old thing back, ya know?"

"Well, ain't that some table turning for ya ass," Bryson said half jokingly.

"You're not helping."

Shrugging, Bryson sipped his beer then cleared his throat of the bitter aftertaste. "Sucks to be you. Just out of curiosity, what have you done to get back into her good graces?"

"I apologized. I've tried to talk to her, but she ignores me. I invited her out to dinner, so we could spend some quality time together, but she turned me down. She did go to church with me last Sunday, but she drove her own car, because she said she had to work afterward, so the only time I had to spend with her was during service."

Sitting back, Bryson shook his head. "She's got you on a ten-foot pole, man." He contemplated something for a moment, then snapped his fingers. "Instead of inviting her, you should set the mood. You know if you ask, she's going to say no, so instead, when she comes home, have some soft romantic music on, have dinner for two ready, and fix a bubble bath or something. Hell, anything at this point."

A slow smile crept onto Michael's face. He looked at his watch, stood, and grabbed his leather jacket. "Will you hit up Stephanie and tell her to cancel my three o'clock? Tell her to push everything back until Monday. I'm taking the rest of the day off."

Bryson fist bumped him. "I got you, man. Go get your wife. Who knows? You may put a baby up in her, after all," he joked.

"From your lips to God's ears."

Chapter 13

The slow hum of the heater was the only noise Karli and Hudson heard while they sat in his office, on opposite sides of the table, in think tank mode. The trial campaign had gone well but had pulled in only about 80 percent of the projected number. They had to go back, revise, and revamp according to what didn't work as intended.

It was only a minor setback, but the creative juices weren't flowing naturally. It was already six p.m. on a Friday night, and Hudson and Karli had dismissed their teams a couple of hours ago. They figured they'd stay and brainstorm and let everyone else begin enjoying their weekend, only they both had gone over the information again and again but had drawn blanks. Even when one of them did think of an idea, the other didn't really see it as the winning formula.

"Adding this might not be so bad," Hudson said as he mulled over an idea proposed by Karli's assistant.

Karli peered over at what he was referring to and cringed a bit. "It doesn't exactly fit the image we had in mind." She sipped her hot tea and sat back, placing her fingertips on the side of her forehead.

"True." Hudson sighed and leaned back, with his hands on top of his head.

Karli stood up and softly paced the floor. Hudson tried hard not to smile at her while she was in her serious think mode—it was cute and admirable—but his eyes mostly traveled to her backside in those formfitting jeans. The long-sleeved cowl-necked sweater and the Jimmy Choo stilettos added a chic sex appeal to her already killer looks.

Rubbing his eyes, Hudson stood and stretched. "Karli, I think we should wrap it up. Clearly, this tea isn't working its mojo, and we're both exhausted from having been at this for seven hours straight. Let's just enjoy our weekend and start fresh on Monday. What do you say?"

She plopped down on his plush ottoman. "Agreed. I need some serious relaxation in my life. I can't wait to settle in with a glass of wine and a good book."

"Really? What genres?"

"Mystery and suspense, contemporary, and some historical. I'm a sucker for a good, juicy autobiography, but I must say my absolute first love is poetry, to read it and to dabble in writing it." She paused. "And erotica," she joked, and instantly, she wished she hadn't.

Hudson saw her sheepish expression and waved his hands. "I like erotica too."

She shot him a look that said she was unconvinced. "The lies you tell."

He howled. "Seriously, what do you know about N'Tyse?"

Karli's eyes bucked briefly. "Hell, what do *you* know about N'Tyse?"

"That she's a helluva writer. Nothing beats *Twisted Seduction*, though. My, oh, man." He shook his head, as if remembering it verbatim.

Grinning, Karli was in awe. "I can't believe you know about that. You should definitely read the entire series, if you haven't. It's a nice pot of steam for you."

"I will." He laughed with her as she gathered her things.

Karli sat down to zip up her bag as she rubbed her neck and tried to stretch it out. Hudson walked around and put his hands on her shoulders to knead away the pain.

Karli was taken aback, but the shoulder rub felt too good for her to protest.

"You're tense. You've been under a lot of stress. A spa day would do you wonders."

"Mmm," she groaned, leaning into his massage. "So how'd you get into urban erotica?"

"An ex." He shrugged. "You take the good with the bad, and you try to learn from every relationship. This one taught me to appreciate a good erotic book." He laughed, and his warm cinnamon breath tickled her earlobe. "What type of poetry do you like?"

Karli closed her eyes and licked her lips. "Sensual poems. One of my favorite poets is Kiana Donae," she said barely above a whisper, giving in to the feeling of his powerful hands.

"Like cherries and cognac you got me laid back feeling some type of way. And as you spread my legs to the first sips of me . . . our tongues dance linguistically. As we explore each other, the liquored kisses you cover my body with are thicker than syrup and sweeter than honeyed combs. And when your lips roam below my bud ripens and blooms like cherry blossomed trees in June," she said softly, reciting "Cherries & Cognac," her favorite poem by the poet.

"Wow," Hudson whispered. "The way you recited that—" Karli suddenly tensed, having become aware of the inappropriateness of the conversation and the neck rub. Her sudden change in demeanor caused Hudson to stop in midsentence, and he also stopped massaging her shoulders. He lightly patted her back. "Have a good weekend, Karli," he whispered huskily.

Flustered, she stood up and tried to grab her laptop bag and purse. She fumbled with her cell. "Yeah, I need to . . . to call my husband," she said nervously as the phone clattered to the floor.

Hudson held up his hand to calm her. He handed her, her purse and laptop bag and then retrieved her fallen cell phone from the floor. While placing it in her hand, he held it briefly and smiled at her. "Clearer heads will prevail on Monday."

Swallowing hard, she nodded, and he began walking her to the door. She spun around before exiting. "Have a good weekend, Hudson."

As she opened the door, one of the women from the cleaning service came by, and Karli fell back to avoid hitting her with the door. Swift with his hands, Hudson caught her.

"*Lo siento mucho!*" the woman said, apologizing frantically. "I so sorry."

"It's fine." Karli waved to her to let her know she was okay.

The woman looked at Hudson.

"You're fine. Please don't worry," he said, then realized there was the language barrier. "Uhhh . . . *fue un accidente. Sin preocupaciones, de veras*," he added, reassuring her that there was no need to worry.

The woman smiled nervously, apologized again, and went about her duties.

He focused on Karli again. "Are you okay? You didn't hurt your ankles, did you?" he asked softly, his voice reverberating in Karli's ear.

"I'm okay," she managed to get out.

He steadied her and turned her around to look at him while still holding her upright. "Are you sure?" he asked. The deep worry lines creasing his face showed he was genuinely concerned.

Neither words nor coherent thoughts came to Karli as she stood engulfed in his powerful arms. Being this close to Hudson allowed her to feel his every cut muscle, even through his Ralph Lauren sweater and True Religion jeans. His scent was breathtaking, and those worried oceanic orbs touched her soul.

Finally, she shook herself out of the trance. "I . . . uh . . . I'm . . . I'm good, Hudson." She braced herself by gripping his masculine shoulders and steadied herself.

Hudson briefly held her about the waist as they both stared intently at each other and breathed deeply. A force beyond their control swirled around them, and it was hard for Karli to focus or move. They both felt a surge of magnetic energy flowing between them. The sudden ringing of Hudson's cell broke them out of their trance and embrace.

"I gotta go," Karli said, then quickly turned around to leave.

Hudson reached into his pocket and snatched the phone, intending to decline the call. "Karli, wait."

It was too late. She'd darted out of the door so fast, she beat the speed of light.

"Damn!" Hudson said in frustration, still holding his ringing phone. "Yes, Hudson Lewis," he answered as he somberly walked back to his desk. He didn't hear a word that came from the other end of the line. His every thought was on Karli.

"Get it together, girl," Karli said aloud, coaching herself, as she steered her car through the traffic.

When she stopped at the red light, she looked at her ring finger, and tears came to her eyes. Her life was a wreck at a time when it should be peaceful and joyful. She wasn't sure of anything anymore: not her marriage, and not whatever the hell was going on with her and Hudson.

"What in the world is wrong with me?" she cried aloud, her private thoughts spilling from her unexpectedly.

Her mind replayed the moments before in Hudson's office, and guilt nearly consumed her. Sure, her marriage was beyond rocky, but there was no way she should be experiencing these emotions over Hudson. She loved Michael still, right? Yes, of course, she did.

This is crazy, she thought, shaking her head. She cleared her thoughts and surmised that she had to be making things up because of her emotional state. *That wealthy white man is not interested in you, only in your abilities*, she thought. Not that it wasn't possible, but a man with that degree of power and influence rarely tasted the color rainbow, at least not publicly, no matter how light, bright, and next to white she was. And she didn't want him to; she was married.

Ten minutes later Karli arrived home. Exhaling, she walked into the house, then placed her car keys in the dish and set her laptop bag and her purse on the foyer table. She leaned against the front door, with her eyes closed, and noticed soft music playing in the background. When she opened her eyes to figure out what was going on, she found Michael standing in front of her, holding a bowl of grapes, with only a pair of basketball shorts on.

"Rough day?" he asked.

She nodded her head, looking confused, and although *rough* wasn't the right word to describe how her day had gone, she couldn't very well tell him the truth, so she rolled with it.

Michael stepped closer to her and took her hand in his. "Let me take your stress away." He released her hand, then wrapped his arm around her waist and gently pulled her close to him. He placed the bowl on the table, picked up a grape, and fed it to Karli.

"Michael, what is this?" she protested after swallowing the grape.

Michael shook his head and placed an index finger to her lips. "Just let me wash away the worries of today." He took her hand and led her into their family room, where the smooth sounds of Raheem DeVaughn were playing.

Karli smelled the sweet aroma of her custom Pomegranate Passion Poetic Soul candles and saw that their family room had been transformed. She took in the tray of fruit and chocolate, and the chilling bottle of wine, then gazed at the fireplace, which was ablaze, and the soft pallet on the floor, all of which created the perfect romantic setting.

Michael took her in his arms and began to sway with her to the rhythm of the music as he held her close. "I love you so much, baby," he whispered in her ear as they swayed.

"Michael, I—"

Before she could finish, he captured her lips in a deep kiss. Sucking his bottom lip after the kiss, he gently held her face between the palms of his hands and stared lovingly into her eyes. "Karli, let's just let this mess go. These past couple of months have been hell for both of us, and I just want my old thing back. I don't want to talk. I don't want to argue. I just want you. That's it."

Without another word, he led her to the pallet, sat her down, and removed her shoes. Karli leaned back against an ottoman as Michael leaned back against the one opposite her, and then she placed her feet in his lap. He began to massage them.

Karli leaned her head back and decided to enjoy the pampering. There was so much that needed to be said, but she held it in, determined to try to enjoy her husband, at least for tonight. She picked up one of the filled wineglasses and a chocolate-covered strawberry from the tray.

Michael smiled to himself as he watched her finally relax in the moment. Silently, he thanked Bryson for the idea. He was going to cook dinner, but he wanted their night to begin with sex. With Karli being so distant, cooking and eating would serve only as an unnecessary distraction, so dinner would have to come later.

Michael noticed Karli's empty glass of wine, and he paused his massage momentarily to refill it. Once she finished off that glass, he got up and washed his hands, then returned with the bowl of grapes from earlier. He sat in front of her and fed her grapes, and she fed them to him. They shared giggles as the juice from the grapes slid down their lips. Michael leaned forward and licked and kissed the juice on her lips.

The wine had begun to creep up on Karli, and she began to sway to the music right where she was sitting. Michael sat back for a moment, admiring his beautiful wife. When "Jupiter Love" by Trey Songz came on, Michael's urges kicked in, and he pulled Karli onto him so that she straddled his lap. He hungrily kissed her about the neck and caressed handfuls of her luscious backside.

The wine and the music had Karli on an orgasmic high, and she didn't even notice that her shirt and bra were off until she felt the warmth of Michael's tongue swirling over and suckling her quickly hardening nipples.

"Mmm," she moaned, enjoying the feeling of the sexual attention she craved. "My jeans. Let me take off my jeans," she breathed heavily.

Karli swung her leg over Michael and kneeled to one side of him, and as she began to unbutton her jeans, Michael sank down and kneeled behind her. He began massaging her neck and shoulders, and instantly, she thought back to Hudson just an hour or so ago. Before she could react, Michael began trailing kisses down her back, sending her libido into a frenzy. Before long, their clothes were off, and Michael was laying her back on the pallet. Her mind was so clouded by the events earlier in the day that she wasn't paying attention when he slid into her. She wrapped her arms around him and closed her eyes. Suddenly, an image of Hudson making love to her flooded her mind. She squeezed Michael tightly, trying to make the thought go away, but the more he moved, the more she imagined Hudson on top of her.

"Damn, baby. You feel so good," Michael said sensually in her ear as he lovingly thrust in and out of her creamy oasis.

His voice brought her back to her reality, and she opened her eyes to see him peering down at her with such a look of pleasure and such intensity. She froze in place and immediately began to run dry.

"Baby, what's wrong?" he asked, noticing the shift and growing limp from the discomfort of the moment.

"Uh . . . um," she stammered, then bit her lip.

Michael bent down to kiss her, but she felt truly uncomfortable, especially after her inappropriate thoughts of Hudson. She cringed, and Michael rolled onto his back beside her. They both knew the moment was over, only Michael didn't know why. Without a word, Karli pulled up the thin blanket, covered them, and rolled onto her side. Confused beyond belief, Michael just lay there.

Michael took a deep breath as he clicked off the television in his home office. He'd come home early with the intention to work in peace, but his mind was so preoccupied that he'd decided to relax first by catching some shows. Unfortunately, that hadn't worked, either. Nothing was working to keep his mind off what was truly bothering him. He simply couldn't block the unwelcome memory that continued to assault his mind.

As Michael revisited the past weekend, he tried to think of a million ways he could've handled what had happened differently, but the truth was he hadn't known what to say to Karli after that debacle of lovemaking they'd experienced, so he hadn't said anything at all. Unsurprisingly, she hadn't spoken about it, either. The entire weekend it had felt like they were walking on eggshells, trying not to address the elephant in the room. Sadly, that had become the norm for them lately.

As he tried to sort it out in his mind now, his cell phone rang, and he saw that it was Bryson calling. He didn't want to answer, but he'd have to deal with his friend eventually. He couldn't put off everyone.

"Yeah, man? What's up?"

"So you blew like a hurricane through the office today. Even Stephanie caught it, and I've never seen you snap at her. What the hell happened? I thought you were supposed to have had a good weekend with your wife."

"Man, it sure started off good, but in the middle of us gettin' it in, she freezes up. I mean straight Sahara!"

"Did you try to talk to her? I mean, maybe she's still juiced up on that ho move you played."

Rubbing his head in frustration, Michael spat, "I didn't want to talk. I wanted to make love to my wife." He huffed. "But, man, it wasn't just that. When I tried to ask her what was wrong or even touch her, she cringed like, like I repulsed her."

Bryson was quiet for a moment. "Did you ask her about it?"

"Are you crazy? Heck no. I'm not going to rush into a conversation about how I don't do it for my wife anymore. I couldn't take it if she told me she didn't want me or, worse yet, didn't love me anymore. I just . . . I can't take that. I think I'm just going to give her a little more time to get over whatever ill feelings she has, and then we'll try again."

Bryson shook his head skeptically, though Michael couldn't see him. "I think you should really talk about what happened that night. Karli loves you. Something isn't right."

"Nah, I'm going to wait it out for a bit. Maybe it was a fluke or just her having to get used to our intimacy again," Michael replied. "I know Karli. She'll get over this, and we'll be fine. Just watch."

Bryson sighed, feeling sorry for his friends and feeling that Michael could be making a huge mistake by not attempting to nip this thing in the bud. "Well, you better find a way to work it out quickly. A marriage is too sacred to leave in shambles. The devil breeds in confusion. Don't dance in his playground."

Michael stared at the phone in disbelief. "Funny, but you sound just like my father, and I'm supposed to be the deacon," he said, thinking back on an earlier conversation he'd had with his dad, who'd given him similar advice.

Chuckling slightly, Bryson quipped, "Well, we both know your father is a bright man who's been married forty years. You should listen to him, and not to toot my own horn, to me too." Sensing Michael's apprehension, Bryson added, "Just think about it."

"It's all I ever think about."

Chapter 14

After the botched reunion last weekend, Karli immersed herself completely in her work. It was the only thing keeping the monkey off her back. She felt horrible and ashamed. How could she talk to her husband about what had happened? What would she say? That in the throes of passion with him, she had imagined having sex with another man, one whom she worked closely with? If Michael hated her new job title already, she shuddered to think how he'd react to that news, even though her thoughts were unintentional.

What surprised her was the fact that Michael hadn't asked about it. If she were in his shoes, she surely would have. Though she was relieved that he hadn't, she couldn't help but feel somewhat bothered that he hadn't even attempted to sort it out. Had he just given up on them? Did he care anymore? Maybe she should have just told him and tried to explain the entire story. At the end of the day, she had no ties to Hudson, and though at times she was smitten with him, there was nothing between them but work. At least that was what she kept telling herself. It was the truth, the only truth she could hold on to.

Delving into work helped her not only personally, but also professionally, as her creative juices were forced to kick into overdrive. During an entire week of work devoted to Lewis Investments, Karli and Hudson's team produced a hugely successful ad campaign. After the celebration dinner, the team met briefly in Lewis

Investments' Manhattan office to go over meetings and schedules for the second phase of the campaign. An hour later, they had wrapped things up as best they could, and everyone began filing out. Hudson and Karli stayed behind in the conference room, discussing particulars for the meetings they had scheduled and making sure all necessary points of discussion were on the agenda.

Karli looked down at her watch. "Oh my goodness! It's after seven o'clock. I better get going, since I have an hour-and-a-half drive to look forward to," she said to Hudson as she rose to her feet.

Just then, Karli's cell rang. It was her assistant, Stacy.

"Hey, Stacy. Did you forget something?" Karli said when she picked up.

"I was just checking on you to see if you were stuck in this traffic too."

"I'm just about to leave. You left two hours ago. You're not home yet?" she asked, and Hudson looked up at Karli with growing concern.

"There is a bad accident on the FDR. The radio is reporting a seven-car pileup. It has traffic backed up for miles. I may be home in another forty-five minutes to an hour, give or take. But if you haven't left yet, you better be prepared for a good four- to five-hour drive back home."

"Shit!" Karli cussed aloud.

"Sorry to be the bearer of bad news. I was calling to see if we could keep each other company, but I think you're going to be worse than me."

Karli waved her hand. "Don't worry about me. You focus on the road, and text me when you make it home."

"Will do. Have a good night, Karli."

When they hung up, Hudson looked at her, waiting to hear the news.

"FDR is backed up from a seven-car pileup. I'll have a good four- or five-hour drive home. If I leave now, I may make it home by midnight."

Hudson stood up. "Nonsense. Just spend the night in Manhattan and leave in the morning."

"My husband would not want me running up a hotel bill by staying here."

"I'd hope he'd be more concerned that his wife is safe and secure at a stable location rather than on the highway by herself in the middle of the night," Hudson huffed, shaking his head. "Besides, if you think I'm going to let you drive back tonight, you must be suffering from exhaustion."

Karli sat down and put her head back in frustration. "I don't have time to be looking for a hotel room—"

Hudson spread his arms out. "Good thing my office is right across the street from a hotel. Problem solved."

Karli looked at him as if he were crazy. "Not that I don't have the money, but that place is like staying in a palace. I'm sorry, but I can't see frivolously throwing away eight hundred dollars for one night's sleep."

"Who said you had to pay anything?"

Karli stood up again, shaking her head. "You will not pay for my room there. No. Absolutely not."

Hudson laughed. "Okay, I won't, and you're still staying."

When she arched her eyebrows, Hudson gathered their things and motioned for her to come with him. They left the building and walked across the street. When they entered the hotel, he led her to the elevators, and they stepped on one together.

Karli turned to him. "Hudson, what are you doing? We bypassed the front desk. We don't even know if they have a vacancy, and I'm too old and too scared of jail to sneak into a hotel room."

Hudson burst into teary-eyed laughter. "That's funny. But don't worry. You don't have to pay, nor are you going to jail."

He pulled out a card, stuck it in a slot on the elevator's panel, punched in a code, and then pressed the letter *P*.

"The penthouse? Why would you reserve the penthouse? Did you plan on staying here?" Karli asked suspiciously, folding her arms.

Hudson shook his head. "No, I planned on leaving to go home, but I'm not chancing the FDR. And I didn't have to reserve the penthouse, because I own the penthouse. I own the hotel," he explained as the elevator doors opened.

They stepped off and Karli realized they were on a floor with a single suite. He put the key in the door, opened it, and allowed Karli to walk inside the penthouse first.

Karli paused in the doorway. She was used to the finer things in life. Her parents were well off. She was on the smaller side of rich, between Michael's salary and her own, but this . . . this was wealth. Hudson was like Bill Gates.

Karli gasped as she took slow steps inside the suite. "Oh my God. Hudson, this is amazing," she said in wonderment. Then she shook her head. "No, I can't do this. I can't be in a hotel . . . your hotel . . . your hotel suite . . . with you."

Hudson turned to the left, then the right. "Seriously, Karli, look at this place. We don't even have to be in the same room if you don't want to be. The amenities are endless. There are three bedrooms, three bathrooms, two living areas, a balcony with a view, and . . . okay, well, only one kitchen, but we literally do not have to be in the same space at the same time. This place spans the entire top floor of the hotel."

Karli bit her lip and began to walk around, admiring the exquisite trim and molding on the walls, the lighting, the paintings, the furniture, and mostly the alluring floor-to-ceiling windows with custom window seating. Hudson removed his scarf and his blazer and draped them on a chair as he watched her move about, her Louboutins gracefully stabbing the floor with each step. She moved to the massive wall of floor-to-ceiling windows in the larger of the two living areas as night began to fall. The view of the city from this vantage point was breathtaking, unlike any she'd ever seen.

So intrigued with the view, she said, "I'll call my husband to let him know what's going on."

"Good. I'm going to change," Hudson said, and then he disappeared into a bedroom.

Karli called Michael to explain what was happening, and he agreed that she should stay in Manhattan for the night. They said their good-byes, and Karli placed her phone on a nearby table, slid off her pumps, and stood barefoot, never taking her gaze off the view from the floor-to-ceiling windows. The skyline and the city lights were mesmerizing. She'd seen the city from high up many times before, but never like this.

"It's gorgeous," she whispered, placing her hand on a windowpane.

"Yes, it is," Hudson said softly. "It's what I mean when I say I see what others don't—"

"What goes beyond the matrix of others' thought processes," she whispered, intercepting his words.

Hudson slowly walked over to Karli. She looked gorgeous in her wrap dress, which clung to every inch and curve of her beautiful body. From her springy curls to her beautiful manicured toes, she was simply divine.

His heartbeat quickened as he got closer. He placed his hand on the pane beside hers, and they took in the soft lights of the skyline as distant lightning and soft, thunderclaps seemed to summon rain. Their breathing grew shallow as raindrops began to streak down the window, and Karli could feel the heat radiating from him.

Leaning in close, he murmured, "See? It's the inner beauty of the thing that I care about."

"Among the hustle and bustle, the bright lights of the big city, this is the calm," Karli mused aloud, lost in the view.

"This is peace. That is the inner beauty of it. In the center of chaos lies peace," Hudson added softly.

Feeling lost in his words, Karli turned, and Hudson hovered in front of her, with both hands on the glass pane, one on either side of her head. Their chests swiftly rose and fell in sync from anxiety and anticipation.

She swallowed hard, staring at those intense crystal blue orbs. "I can't, Hudson. I'm married. My husband . . ."

"Is a damn fool," Hudson said, finishing for her. "Not for letting you stay here, but for not loving the inner beauty of you. For not appreciating the one thing that men—men like me—crave."

"He appreciates me. He loves me," she protested weakly.

"Tell me how. For two months, I've been with you nearly every day, and not once has he called to check on you. Not once has he invited you to lunch or shown up to say hello. The only interaction you've had with him in front of me was tonight, and the conversation was so short, you would think you were checking in at the office. If you were mine, there's no way in hell you would've gotten off that phone with me."

He caressed the side of her face, and she leaned into his touch. He went on. "I would've stayed on the phone with you all night, making you cum just from the sound of my voice, leaving you so on fire that you'd rush out the next morning just to get to the real thing. You're married to him, but he's not taking care of you. Let me take care of you."

Karli was nearly hyperventilating from his words and the dangerous level of attraction she was feeling. "But, but I'm married."

Hudson smiled wickedly. "The only thing saying that is your mouth. No part of you believes that." He touched her eyebrow. "Your eyes," he said, sliding his fingers down her chest. "Your body." He leaned in close to her neck. "Even your scent." His lips grazed her ear as he whispered, "I'm not going to do anything you don't want. If you still want to be his wife, you can, but do what you need to do for you. Let me take care of you, because I definitely want you to take care of me."

He kissed her lips softly, then pulled back and looked into her eyes. Karli wrapped her arms around his neck and pulled him into a deep kiss. Hungrily, he unfastened the tie of her dress, and as the garment fell off, she reached for the waistband of his sweats. He stepped out of them and pulled his shirt over his head.

Still kissing her lips as they hungrily tasted each other, he slid his fingers into her thong and then slid it off as he lowered himself to his knees. Karli couldn't believe what was happening, but she didn't fight it when Hudson lifted one of her legs onto his shoulder and planted his face in her neatly shaven essence. As Hudson's tongue sensually connected with her love button, the fight in her was completely gone, and she gave in to the desire that she'd been desperately trying to ignore. Her juices flowed as his tongue encircled her throbbing bud. She held his head tightly in place, savoring every second of pleasure he gave.

"Mmm, Hudson," she moaned, running her fingers through his curly mess of blond hair.

"My pussy tastes so sweet," he groaned in ecstasy.

Karli's wetness flowed like the Hudson River into his awaiting mouth. He stood, then picked her up by her waist and pushed her back against the windowpane. She pulled down the cups of her bra and allowed her melons to topple out. Hudson captured each one in his mouth, savored every inch of them as her moans grew stronger and louder.

He lifted his head up and whispered, "One moment, baby," then surveyed the room. He turned quickly and reached for his blazer, which was draped on a nearby chair. After pulling out his wallet, he retrieved a gold wrapper from it. Bracing her against the window, he protected his massive shaft, then slid into her awaiting ocean.

Karli gasped at his girth. He was as thick as her husband, but he had to be at least an inch longer. Comfortably inside her, like a hand in a glove, he swirled methodically inside her. Her back lightly thumped against the window, taking turns with the rolling thunder and the rain. With each stroke, their passion grew to unimaginable heights. Karli's insides began to tremble as a monstrous orgasm built in her core. Feeling her impending climax, Hudson gripped her hips and thrust longer and deeper into her center, so deep it appeared as if they were conjoined. Karli gripped his muscular back, digging her nails deep, as her toes curled and her legs shook uncontrollably.

"Ooh, Hudson. Hudson. Oh, Hudson," she roared. Sweat beaded down her forehead, and tears cascaded out of her eyes.

Hudson reached behind him and unwrapped her legs from his waist. He held her steady on her weak legs and then turned her around and pressed the front of her body against the pane. Karli placed one foot on the cushioned window seat as they interlocked fingers, and he slid back into his new place called home and continued his masterful motions with endless pleasure. Karli was on a euphoric high as she continued to receive everything Hudson delivered.

He slowly massaged her luscious mounds with his hands and then pulled her hips to bounce her against him, making her derriere jiggle. The sight heightened Hudson's arousal, and Karli felt him stiffen and extend a bit more. Arching her back, she dropped her head down a bit and threw her back into him. Hudson let out a deep groan from the pleasure Karli was giving him. He was skilled, but her love nest was taking him to a place of ecstasy he had never been to, and he pushed past to her soft, gushy center. A deep orgasm, one Karli had never felt before, overtook her, and her body released a powerful rain shower against Hudson.

"Oh God. Shit! Hudson. Hudson, take it. Daddy, it's yours," she moaned sexily.

"Ooh, Karli, baby. Oh, baby."

Hudson could no longer restrain himself and he buried himself deep in her crevices. Then, with a deep growl, he released so hard, he had to brace against her to keep from falling over.

Barely able to move, Hudson stood still until every wave of pleasure had passed. When he could finally move, he walked a few paces and pulled over a big cushioned chair. He sat down in it and pulled her into his arms, and they leaned back together, holding each other, and stared at the view of the city through the rain and listened to the rise and fall of each other's breathing before they drifted off to sleep.

Several feelings washed over Karli that she hadn't felt in a long time. Calm, rest, pleasure, and satisfaction. When the light filtering into the room awoke her from her restful slumber, she stretched, feeling the plush bed and pillows.

"Mmm," she moaned, turning on her side.

Suddenly, she remembered the previous night and where she was, and she bolted upright, clutching the sheet in front of her. Instinctively, she turned to look at the time on the clock. It read 8:32 a.m.

"Shit!" she said frantically, about to throw the covers off her body.

"Calm down, Karli." Hudson's voice resonated from the opposite corner of the room.

Karli jumped and turned to look at him. He was sitting in a chair, clad only in a pair of sweatpants, and was holding a cup of tea and gazing at her with those brilliant crystal blues. The red marks on his chiseled chest, his messy blond curls, and his five o'clock shadow told the tale of the intense, long night before.

"Calm down? Are you serious? I haven't been home. Oh my God! My husband. He's probably freaking out. What the hell did I do?" she yelled in a panic. She looked around frantically as all the other issues surrounding her night of passion invaded her mind. "I was supposed to be at work a half an hour ago, and I have no clothes except the ones from yesterday." She jumped up from the bed and scurried toward the door. "And how the hell did I even end up in bed? We fell asleep in the chair."

Hudson placed his tea down on a little table by the chair and met her before she bolted out the door. Gently yet sternly holding her by the shoulders, Hudson forced her to stare into his eyes. "Calm down, Karli."

She exhaled. "You don't understand—"

"I called Jack and let him know that your phone was dead and that we had an early morning meeting. Your phone rang only once, and I didn't answer it, nor did I check it. I assume your husband just wants to know if you're okay. You can tell him you overslept, which is not a lie. You got in the bed because I woke up in the middle of the night and placed you there. And I took the liberty of having the hotel boutique bring you up a pantsuit. Size ten, right?"

She nodded.

He went on. "So please calm down. Everything is under control."

After walking back to the bed, with the sheet still wrapped around her naked body, she sat down and dropped her head in her hands. Her internal struggle was intense. She had never done anything like this in her life. She'd prided herself on doing the right things, and now here she was with Hudson. What bothered her the most was that while she was worried about her husband and concerned about her marriage, being with Hudson felt good. It felt as if Hudson had breathed life into her at a time when she felt dead inside and unwanted. Sadly, the pleasure felt just as good to her as the guilt felt bad.

Hudson sat down beside her and pulled her hand into his. "Are you okay? How was last night?"

Karli scoffed. "I'm worried about the state of my marriage, and you're asking me about last night?" she said, side eyeing him in disbelief.

He nodded, with a smirk. "Yep. Yes, I am." He rubbed the back of her hand. "So how was it?"

She shrugged, tears threatening her eyes. "Hudson, I'm a married woman. Last night wasn't even supposed to happen." She sighed, looking into those deep ocean-blue eyes, and for some reason, a wave of calm washed over her. "But I can't deny that last night was . . . You know that last night was amazing."

Biting his lip, he caressed the side of her face. "So if you enjoyed it, then why change it? You're covered at work. You can check in to make your husband feel better and spend the day with me. I can make last night last all day."

Karli groaned deeply. The struggle was already beyond real, and now he was tempting her with forbidden fruit. Fruit that she'd already tasted and enjoyed. Surely,

Hudson was igniting something inside her that she'd never known existed. These feelings, emotions, and pleasures were begging her to let him set her free, but her heart felt guilty. Rational thoughts mixed with irrational emotions was not a winning combination.

"Hudson, last night may have been something I wanted, but I can't do this. I can't trade my marriage for something that's meaningless," she told him. "I mean, you're only attracted to what's behind closed doors, and I can't sell myself short as your honey pot for hire."

Hudson stood, placed his hands in his pockets, and hovered in front of her. "Karli, my attraction to you was instant. When I walked into that conference room and saw your high-powered suit and those Louboutins on your feet, your hazel eyes and beautiful body, everything inside me lit up. But I didn't approach you, and do you want to know why?"

When she nodded, he continued. "Because you were married, for one. And because I am a multimillionaire, a good-looking woman comes my way every fifteen minutes, sometimes out of want, most times out of need. I say that to convey that if looks were all that mattered to me, then you would not be the woman in my bed right now. The hotel desk clerk could be in my bed, that cute office assistant of yours could be in my bed, and the hotel boutique owner could be in my bed. Lacking a woman in my bed is not my problem, and a honey pot for hire you are not and never will be. I'm attracted to what makes you shine from the inside. The way you asked me about me. The way you're concerned if I made it home after our late-night meetings. Or when you make it a point to bring hot tea, because you know I like it. Or the way you fight for a marriage and a man who hasn't even called yet to see if you're okay. Yes, I lied when I said that I hadn't checked, but damn that."

He paused for a moment and took a deep breath. Then he went on. "Your intellect, your fire and passion for what you do, and the way you care are what attracts me to you. If I have to get used to the fact that this is all there is, I can try my damnedest to do that, but know the reason why first. And to clear up the 'behind closed doors' comment, every woman I have ever dated was black, because that is what I prefer, and if I ever go outside the confines of the four walls with you or any other brown-skinned beauty, I will definitely not be ashamed of that." He stood back to allow Karli to make her decision.

Karli couldn't help herself and tried to stifle a grin, until she couldn't and laughed aloud. Although Hudson was being dead serious, he couldn't help but laugh with her.

"I'm sorry." She put her hand up. "That just explains a helluva lot."

Realizing what she meant, he kneeled in front of her so that they were eye to eye. "You like the motion in that stroke, huh?"

Karli giggled. "Can't deny that." She grew serious and looked at him sorrowfully. "I'm sorry." Karli got up, and Hudson moved to the side and retrieved her cell for her. She unlocked it and found that the only missed calls were from work and Catrina, and the only text she'd received was from Stacy, who'd texted her when she got home.

Disappointed, she sighed and sent a text to Michael, telling him that she was okay and that she would see him later on. She'd expected Hudson to be wrong about her husband not contacting her, figuring that he hadn't recognized the text or he'd overlooked Michael's call from the preview. Yet he was right. There were many things that she could say were lacking in her marriage these days, but the foundational values—love, caring, protectiveness—were ones she had been holding on to.

Even if everything else was failing in her marriage, she had thought she could at least fall back on that foundation. But knowing that her husband hadn't even been concerned enough to check on her, despite the fact that he was aware that she had unexpectedly spent the night in another city, away from their bed, made her feel that their marriage had hit an all-time low. The foundation was officially cracked, and she was unsure if there was any coming back from that.

Usually, it wouldn't bother Hudson if a female wanted to walk away. It meant fewer complications and less drama, and in this situation, he definitely didn't need the drama. However, watching her preparing to leave him did something to him. Hudson couldn't believe the power that she held over him, and she didn't even know it. Surely, it was something he couldn't reveal to her.

After some deep contemplation, Karli sat her phone down on the nightstand and walked to the doorway, still clutching the sheet around her. She leaned against the doorframe that separated the bedroom from the larger living area and peered out the wall of windows across the room, taking in the view. So many things were in chaos, but one thing was surely crystal clear. She would no longer fight against the one thing that she was sure of. She needed her peace in the midst of the storm.

Looking back and seeing Hudson with his head down, she smiled. "I wonder what the view is like during the day," she said aloud.

Hudson peered up. "What?"

After turning her back to him, she looked over her shoulder at him. "You said you could make last night last all day, so I wonder what the view is like during the day. There is only one way to find out," she said devilishly as she dropped the sheet on the floor and walked into the living area.

Hudson joined her at the windows, pulled her to him by the waist, and kissed the nape of her neck. She moaned and reached back and caressed the side of his face.

"Let me make—"

"Hudson," she said sexily, interrupting whatever he was about to say.

"Yes, baby?"

"I need you to fuck me," she muttered breathlessly.

Hudson groaned and instantly grew rock solid. Karli turned to face him and helped him slide out of his sweats as they kissed feverishly. As soon as the protector was on tight, Hudson turned her around and guided her over to the window seat while kissing her neck and shoulders. He gently pushed her forward so that she was kneeling on the window seat. Smoothing his hands across her bodacious behind, he gave her three gentle love taps as she moaned with excited anticipation.

He leaned toward her and slid inside. As they united, they both had to pause and let the moment soak in. It was electrifying to both of them.

Hudson leaned forward and whispered, "I'm about to beat it up."

Karli braced herself as he slid easily in and out and then increased his speed, gripping handfuls of her backside and power driving his way to home plate. The view made her feel free to enjoy the moment, and though she was full monty, no one could actually see her. Her body rippled with pleasure as Hudson made her booty bounce in delight. Squeezing her eyes tight, she bit on her lip as Hudson delivered hard thrusting pleasure and tapped roughly on her G-spot. Gripping the seat cushion with all her might, she knew that his powerful dives would soon make her come undone. It felt too good to hold on to. Karli began to feel her pressure mount, and Hudson thickened. As they released together, they let out wails that surely would've made the entire hotel vibrate if they were not on the penthouse floor.

Collapsing into a nearby chair, Hudson panted heavily and eyed Karli as she turned and sat on the seat facing him.

"Karli. My Karli." He grinned at her.

She leaned forward, lifted the arm on which he wore his watch, and peered at the time. It was 10:00 a.m. She looked up at him with a sneaky and sexy look in her eyes.

He smiled at her. "What's on your mind?"

Biting her lip, she held up three fingers. "Round three?" she asked.

Hudson winked at her and waved her over. "Come over here."

Chapter 15

"So I say to you, who here is so perfect that they can cast the first stone?" Pastor Monroe asked. "That's right. None of you. Do you want to know what most Christians' hang-up is? They get so caught up in religion, in being 'Christians,' that they forget the purpose is to be Christlike. No one is perfect, not even Christians. We just accept God's perfect love of our imperfect selves. So if we ask God, who is omnipotent, to accept us, then who are we to not be loving and accepting of others? How dare we, with our imperfect selves, claim self-righteousness? Are we to be examples? Yes. But we have to remember that we are examples of Christlike behavior, not a replacement for Christ."

Michael zoned out as he listened to the words of his pastor. His message resonated so clearly with him. Here he was, mistreating his wife and judging her when she'd never mistreated or judged him. Last weekend had been a sexual disaster, and it seemed that this week they had only gotten worse. Ever since this weekend had started, Karli seemed to be avoiding him altogether. He knew it was his fault, and he had to find a way to make it right. She wasn't even at church with him again today. She'd claimed she was tired, but he knew better. She didn't want to be around him. How could he blame her? It was time to let it go and get his wife back. When he knelt at the altar, he received prayer, because God knows he was going to need it.

When Michael arrived home from church, he found Karli sitting on the bed in some leggings and a long T-shirt, watching television. She looked up at him, shocked that he was standing in their bedroom, since he still had not moved back into it.

Not knowing what to do, she quickly dismissed his presence by focusing back on the program she was watching. Michael stood there, flabbergasted that she'd truly dismissed him. He pulled off his suit jacket and tie, threw them on the foot of the bed, and stood in front of the television.

Karli threw up her hands. "Seriously, are we getting this petty now?" Rolling her eyes, she reached over to the nightstand and picked up a poetry book entitled *Timeless Ink*, which she'd been reading lately. Before she delved into the book, she looked up at him, unable to resist giving him the third degree. "What are you even doing in here, Michael? Your room is down the hall."

Calmly, he held his hands out to her. "I don't want to argue, Karli—"

"Or talk," she snapped, then refocused on the book.

He nodded. "I deserved that."

Karli placed the book down on the bed and massaged her temples. "Why are you here, Michael?"

He took Karli in and realized that in a few short months, he didn't even know his wife anymore. Sure, she was the same person, but the closeness, the warmth, the love, none of it was there. Her eyes were so cold to him. It was like looking at ice.

Knowing what he had done to them, he allowed uncontrollable tears to well up in his eyes, and he began to sob profusely. He fell to his knees and wailed out in pain.

Instinctively, Karli hopped off the bed, unsure of what was going on. She ran over to him and knelt down beside him on the floor. "Michael, what's wrong? Oh God. What happened?"

"I . . . I . . . am . . . so . . . sor . . . sorry," he struggled to get out. He reached up and hugged her tightly. "I miss you. I love you, and I'm sorry about what I did to us. I'm sorry. We can talk. Whatever you want. I just want you to forgive me. Please forgive me. Please take me back, Karli. I can't. I can't."

Karli held him as he sobbed in her chest. The sincerity in his voice filled her with guilt. True, his actions had driven the wedge between them, but her actions had kept it there. How could she not forgive him when she definitely had done something she needed forgiveness for? Just two days ago, she'd been in another man's bed.

She lifted his face to hers, and all the hurt and pain just seemed to flow from him. Her heart melted as she palmed his face.

"Please, Karli. I was wrong. I need you back. I need my old thing back."

She nodded. "Okay, it's okay, Michael. I forgive you for that. We don't have to talk about it. We'll let it go. All of it."

Those words were music to his ears as he leaned on her and poured all his tears into her. She held him in her arms as they sat on the floor, rocking back and forth. When his tears subsided, they got up, he changed into his sweats, and they lay in their bed and held each other for the rest of the day, in silence.

Chapter 16

Sitting at her desk, going over paperwork for another client, Karli let out a nervous sigh when her cell phone buzzed. It was another phone call from Hudson. Suffice it to say, she'd been ignoring him for the past two weeks. She figured that if it were truly work related, he'd call the office. Since he had no reason to, given the recent success of his campaigns, she knew he was calling because she'd ignored all ten voice mails, fifteen emails, twenty texts, and now thirty phone calls from him.

When she'd parted ways from Hudson late that Friday afternoon, they'd vowed to keep in contact, but she'd explained that she was going to try to limit their fling to that one time. He'd promised that he wouldn't pressure her, but he'd also told her that he'd be available whenever she was ready, because he felt that she wouldn't be able to hold true to her own demands, and he'd even given her the spare elevator key card for the penthouse as added assurance.

She hadn't let on that she felt he was correct in his assessment, because she wanted to prove herself wrong, and if she couldn't resist him, there was no harm in making him sweat about it. She had pondered what she would do the next time they were face-to-face, and after a hot and steamy phone conversation on Saturday, she'd been convinced that she wouldn't be able to resist the sexual tension between them. The only issue she'd been having trouble deciding on was when she would give in. That was until Sunday afternoon.

She'd all but written off her marriage until Michael fell down on his knees in tears. It was as if all the love that she ever had for him had rushed back into her like a tidal wave, and she had known in that moment she couldn't leave him. She had to fight for her marriage, and now that she knew Michael wanted the same, Hudson had to go. It was better to cut it off before either one of them was too vested in a side relationship that was doomed for failure, anyway. But she damn sure missed their sex.

She and Michael had not made love, because they were trying to learn to talk again and be friends. They were working on them, so while she missed the loving that Hudson had given her, she refused to get sucked into another whirlwind tryst with that man. She'd be lying if she said she didn't think of him often. Of course, he didn't make it any easier with the constant attempts to reach out to her. However, she owed it to her husband to make their marriage work, and work it would not if she answered even one personal call from Hudson. She was weak for that man. Too weak. Until she could build up her resilience, she had to stay clear of any personal contact with him, and the only way to do that was to flat-out ignore him.

As she sat there signing off on paperwork, a knock came on her office door. "Come in," she called out as she stood and turned to pull out some files in her filing cabinet.

The door opened and shut, and when no one said anything, Karli turned around to see who it was. Hudson was standing in her office.

"How in the—"

"I told your receptionist that we had an impromptu meeting. Since I'm your number one client, she believed me and told me it was clear to come to your office. Why have you been ignoring my calls, Karli?"

A full gamut of emotions coursed through Karli as she stood there, stunned and frozen in place. The mere sight of Hudson made her body pulse with an excitement that, at one time, only Michael had been able to elicit. So much so that it scared her. She was torn between wanting to run into his arms and wanting to run for the hills. Just as quickly, her emotions turned into anger. Someone was going to be held responsible for this unwarranted assault on her emotions.

Fuming, Karli threw the files on her desk and headed straight out of her office to confront her new receptionist. Hudson knew what she was about to do and stopped her by grabbing her by the waist and pulling her into his arms.

"Oh no, you don't. I put her in this position. Don't hold her accountable for my dishonest actions." Lifting her chin, he asked gently, "Why are you ignoring me? Why are you running from me?"

It took the strength of Job, but somehow Karli cleared her throat and found the courage to step back out of his embrace. She folded her arms and looked nervously at him and back down at her feet. "Look, Hudson, if it's not work related, I can't speak with you. Please stop contacting me unless it's about business."

Hudson took a step back. Normally, he wouldn't care this much about a woman. He wasn't a player, but having a woman was the least of his problems. That, in turn, was the problem. He didn't want just any woman. He wanted Karli. She'd done something to him that he couldn't shake. He knew she was right, but he couldn't help himself when it came to her. He needed her like he needed air. The past two weeks without her had almost driven him insane from worry and jealousy. She consumed his every thought, and now she was pushing him away and out of her life for good, and he didn't know why. Well, he knew why, but it was hard to understand, because he knew she wanted the same thing, and it was even harder to accept.

Getting choked up, he pleaded with her. "Please, Karli. I know I have no rights to you, but please don't ask me to let go of you."

Running her hand through her hair, she shook her head. "I can't, Hudson. I'm married, and my husband and I want to work on our marriage. I made my vows to him, not you. I owe him, not you. I'm sorry to drag you into my mess. I'm sorry to get you involved, but I need you to understand that I'm not available to you like that anymore. We had what we had, and it was good, but my marriage is what's real. Please respect that."

The words cut deeper than any physical wound ever could. Thick emotion filled Hudson's throat, and he fought hard against the burning sensation in his eyes. He couldn't knock the fact that she was trying to be loyal. But he felt her loyalty was misplaced, but who was he to tell her that?

Hudson took another step back, trying unsuccessfully to mask his hurt. "I apologize, Karli. I will leave you alone unless it's business related. Have a nice day and a nice life." With that, he turned to leave.

Karli reached out to him and touched his arm. He withdrew from her, unable to control his hurt and disappointment.

"I'm sorry, Hudson. I swear, I really am," she said in a low voice.

Taking a deep breath, Hudson turned to face her before he opened the door. "No you're not, but it's okay. You belong to him, so don't concern yourself with me. I'll check in with Carl and Stacy from now on. Goodbye, Karli."

With that, he opened the door and left. Karli plopped down in her seat and cried a good cry. She was so wrong on so many levels. All she wanted was to get back to that happy place in her life, and she prayed that her marriage would work out. Yet she couldn't help but feel that maybe a slice of her happiness had just walked out the door.

How did things get so messy and confusing? she thought as her mind drifted back to the look of sheer devastation on Hudson's face. She had done only what she felt was right—what she had vowed to do—but now she'd successfully crushed Hudson in the process. She loved her husband, but she felt hurt that she might have misled Hudson in some way.

Chapter 17

"I'm so glad you and Michael came over for dinner tonight. I've been feeling so bad about the whole debacle at your announcement dinner, and I know you all have been going through it," Karli's mom said as she and Karli prepped the salads.

Karli looked up. "And just how do you know that?"

Her mother stopped chopping up the tomatoes and looked at her daughter. A flushed look came over her face. "Catrina told me. Please don't be upset with her."

Shaking her head, Karli continued chopping the eggs to place in the salad. "It's okay now. We're getting back to us."

"I was worried, and so were Michael's parents—"

Karli shot her a glare. "Ma! You told them?"

"Don't take that tone with me, young lady," she huffed, and Karli recoiled. "No, Michael confessed to them about your marital issues, and they called me to see if we knew what was going on. I figured I'd interfered enough, so I wasn't going to butt in."

Karli laughed on the inside. That was code for her dad told her mom to leave them alone. When it came to other people's business, her parents were polar opposites. Her dad had his hands full trying to keep her mom in line, but he managed to do so, for the most part; and if anyone appreciated that right now, it was Karli. Her mother was the best at getting information, and the last thing she needed was for her mom to get wind of Hudson.

"So how is your new position coming along?" Karli's mom asked.

Speak of the devil.

"It's going great. My accounts have been extremely successful."

"As they should be," Michael said, entering the kitchen. "She's been burning the midnight oil, like, literally every day."

"Really?" Karli's mom said with surprise.

Michael nodded, picked up a cucumber slice, and stuffed it in his mouth. "Even had to spend the night in the city a month or so ago, as she'd been working so late."

Karli's mom looked over at Karli with a raised eyebrow. "Really?"

Karli shook her head and put her hand up. "I worked late, and there was a bad wreck on the FDR. That's the reason why. It's no big deal."

Her mom shrugged and shot a side glance at Karli.

Karli shrugged and began dumping the remaining toppings into the salad bowl.

"Baby, will you and Dad set the plates?" Karli asked Michael.

Michael bent down and pecked her on the lips. "Anything for you, baby."

Once he left the kitchen, Karli turned, and her mom was standing there, holding a bowl in her hands. She gave Karli a blank stare.

"Here. Make sure this is on the table. And make sure that work is not interfering in your marriage."

After taking the bowl, Karli walked out and muttered, "I already did."

Dinner with her parents was great. As usual, Karli and her dad went back and forth about politics and work, and then her dad and Michael got into their usual banter about football. As the men enjoyed themselves, Karli helped her mother clean up the kitchen.

"So how are things really going between you and Michael?" her mom asked.

Karli shrugged as she rinsed a plate. "It's going. Like I said earlier, we're trying to get back to us. It takes time."

Her mom nodded. "That it does, but if there's one thing I know, it's that that man loves himself some you. I'm not saying not to take your time with things. I'm just saying to remember the love."

Rolling her eyes, Karli turned to face her. "I do remember the love. That's why we're trying."

Her mom sighed. "You're so much like your father, so rational. Love isn't rational, Karli. Love just is. Remember that."

Karli decided not to say anything more, and they finished up in silence.

Although dinner had been great, Karli felt drained afterward. Her mother always had a way of prying that kept her on edge. With all that had happened with Hudson, she really couldn't tolerate the third degree from her mom. As soon as she got the opportunity, she was definitely going to talk to her little hummingbird friend about keeping her business to herself.

While Michael handled a last-minute business call, she decided to jump in the shower. As the water from the showerheads cascaded down her back, her mind roamed back to Hudson. She tried to block her thoughts of him, but the ache in her honey pot sent thoughts of him crashing into her mind. She hadn't been with him in a month, hadn't seen him privately in a month, and had talked to him only twice, both times in a group setting and about business, but the treasure between her legs remembered him like it was yesterday. It didn't help that she and Michael had agreed not to have sex in order to reestablish their relationship and closeness. Right now, the only closeness she needed was the warmth of girth between her legs.

As thoughts of Hudson consumed her, she toyed with her nipples, gliding her fingers back and forth over them as they hardened. Imagining his lips on her breasts, she cupped her left one, tilted it upward to meet her mouth, and sucked gently on it. A low moan escaped her lips as she imagined it was Hudson's mouth encircling her aching melons. Cupping her breasts and moving from the left one to the right, she continued her playful taste test as her flower began to thump between her legs.

"Mmm," she moaned, closing her eyes and leaning against the tile wall of the shower. After propping her foot on the shower seat and bracing one hand on the glass, she placed her free hand between her thighs and swirled her forefinger around her bud. The motion enhanced her senses, and she stuck her middle finger inside her wetness.

"Ooh . . . aah," she moaned softly, working the middle.

She removed her finger, placed it in her mouth, and suckled it. Her juices tasted so good to her. An image of Hudson appeared in her mind, and she inserted three fingers and began working her center rapidly. Her climax rumbled as she began creaming, and her essence dripped down her hand. Her breathing turned hard and labored as she felt a mini explosion about to happen.

She let out a low growl, then hissed, "Hudson," softly as she reached her peak.

Her eyes were closed so tight that she was beginning to see spots. She carefully put her foot down to balance her weakened legs. She was literally delirious from satisfaction, but now she was truly on fire. She hurriedly finished her shower. She had to clear her mind, because thoughts of Hudson had her ready to go AWOL from her marriage, and she couldn't do that to Michael.

After moisturizing her skin, she wrapped herself in a towel and went into the closet to put on a fresh pajama set. She didn't even hear anything when Michael entered the closet. He walked up to her and kissed the side of her neck.

"Hmm, what a beautiful sight to see," he whispered in her ear.

Instantly, her bud thumped again, and though she knew it was wrong, she would have to make love to Michael tonight to clear her head, satisfy her urges, and solidify their marriage. Without warning, she turned, dropped her towel, pulled him to her, and kissed him hungrily.

Michael moaned against her. "Baby, not that I don't want this," he said as he watched her unbuckling his pants, "but I thought we were going to wait."

"The wait is over." She giggled huskily as his pants fell to his ankles. Before he could say another word, she pulled his face to hers and captured his lips in a deep kiss filled with longing.

Michael kicked out of his pants, getting sucked up into the moment with her. His breathing turned rapid as Karli wrapped her arms around his neck. After he placed his hands around her butt and picked her up, Karli wrapped her legs around his waist, and they continued their feverish kissing. He carried her into their bedroom, placed Karli on her back on the bed, and hurriedly began to take off his sweater and boxer briefs. Karli decided to give her man a little show, and she spread her legs and began massaging her clit as he watched with lustful eyes.

"Karli," he said, his voice deep. "What are you doing?"

"Giving you a show." She giggled sexily. "You like?"

Inhaling, he could only nod as he peeled off his remaining clothes and climbed in the bed with his wife. Holding her close, he traced his finger along her jawline. "I love you, baby. I'm gonna make love—"

Karli interrupted him by placed her index finger on his lips. She replaced it with a sensual kiss and skillfully flipped Michael on his back. There would be time for lovemaking. Right now, she just needed a good ride on his stick. Something she'd never gotten a chance to experience. She straddled him, and Michael gripped her hands to stop her from slipping him inside her.

"Karli, I want to make love to you. What are you doing?"

"Call it making love, Michael," she said, getting a little irritated. "Let me do this. Let's try something new."

He shook his head. "New, but not this, Karli. We can do something else. Foreplay or something."

Karli snaked her hands around his neck. "Come on, baby. It might be fun."

Michael removed her hands from around his neck. "No, Karli, let's just do our thing. It's our first time in so long. Let's keep it sweet and special."

Karli pulled her arms back and rubbed her forehead. "Okay, what is your problem with any of this? I mean really, Michael."

Michael moved her off him. "Are we seriously going to have a discussion about this?" He got out of the bed and looked back at her.

She threw her hands on her hips. "Yes, we are. I need to know what the problem is so we can try to get back to us."

"That's the problem," he hollered. "This ain't us! You're fondling yourself and wanting to do all kinds of freaky stuff. I like freaky stuff. I'm a man, but I didn't marry a freak. I married a woman. You're my wife, Karli, not some ho I wanna beat down!"

"You had no problem treating me like a ho that night you demanded and took sex from me like I was a trick!" she yelled, jumping out of bed.

Michael shook his head. "Wow. So we're back to this. I've apologized, and you said you'd forgiven me and let it go, but now you want to throw it in my face just because I'm telling you that's how I don't want to treat you."

Karli threw up her hands. "I did forgive you for it, Michael. It's not about that. There's a difference when I want to satisfy you. You're the one making a big deal out of me wanting to please you. I'm your wife, Michael. That's my job."

Michael sighed and approached her, then pulled her to him by the waist. "You do please me. That's why I said you don't need to do all of that. Let's just do our thing. This isn't us. Let me put it on you and knock you out the way only I know how to do."

How could she tell her husband that she wasn't satisfied? That she was sexually frustrated? She wanted to be with him, but that old-school missionary style was old and tired. She needed to feel wanted and like she was pleasing both of their desires to be fulfilled. It bothered her that other women he'd been with had gotten to experiment and try new things with her husband, but she had never even gone for a ride on his magic stick. He cherished her so much that he was smothering her.

Feeling as though her pleas would be ignored, she simply agreed, and Michael smiled brightly and kissed her with vigor. He picked her up and laid her back on the bed. Admiring his wife, he lay on top of her and slid into home. Karli could only close her eyes and imagine that she was enjoying it, so that she could satisfy her husband. Too bad it was unfulfilling for her.

Michael rubbed his eyes as the constant vibrating of his cell startled him. Focusing, he reached for the phone just as memories of last night invaded his mind. He smiled as he thought of the passionate love he'd made to his wife.

"Yeah?" he answered groggily.

"From the sounds of it, you're still asleep, so I guess I should assume you have no plans to come in today, right?" Bryson asked. "Sounds like you had a good night." He chuckled.

Michael jumped up and looked at the clock. It was 9:30 a.m. He hit his forehead and looked over at Karli's empty side of the bed. Apparently, she was up and out and had left him in bed, asleep. He smiled to himself and lay back against the pillows.

"Yeah, man. My bad. I'll be in at about noon. Tell Stephanie to reschedule my appointments today."

"Who's your man?" Bryson quipped. "It's already done. And you didn't answer my question about last night."

"That's 'cause you didn't ask one," Michael joked as he rubbed his hand down his face. "All I'm gonna say is Karli and I are all good."

Bryson howled. "My man! You're back in there!"

They laughed in unison.

"So where is she?" Bryson asked. "I don't want to wake up Sleeping Beauty."

Michael sighed. "She left for work already. I'm just here recuperating."

Bryson paused. "Not knocking your skills, but ain't that supposed to be the other way around?"

"Fu . . . You almost made me lose my religion! *Forget* you, man!" Michael laughed. "You know this new position has her stretched out. Besides, I was putting in a lot of work."

"A'ight! A'ight! I feel you," Bryson joked and then got serious. "Seriously, though, are you sure you two are goody?"

"Yeah, man. We're all good. Karli and Michael are back."

"Good, bro! I'm glad, for real. Listen, get your beauty rest, and I'll see you in a bit."

"Funny! Bye, ninja."

Michael hung up, sat on the edge of the bed, and checked his phone. No texts or calls from Karli. Not even a note. If she weren't his wife, he'd feel like a one-night stand. He shook his head. After last night he was sure things would get back on track, but he had a sinking feeling that things still weren't quite right between them. He just couldn't get down with this new Karli and wished she'd get back to the wholesome, sweet, demure woman he'd married. Maybe he was tripping because they had been so out of touch lately. Taking a deep breath, he prayed that he was wrong and that everything he'd just told Bryson was the truth.

Chapter 18

Today was the monthly follow-up meeting with Lewis Investments. Karli and her team went over the expectations and the new research for the upcoming campaign with the Lewis team members. Karli was happy that Hudson had chosen to sit this meeting out. After her devastating sexual encounter with her husband a week ago, she was sexually frustrated and on edge. Michael was pleased, but she was losing her sanity, trying not to think of Hudson, so the fact that he wasn't at the meeting calmed her down.

"So unless there are any questions thus far, we can move into the wrap-up portion, and we'll be out of here in ten minutes," Karli said to everyone in the conference room.

Suddenly, the door opened, and in walked Hudson. Lawd, have mercy! He was looking all kinds of fine in a crisp Brioni suit, with diamond cuff links and a silk necktie. He sported a freshly trimmed goatee, neatly cut and slightly spiked blond hair, and his gorgeous blue eyes were shining ever so brightly.

"Pardon my interruption. I just wanted to stop by and get filled in," Hudson said as he walked around the table, shaking everyone's hand. When he got to Karli, he shook her hand, leaned in, and gave her a small embrace. "Karli, good to see you."

He pulled away quickly, but his Armani cologne lingered in Karli's nostrils. Shifting in her seat, she invited

Hudson to sit as she was preparing the wrap-up. He had only a few questions, but every time he asked one, his stare almost bored a hole in Karli. Her honey pot was twitching with each smile he gave and each glance of those crystal blues. She crossed her legs and squeezed tight to keep from climaxing on herself right then and there.

"Sounds great, as usual!" Hudson said as they adjourned the meeting.

Everyone said their good-byes, and Karli asked Hudson if he would stay behind for a moment. He agreed, and everyone else filed out of the conference room.

Biting her lip, she looked at him. "So how have you been?"

Hudson laughed smugly. "What is this?"

Looking confused, Karli asked, "What? What do you mean?"

Hudson cleared his throat and spoke low but clearly. "The last time we actually spoke, you told me to back off and not speak to you unless it was related to business. I respected that, so why are you speaking to me now if it's clearly not about business?"

"I only wanted to check on you." She held up her hands. "I apologize. You're right. I changed our dynamic, so I must adhere to it as well."

Hudson nodded. "Good day, Karli."

"Good day," she said and watched him walk out of the conference room.

Karli returned to her office, but she was no good. She couldn't keep still and could barely contain her composure. She shifted and danced in her desk chair for nearly an hour before she finally picked up the phone.

"Hudson Lewis," he answered on the second ring, obviously not paying attention to the number on his cell phone's screen.

"Hudson, it's Karli."

Holding up his finger, he looked over at his employee. "Sue, give me one moment," he said. Then he moved into an empty office and closed the door.

"Did I forget something?" he asked Karli.

Karli breathed heavily into the phone, squeezing her legs together and chewing on her bottom lip. "I need to see you."

"About work?"

"No."

He sighed. "Karli—"

"I need you, Hudson."

He paused for a moment. "Where?"

"At the view, right now."

"I'm on my way."

As Hudson waited in his penthouse, he paced back and forth. He hated being vulnerable to Karli in this way. She'd been right to let him go, and just when he was beginning to come to terms with her decision, he got a phone call. It excited him and slightly angered him. He didn't want to play with her emotions, and he wasn't going to allow her to play with his. He refused to be at her beck and call when she had explicitly told him to leave her alone. He couldn't take her coming in and out of his life like that. It pissed him off, because Karli was the first woman who had turned on his emotions as well as his loins, and these feelings were for the birds.

He was still practicing his high-and-mighty speech when there was a knock on the door. He answered the door then slipped his hands in his suit pants pockets.

"Karli," he said as he let her inside. He walked away as she stepped inside and closed the door. "I can't keep doing this back-and-forth with you. If you want to be with your husband, then you're going to have to be with him. I won't allow you to treat me like an afterthought," he explained as he finally turned to face her.

His eyes nearly popped out of his head. Karli stood before him, naked as the day she was born. A deep groan escaped his lips as she closed the space between them. Gripping his blond hair in her hands, she brought his face to hers for a succulent kiss.

"You were saying?"

"I . . . uh . . . Karli."

Placing her index finger on his lips, she silenced him. "Hudson, I don't want to talk right now. I promise you we can talk later, but right now, I need you."

That was all that needed to be said. He stared at her with lustful eyes while he removed his suit jacket, and he watched in excitement as she unbuttoned his shirt and pants and removed them for him. As they stood there in all their naked glory, they took a few moments to truly take each other in. A new and unspoken appreciation for their rekindling passed between them.

Without another word, Hudson picked up Karli by her bodacious mounds and carried her to her favorite spot, kissing her neck and lips the entire way.

Before he sat her down, she stopped him. "I want to ride. Can you let me do that?"

More than happy to oblige, he sat down on the window seat and allowed her to straddle him. She held her arms around his neck, and he noticed the nervous expression flash across her face. Gripping her in place with one hand, he used the other to guide himself inside her warmth. She grunted and gasped at the connection, and it dawned on him that this was new to her. Holding the sides of her hips, he stared into her eyes, willing her to follow his motion. Soon, she found her rhythm, and he allowed her to take control, only holding her in place to balance their weight.

"Mmm. Oh God!" she moaned, tilting her head back in pleasure, as she began to ride him like a stallion. The murmurs of their lovemaking increased as Karli began to fully enjoy this newfound thrill ride. Her wetness and excitement heightened Hudson's passion as he gripped her in place and forced himself deeper and deeper inside her.

"Damn, Karli. You feel so fucking good," he bit out. She had him on fire, and he'd never felt this good and this out of control of his body or emotions. "Baby, I'm about to cum," he huffed breathlessly.

She locked her legs around his waist, and her arms around his back. "Me too. Come with me, Hudson. Oh, baby!" she hollered, and they hit their crescendo in unison.

Hudson looked up into her eyes and couldn't help it; he kissed her with everything in him. He wanted this woman. He didn't give a damn if he had to be at her beck and call as long as she didn't let him go again. He couldn't handle that.

Karli leaned her head on his shoulder, and they play-fully toyed with each other's fingers until they interlocked them together.

"So this was your first time in this position, huh?"

Karli simply nodded. He'd figured it out. She could tell by the way that he had guided her from the beginning. For the first time, she was ready for an honest talk with him. "Can we be honest with each other?"

"Please. I would appreciate that."

Sighing, Karli began her confession. "Don't think that my husband is a bad man. He's good. He loves me, and our marriage was rock solid up until a few months ago." Karli paused and then huffed in exasperation. "God, I should feel so horrible for telling you this, and even worse for doing this, but I can't lie. I honestly don't. I've tried to mend things, to guide him and even talk to him about how I feel and what's bothering me, but he doesn't listen. He never listens. He smothers me with what he wants for me with no consideration for what I want. Like with sex, he thinks that missionary is more 'wifely' and that I'd be acting whorish if I tried something new. How is it fair that all the women he used to sleep with before we got married get to experience all these pleasures with him, but not me? I'm his wife. If anything, he should've reserved it for me. I reserved myself for him ,and now I'm stuck wanting more than he's willing to give."

Hudson looked over at her in shock. Not because of what she had said about her husband—a lot of men felt that freakiness made their wives impure—but because Karli had revealed that she was a virgin when they married, if he was reading into what she had said correctly.

Karli looked at him and smiled. "Yes, I was a virgin when I married my husband."

Suddenly, Hudson's face turned into another question, and she answered that one too.

"And yes, you are the only other man I've slept with besides my husband."

Any feelings that Hudson thought he felt for Karli were confirmed. He couldn't show it, but if she wanted to leave her husband this instant, he'd move her into his home and pay for the divorce himself.

After moving her hair out of her face, Hudson lifted her chin so that she would look at him. "Wow. Karli, I didn't know. When I first approached you, I'd only had a feeling that you weren't being taken care of. I must say I agree with you. If you were my wife, then you absolutely would be the one I'd give all of myself to in that manner. Your spouse should be that person that you can release all your inhibitions with. I know some men with your husband's perspective, but I don't agree. Why would you enjoy all those moments with someone else instead of with the person you pledged your life to?"

Karli sighed in relief. "Thank you. I thought I sounded crazy."

Hudson laughed. "No, you're normal. To me, his thought process is crazy. I sound hypocritical saying this, considering you're sharing this moment with me, but I'm willing to give you what your husband can't or won't."

Karli shrugged. "I hate to sound like a broken record, because I know that I should feel bad. I did, at first, but I've tried, Hudson. You know I walked away. I tried to give him what I have with you, and he's just not getting it. And how can something that feels so right be wrong? I don't even know what I want anymore. I love my husband, but I can't let go of what you and I have, either."

"Then don't. I'm not forcing you to leave him for me. I'm simply letting you know that I'm here for you any way you want me to be, but you have to promise me that you won't push me away again. I'm willing to be on your terms, but I can't be thrown to the side unless we're completely done for good," Hudson said confidently, cupping her face in his hands.

A moment went by as Karli considered what he was asking of her. If she continued this with Hudson, she'd be signing up for an affair. Not a one-night stand. Not a "mistake." A full-blown affair. And before she risked it all and gave him her decision, she had a few questions herself.

"And I can't agree to this unless I know that if I do, I'm the only one who has you. I need you to be open and honest with me. I never asked before, but do you have someone?"

Hudson shifted her as he wrapped both arms around her waist so that they were clearly eye to eye. "The only woman in my life or in my bed is you. With me, what you see is what you get. I'm always going to be open and honest with you about everything. So when I say it's just me and you, I mean just that. I know I have to share, but I accept that, because I want to." He bit his lip as his intense blue eyes stared at her. "I just need to know that you're all in with this with me."

With a grin, Karli winked. "I'm all in with you. In fact, let me show you how much."

She kneeled down, then took his manhood in her hand and massaged it. She could smell her sweet essence lingering on him, and her mouth watered for a taste. Licking her lips, she bent down and gave his manhood a few quick pecks and sucks as it throbbed and jumped with anticipation.

"Teach me how to please you. Teach me how to suck you," she commanded sexily.

His eyes rolled back as he lightly held her head and guided himself inside her awaiting mouth. Breathing huskily, he murmured, "Just keep wetting it and slurping like that."

For the next half hour, Hudson taught her the art of sucking dick, and in turn, he enjoyed yet another heart-pumping climax inside her warm mouth.

Chapter 19

"As much as I love our family and friends, I am so glad everyone decided to call it a day early. I can barely keep my eyes open to watch the games," Michael joked after he walked into the kitchen and wrapped his arms around Karli's waist. Smiling down at her, he kissed her on the cheek. "Thanksgiving dinner was great. You did an excellent job, and you were a wonderful hostess."

Karli smiled and patted his arm. "Thank you, sweetie."

Michael looked around and saw that she had cleaned up nearly all the dishes and had packed away the food in containers. He picked up a couple of the containers and began to walk toward the refrigerator.

"No, baby. Those don't go in the fridge." She pointed to the breakfast table. "Those over there go in the fridge. You can put those away."

Michael sat down the containers he was holding and walked to the breakfast table. He picked up the containers there and headed back to the refrigerator, looking confused. "So who are those other ones for? I thought everyone took plates with them when they left."

Karli turned on the water in the sink to rinse off the sponge. "Those are for one of my new employees. They just recently moved and had no one to cook for them. I told them I'd bring them some of our food."

Michael smiled. "That's sweet. You could've invited them over."

She put away the dish detergent and the sponge before she looked over at Michael. "I did. They didn't want to intrude, but I insisted on bringing them food, which they gladly accepted."

Michael shrugged and continued putting away the food as Karli ran upstairs to change. She slipped on her low-rise jeans, her UGG boots, and a wrap sweater and checked herself in the mirror. She sprayed on some perfume and headed back downstairs. She passed by Michael, who was now sitting on the sofa, watching football.

"Whoa! Wait. You're leaving tonight to take them the food?" he asked with a slight attitude.

Karli paused, turned, and walked back over to the sofa. "Be nice. It's Thanksgiving. I want to spend a little time and give them the food while it's still fresh."

Karli noticed that Michael was about to protest, so she bent over and delivered a supple kiss on his lips. "I shouldn't be too terribly long."

"I know. I just wanted to snuggle up with you and have our own alone time."

He sighed and decided to give up his argument. He knew it'd be a losing battle, anyway. Even though they had supposedly forgiven each other, made love, and were now talking to each other, their relationship was still extremely rocky. Michael had hoped the bad times were all behind them, but even the simplest of mishaps tended to spark intense arguments and snappy attitudes. At least **for the** holiday, he wanted peace in their house and no **arguing** with his wife. God, how he wished he could have his old thing back.

He rubbed his forefinger along her chin. "You're right. You're mine anytime I want. You're so sweet and amazing. Go ahead and be the Good Samaritan, and I'll be waiting for you when you return."

She smiled and pecked him on the lips again before going into the kitchen, bagging the items, and leaving the house. Once she was out of the driveway, she rolled her eyes toward the house and sent a quick text before making the forty-minute drive. Once she arrived at her destination, she got out of the car, pulled out the items she'd packed, and went to the door. She was about to ring the bell when she smiled to herself and pulled out her key ring to let herself in.

"Hudson!" she called out as she made her way into the kitchen. "Hudson!"

She put the bag down on the kitchen counter, kicked off her boots, and began to walk to the long staircase. In the distance, she could hear the shower running. She giggled to herself, knowing he was freshening up for her, and went back to the kitchen to reheat their food.

Karli stood in the kitchen and prepped their dinner. With her earbuds in, she pranced around, listening to one of her new favorite songs, "Hit 'Em" by Frankie Storm.

A few minutes later, Hudson came up behind her and kissed her neck, startling her.

"Hudson!"

Laughing, he turned her around as she removed her earbuds. She couldn't help but smile demurely as he wrapped his hands around her waist and pulled her close to him. "Sorry to interrupt your little party. Everything smells good. I apologize for not meeting you, but I was trying to freshen up for you," he said, licking his lips.

She playfully tapped him. "I guess I forgive you this time, since you're looking and smelling all good for me."

"Is that right?" He bent over and playfully kissed her neck and tickled her.

She giggled loudly. "That's right."

"Mmm," he murmured against the nape of her neck. "You smell so good. I'm starving, but I don't think I want that food right now."

"Eat. You need sustenance." She pulled away and scooped a spoonful of dressing, then turned to face him. "Open up."

He smiled and did as she said, and she placed the food in his mouth. As he nodded his head, his face contorted into a look of euphoria, and he patted his stomach. "Damn, baby. This does taste really good. I think I'll go ahead and take that plate of food, if you don't mind."

Laughing, Karli gave him the eye. "Mmm-hmm. I know I did that, baby. Sit. I'll make your plate for you."

Hudson raised his hands in surrender and did as he was told.

Two months had gone by, and their relationship had developed tremendously. They had gone from getting it in at his penthouse to getting it in on the terrace of his bedroom at his main house. She'd become a permanent fixture in his life. At this point, he was seeing her almost as much as her husband did, and she even had his spare house key, a garage opener, the security codes, the gate codes, and even a spare key fob to his favorite car, his Audi A8.

Hudson had made plans to go out of town to visit his dad for Thanksgiving, since he had figured Karli would want to spend quality time with her husband and family. Although their relationship was strained, his dad was the only family he had, since his mother had passed away several years ago. However, Karli had balked at the idea. She'd promised him that part of his Thanksgiving would be spent with her and that she'd be sure to bring him a home-cooked meal. She had kept her promise, much to his surprise, but then again she was full of surprises— good surprises. He swallowed the lump in his throat now as she prepared his plate. He had to remember this was only temporary.

"Here you go," she said, placing his plate in front of him and placing a small plate down on the table for herself. She'd eaten only a little bit at dinner so that she could eat with Hudson.

It may have seemed odd, but they actually held hands, prayed, and thanked God for their blessings and for each other. As they ate, they took the time to enjoy each other's company and talked about their lives. Hudson shared with her other business plans, gathering her opinion and ideas, and she confided in him about her latest poetry. They ate and carried on a conversation that flowed between jokes, books, and life in general.

"That food was so good, Karli. You and your mother did your thang." They shared a laugh, and he rubbed his stomach. "I'm still a little hungry, though."

Karli stood, walked up to him, and straddled him. "That's because I didn't want you to have a full stomach. You must save room for dessert."

With that, she wrapped her arms around his neck, and they gave each other intimate kisses. The attraction heightened, and Hudson stood, holding her to him, but he made it only as far as his living room before they were consumed with passion. After placing her on the sofa in front of the huge fireplace, he slowly slid off her jeans. She didn't have on any panties, and he instantly rocked up as he pulled off his jeans and T-shirt.

"How long do we have?" Hudson asked huskily as he kneeled on the floor.

Glancing at the clock on the wall, Karli did some calculations. "I've only been here an hour. So about an hour, hour and a half, so I can get home at a decent time to keep everything on the up-and-up."

Hudson only nodded, unconcerned about Karli's marriage. He just wanted to keep her safe and protected, but right now, his only thought was pleasing her. Spreading her legs open, he licked his lips, and then he dove face-first into his creamy oasis.

"Mmm. I swear to God, you taste like heaven," he murmured, in the throes of love.

Karli couldn't respond, as her head was tilted backward as she received all his glorious treasure. She moaned heavily as his tongue flickered against her throbbing bud. Enveloped in complete ecstasy, she tightened her grip around his neck with her legs. She pushed his head farther down, determined to make sure he licked every corner and all the gushy center.

"Shit! Hudson, baby," she wailed out. "I'm about to cum!" She exploded, and her climax was so powerful, it made Hudson extend another inch.

He carried her to the love seat and positioned it to where she could get a partial view of the night lights taking over the city—it wasn't the view from the penthouse, but she loved it just as much. He pulled her to the edge of the cushioned seat, positioned her legs in a V shape, and pushed back as far back as they could go. He delivered a rough but feel-good power drive inside her. She wailed with passion as her body instantly slicked him with a rain shower. Faster, deeper, longer, and harder, he dove, working her like a porn star. His thickness was opening her up, and she took pleasure in him removing his wood and sticking it in her mouth to suck, then pushing back inside her.

"Karli! Karli, I can't hold it. I'm slipping," Hudson said, barely above a whisper.

He attempted to pull back, and Karli gripped him and held him in place. "I want to feel it inside me when you cum," she said seductively.

That was all it took. Hudson pumped faster, and then he gripped Karli tightly and released hard. "Oh my God! Mmm, baby. You feel so damn good. So good," Hudson hollered.

After a minute, he was able to move, and he lay down on the plush carpet. Karli got up and lay with him, and he wrapped his arms around her. He'd give anything to stay like this. They lay there for a few minutes, just listening to the rise and fall of each other's breathing.

"What's on your mind?" he asked, breaking the silence.

Karli toyed with his fingers and looked up into his crystal blue eyes, which always pulled her in. "What's your fantasy?"

"What do you mean?" He blushed coyly.

Karli sat up and kissed him. Rubbing on his chest, she asked again. "What's your sexual fantasy? You can tell me."

"You're my dream."

"I didn't ask you about a dream, Hudson." She straddled him. "I asked about your fantasy. What's your fantasy?"

Hudson eyed her suspiciously. "I'm just asking. Where is this coming from?"

Karli bit her lip. "Hudson, you've opened me up in ways I never dreamed possible. Because of you, I'm free. Free to be me. Free to be who I am and to do what I want for me. You've made my wildest fantasies and dreams come true, so I want to do something for you. What's your fantasy?"

Hudson tapped his chin and gazed at her. She was serious. This woman couldn't get any better to him. Here she was, literally devoted to someone else, yet wanting to please him in every sense of the word. Hell, his ultimate fantasy was to kick that damn Michael dude to the curb and take his woman permanently, but he digressed and told her his second all-time fantasy.

"The same as every man's fantasy—two women at the same time." He pulled her into an embrace before continuing. "But I wouldn't ask you to do that with me. I respect your limits."

Karli pulled back and stared down at him, in deep thought. Then she smiled. "With you, there are no limits. For you, I want to make that happen. If you find a woman, I'd be interested. I'd make that happen for you."

Hudson gasped, realizing how truly selfless she was. He knew she wasn't bisexual, so what she was willing to do just to please him spoke volumes.

"Karli, please don't feel pressured to do something. I want you regardless—"

She planted a soft kiss on his lips. "No pressure. No ill feelings. Just a one-time 'fulfill your fantasy' event. Call it a Christmas gift from me to you. You share me, so it's only fair that you get something in return, but I want to stress that it's only once. For me and for her. I'm not sharing you for more than one night. Besides, it'll be fun to discard these sexual inhibitions. Through your eyes, I see a whole new world, one that I've been shielded from. You make me embrace my sexuality in ways I never dreamed of. I told you, with you, I'm free, and you're the only one I want to share this freedom with."

"Wow," he said before kissing her and staring into her eyes. "You're amazing, you know that?"

Winking at him, she giggled. "I try."

Hudson nodded. "I know the perfect person."

When Karli eyed him, he explained.

"My ex." He held up his hand, because he saw her beginning to protest. "She's a lesbian. She was bisexual when we dated, and we used to do things together like this with one of her friends. Somewhere along the way, I was cut out of the equation, and the next thing I knew, she was leaving me for her. As long as you promise not to get caught up and leave me for her, I'll ask her."

She laughed and hit him. "Uh no, sorry. I'm all for exploration, but this is for you and only for you. This kitty is too addicted to the dick."

"I love it when you talk nasty to me." He kissed her neck, causing a giggle to escape her lips.

"How do you know she'll go for it, though? I mean, she may be serious with her lady."

Hudson laughed. "Because money talks and bullshit walks. If she says no, money will sucker her in. She is as big a gold digger as she is a lesbian. If it doesn't work . . . Oh well, we tried. It's not like I have to have her. I've already tapped that. I'm into my new thing now." He caressed her face.

Lying on his chest, Karli swallowed the lump forming in her throat. His comment reminded her of Michael, who was waiting at home for her. She loved him, but she couldn't lie. What she had with Hudson was stronger than she had anticipated. She couldn't say it aloud, for fear the feelings would take root and would grow even more, but everything about him tugged at her heartstrings.

"I wish I could spend the night," Karli said sweetly as they lay basking in their afterglow.

Hudson parted his lips, about to say something, but then stopped himself. He settled on saying, "Yeah, but you have to go back to your life."

Together, they sighed at the thought.

Without another word, she stood up slowly and then headed up the staircase to shower. He watched her ascend and resisted the urge to beg her to stay.

Chapter 20

Michael fumed as Karli packed her luggage. He couldn't believe the gall of her boss, or her at this point. Sure, their relationship had been strained lately, to say the least, but never in a million years could he have anticipated that she'd pack up and leave for the holidays. During the five years they'd been together, this sort of thing had never happened, and Michael wasn't pleased at all.

"Why in the world would your boss want you to go out of town two days before Christmas, Karli? It's the damn holidays!"

Karli shrugged. "Oh, I don't know . . . Because I'm the new senior executive marketing director, and it's my job?"

"You're being sarcastic, but this is our time. We were both supposed to be on vacation and spending time together. What about our traditional gift wrapping and drinking eggnog while watching Christmas movies?"

She was so happy her back was to him so he didn't have to see her rolling her eyes. Why he chose to act as if they were the perfect couple anymore was beyond her comprehension. Sex with Michael had become a mundane and mind-numbing chore. Did she still love him? Yes, and she was sure he still loved her, but she could no longer ignore the fact that everything that had transpired had taken a toll on their relationship.

The biggest issue was that he wanted his old thing back, but the old thing was tired, boring, and unfulfilling.

Honestly, even though they'd supposedly moved on from the baby issue, it was still an issue. He'd only moved from trying to control her body through a baby to trying to control her body through sex. At the end of the day, control was still control.

Karli stuffed her toiletries into a plastic bag. "We can still drink eggnog and watch Christmas movies on Christmas Day. I'll be back that morning, and I've already gift wrapped my presents. I placed them under the tree this morning."

Michael huffed. "You know what I mean."

"So what do you suppose I do, Michael? Tell my boss no and run the risk of being written up or demoted? I'm sure that's what you want." Her anger caused her to let that last part slip out.

Throwing up his hands, Michael seethed, "So we're back to this again. Just when I thought you'd forgiven me. Thanks for that, Karli. Good way for us to move on."

She wanted to yell, "If the shoe fits," but she refrained and walked up to him, looked at him with apologetic eyes. "I'm sorry. I was wrong." She held his face in her hands. "Michael, I don't want to argue with you. My position requires me to do things a bit differently now. It may make us uncomfortable at first, but I'm trying to keep a balance. I just can't have you battling every little thing because it makes you uncomfortable. If you want to work on us, you have to work on being more understanding."

Closing his eyes and taking a deep breath, Michael took in what Karli had said. He realized she was right. She didn't own her own business like he did, and like it or not, she had that senior position now, so when she was called upon, she was required to spring into action.

After pulling her close, he leaned his forehead against hers. "You're right, Karli. Absolutely. I promise you, I will try harder, if you promise me that before you leave, I'll get an early Christmas gift."

Forcing a smile, Karli nodded. She knew this was the only way that Michael would ease up, and she was tired of the constant tug-of-war. It was making it harder for her to hold on to their marriage, especially while having someone like Hudson on the side.

"Just let me finish up my packing." She gazed into his eyes as they wrapped their arms around each other.

Holding her a little closer, Michael breathed deeply and kissed her lips so passionately that Karli swooned. "You do know that I love you, right?"

Unable to answer, she gave a slight nod, still enveloped in the afterglow of the kiss.

"I know I'm to blame for all that's happened, and I promise I'm trying to get it right," Michael told her. "Just please don't give up on me, Karli. Please."

Tears glossed over Karli's eyes, and she sniffed and wiped them away. This was probably the most sincere moment they'd shared in a long time, and it touched Karli in a way she hadn't felt in forever. They stood in the embrace for a few minutes longer before they pulled apart so that she could finish packing her clothes.

Once she was finished, she stripped down and put on her robe, then sat on the edge of the bed, waiting for Michael to come out of the shower for their lovemaking session. Even though it was going to be old missionary, she actually looked forward to the connection with her husband for the first time in such a long time.

"Karli!" Michael called from the bathroom.

Shaking her head, Karli couldn't help but grin. Michael always forgot his soap when he showered, and usually called her and asked her to bring it to him so he didn't have to step out of the warm water. She entered the bathroom, went to his sink drawer, and removed a fresh bar. She walked over to the shower and gently tapped on the door.

"Here's your soap," she said softly.

He opened the door, and instead of taking the soap, he gently grabbed Karli's hand and pulled her into the shower with him. Karli jumped as he shut the door, and then he held her close as her hair and robe got soaked with water.

"Michael, what are you doing?" she asked. "I'm getting—"

He interrupted her with a deep, passionate kiss. In one swoop, Michael untied her robe, let it fall, and slid his fingers inside her honey pot. "Wet. You're getting wet," he said huskily against her lips as he teased her clit with his powerful fingers.

Karli took labored breaths as she held on to him, and got lost in the moment, which felt so good. "Ooh, Michael," she whimpered.

He hardened against her at the emotion in her tone. "I love it when you say my name like that. I haven't heard that in so long."

Karli let out a sexy moan, and it was music to Michael's ears. After easing Karli's back against the wall, he kneeled down, gently lifted her leg over his shoulder, and sensually licked her succulent juices. Holding on to Michael for dear life, Karli panted and writhed under his masterful licks. Their moans grew as Karli's climax neared, and when her sugary syrup was released into his mouth, Michael could no longer hold back. An animalistic nature took over him as he stood and turned Karli so that she faced the shower wall. Bracing himself and her, he entered her wetness from behind and held her tight as they wound and pumped together methodically. Her body felt like home. The familiarity they'd both known was back, and the mounting pleasure was greater than at any moment he'd ever shared with her.

"Mmm. Shit, Karli," he groaned, unafraid of his emotions. "Ooh, this shit feels . . . feels . . . good."

This routine was out of the norm for Michael, but desperate times called for desperate measures. He didn't want to treat her like a jump-off or like some ho he used to deal with, but he figured he'd try to incorporate some things that he was comfortable with, and hopefully, he would please his wife. To his surprise, he was really pleased himself.

All this time, this was what she'd been begging Michael for, and he was finally giving it to her. Lost in the moment, nothing else and no one else mattered to Karli, only Michael and her. The feeling of him inside her grew, and she bent down, braced herself against his thrusts on the shower seat. The moment she did, she began throwing her back into him, and Michael let out a roar, gripping her about the waist.

As her luscious backside jiggled against him, Michael groaned deeper and began to deliver long strokes, going as deep as he could.

"Fuck! Work that shit. Just like that, baby. Fuck Daddy," he yelled before he knew it.

Karli matched his speed as she arched her back and gave him her all. Months of pain and aggression oozed from both of them as they surrendered to the powerful love swirling between them. Grunts and moans could be heard throughout the house as their desire kicked into overdrive.

"Yes, Daddy. Fuck, yes," Karli wailed as she reached her climax.

As soon as she did, Michael shot his hot load deep inside her. "Ahh! Argh!" he yelled.

He paused before removing himself, and then, without any energy left, he sat on the floor of the shower. Karli eased herself down and sat on top of him. Basking in the glory of their moment, Karli had a million thoughts running through her mind. The first one was that after tonight she'd have to end things with Hudson. Her husband had finally come around, and she truly had to devote herself to rebuilding and restoring what was lost, and embracing what was new. She was so happy, and she was actually relieved that Michael had finally seen the light. This was the man she'd vowed her life to, and she was happy that the old and the new him had finally merged and brought back her old thing.

"You good?" Michael grinned and slid his hand up and down her back.

"Better than good. I'm great." She kissed his neck, nuzzling close to him. "Mmm, baby. You were so amazing. We can think of so many ways to—"

Michael kissed her forehead. "That was so great, baby, but it was a one-time deal. We both needed this, but I can't be around here putting ho moves on you. Let's just enjoy the moment for what it is now."

Karli was so distraught she couldn't even open her mouth to protest. She sat there for few minutes, stuck between satisfaction and sheer pisstivity. Just when she thought they'd taken two steps forward, they took ten steps back.

"Let's finish the shower," she said. She wanted nothing more than to shower and go straight to bed—and to forget this moment had ever happened.

***

Karli rushed in and greeted Hudson with a deep kiss of longing.

"Well, Happy pre–Christmas Eve to you too," he greeted with a laugh. "I must say, I love it."

Karli dropped her bags at the door and tossed her keys on a nearby table as Hudson closed the door. She headed directly to her favorite spot in the penthouse and peered out.

Eyeing her closely, he could tell something was off with her. He picked up her bags, carried them into the master bedroom, and walked back into the living room, stopping only to turn on some soft music. For a moment, he stood back and just drank in her features. Then he slowly came up behind her and kissed her neck. Holding her close, he swayed with her to the music, and Karli closed her eyes, loving the feeling of him on her.

"What's on your mind?" he whispered.

Karli let out a weighty sigh.

"Tell me. You know you can talk to me about anything."

"Michael and I made love last night, and I almost called things off with us," she blurted out before she lost the nerve to say it. Confused and dazed, Hudson went to pull back, but Karli gripped his arm and held it in place. She needed him near. "It was just a front. He was trying to lure me in. I held on to my love for him and my devotion to my marriage because it was the only way in my mind that I could justify being with you. Ya know? I was telling myself, 'Well, I'm technically not cheating if I'm still willing to be there, and I can stop being with Hudson whenever my marriage gets on track.' But last night showed me that the only person who has been holding on and waiting for something to ignite is me. I swear to God, Hudson, he almost had me. I was so close to giving in."

This was a pivotal moment to Hudson. He was pissed because she had said this as if he meant absolutely nothing to her, whereas she meant everything to him. Yet he had to consider the fact that she was married and had never given up her devotion to her husband. If they were married, wouldn't he want her to reserve her best for him? Of course, the answer was yes, but that didn't make her words hurt any less.

"I've hurt your feelings, and I'm sorry," Karli said.

Exhaling, Hudson decided to take the high road. "It does hurt, but I can't blame you for trying to love your husband. I just need to know if I need to be holding on anymore."

Karli turned to face him for the first time and brushed his face with the back side of her hand. Staring into his intense crystal blues, she smiled. "Please hold on to me. I need you, Hudson. You're the only thing that's real to me."

Her pleas were so sincere that he rested his forehead against hers, and before he knew it, he finally revealed how he felt. "I *can't* let go of you. I'm so all in, it's not even funny. Forget the sneaking around and making up work-related excuses. Leave him, Karli. Leave him and be with me."

She bit her lip, unsure of herself and of him. He was speaking about her terminating her relationship with the man whom she'd vowed to spend the rest of her life with. On top of that, she wasn't quite sure of Hudson's actual feelings toward her.

Noticing her inner turbulence, he placed a soft kiss on her lips and said, "Just think about it."

She ran her fingers through his short blond curls and pulled him to her for a passionate kiss. As their tongues tasted and teased each other, Hudson unbuttoned his pants and let them fall to his ankles. He felt nothing but bare skin as he trailed his hands up the backs of her thighs and underneath her dress. He couldn't hold back. He lifted Karli up on his waist and slid into her moistness. Bouncing her up and down on his shaft, he gave all of himself to her. The lovemaking was wild and uninhibited as he softly slammed her against the windowpane, filling her up to the max.

"Hudson," she moaned, her eyes closed, consumed with unwavering desire.

She opened her eyes to find him staring directly at her, as if willing her to look into his eyes and see his very soul. Everything that he'd kept hidden from Karli was suddenly clear. In that moment, no words were needed. She understood with complete clarity that he wanted her for himself.

As Karli stared back at him, she felt herself slicking his muscle with her climactic juices, and a gut-wrenching moan escaped her lips. Gripping her tightly about the waist, Hudson let out a yelp from the pit of his soul. He gave way to his climatic urges and released himself deep inside her love nest before he collapsed on the window seat, taking her with him.

"Karli! I love you!"

Karli eased herself off him and sat on the window seat. Slowly she took him into her mouth and worked him until another explosion erupted. She swallowed his full load and polished him clean.

Suddenly, they both became aware of the constant knocking at the door. Without bothering to fix himself, Hudson stalked to the door and opened it. There stood his ex, Tya.

"Damn, Hud. Yous guys getting started without me? I could hear you clear out in the hallway. Good thing you have the penthouse," she joked as he moved to the side, allowing her in.

As soon as Tya stepped inside, she spotted Karli, and her mouth instantly watered. She wanted every drop of Karli. She could fully see why he'd just professed his love to her. Hell, she was practically in love with her at first sight. Karli was a goddess of perfection. Even though Tya and her girlfriend, Ximena, were on shaky ground, Tya had still allowed Hudson to pay her for this impromptu tryst. He was a multimillionaire, and she was a girl who loved money, but looking at Karli, she definitely would've done this for free.

Hudson leaned over and whispered in Tya's ear, "Don't get any ideas. She's not up for grabs."

Tya eyed him and shrugged. "Doesn't mean we won't have plenty of fun. I know I will." She sashayed over to a nervous Karli, who kept looking downward. She ran her fingers through Karli's hair and lifted her chin so that they were eye to eye. "I'm Tya, sweetie. Don't worry. I'll take good care of you."

Hudson walked over to the two ladies, stepped in between them, and faced Karli. "And I'm going to make sure she does. Remember, you don't have to go through with this. Anytime you want to stop, say the word and she's gone. My only concern is for you," he said sincerely, staring lovingly into her eyes.

Tya was impressed. One of the reasons she had decided to pursue Ximena solely, despite her obvious obsession with women, was because Ximena loved her. Even though Hudson had money, which was one of the perks of being with him, no amount of money in the world could get her to stay with him when he was incapable of loving her. At some point, a girl just had to feel loved, and Tya could never get those emotions from him. Hudson was nice, caring, and honest, but love her, he did not. For Karli, he wore his emotions on the sleeve of his arm. He was completely smitten with her, and for the first time, she saw love in his eyes. She couldn't deny that it gave her a twinge of jealousy, but it wasn't enough to make her truly care or not want to enjoy this moment.

Karli cupped his face in her hands. "You're so sweet. Remember, this is your gift, and I freely give it to you. No holds barred, no regrets. Merry Christmas, Hudson."

Tya smiled inside. Now she could see how he had fallen for her. She loved him too. Tya didn't know if Karli had admitted that to him or not, but it underpinned every word she spoke. Hudson loved Karli, and Karli, in turn, loved him.

With that, Karli lifted her dress above her head and let it fall to the floor, exposing all her naked glory. With determination and lust in her eyes, she turned her focus to Tya. Karli gently took Tya by her hand and led her into the master bedroom, with Hudson fresh on their heels.

Tya removed her coat, heels, and dress as Karli lay back on the bed. Hudson sat on his knees above her head. He lovingly ran his fingers through her hair, and she glided her fingertips up and down his thighs.

Tya slid her body between Karli's legs and traced soft kisses from her thighs, up her stomach, to her nipples. Their moans began to mix as Hudson grew, and he began massaging his muscle as he watched the connection grow between the women. Tya moved up to Karli's neck and suckled her earlobes as she eased her hand between Karli's folds and strummed her love button. Karli's moans reverberated in Hudson's ears, and he bent down and lovingly kissed her as he watched Tya masterfully give Karli hand action.

Tya leaned forward and whispered in Karli's ear, "Your pussy is so pretty."

Positioning herself sideways between Karli's legs, she placed her honey pot close to Karli's and slid back and forth, connecting their clits. The wetness and intensity of their love buttons touching caused their moans to get louder, and Karli rubbed and gripped Tya's butt, engulfed in pleasure.

Hudson couldn't deny that seeing the woman he loved pleasured in this way was truly turning him on. He leaned over and began sucking Karli's nipples as Tya pulled on his manhood.

Tya was so worked up at that point that she could no longer resist. She eased down between Karli's legs and slipped her fingers inside her creamy folds. The pleasure Karli was feeling from both Hudson's and Tya's treatment of her body was almost overwhelming. Realizing that her hand work might bring Karli to completion, Tya slipped her face between her legs and swirled her tongue around, tasting Karli's delectable juices.

Karli instantly grabbed Tya's head and pushed her farther inside, forcing her to suckle deeper and harder. Hudson couldn't take it and rose up, then placed his muscle inside Karli's mouth. Karli pulled and slurped on him with vigor as Tya continued to unleash a fury of sensational licks on her clit.

"Suck it. Ooh, like that. Karli," Hudson choked out, his head tilted back in delight, as he massaged her breasts.

Hudson's moans sent both women over the edge, and Tya slipped her fingers to her own clit and rubbed while licking Karli to a completion. Karli stopped sucking on Hudson as she exploded in Tya's mouth. Tya rose up, licking her lips, and Karli immediately flipped on all fours, took Hudson in her hand, and slipped him inside her mouth. Hudson lovingly rubbed her hair as he guided himself in and out of her mouth. Looking over at Tya, who was massaging her breasts and clit as she watched them, Hudson motioned for her to lick Karli from behind. She obliged and planted her tongue on Karli's clit while rubbing on her juicy derriere. They all moaned simultaneously at the pleasure being unleashed.

Hudson could no longer hold on as he held Karli's face between his hands and slid in and out. He released deep into her throat. A beastlike roar escaped from Hudson as he held her in place until all the remnants had been swallowed. After pulling out, he gently pulled Karli up and kissed her deeply on the mouth.

Fully into the moment, Karli slid her tongue around Hudson's lips as they held each other in an embrace. "I want to taste her," she whispered as they both looked back at Tya, who was sexily eyeing them both.

Hudson nodded and pointed to Tya. "Lie down on your back."

Tya lay down, and Karli slipped between her legs. Hudson eased behind Karli, and she looked back at him. Touching her shoulder softly, he whispered to her, "This is a judgment-free zone. I want you whether you do or don't. My fantasy is complete."

Karli smiled devilishly at him and then back at Tya, who gave her the same look. Karli looked back at Hudson and smiled wickedly.

"Eat her real good, baby," he instructed.

Karli lifted Tya's legs and placed her face between her folds. There was no turning back now. As Karli tasted of the forbidden fruit, Tya let out a pleasure-filled groan, and that urged Karli on full force. She began swirling her tongue around and tasting Tya's sweet nectar. Hudson had thought the sight of Karli being pleasured turned him on, but watching Karli give the pleasure released the beast in him. He buried his muscle inside Karli's dripping wet spot and pumped harder than he'd ever had. Her ass bounced back to meet him, causing it to jiggle, with strong ripples. Tya screamed and moaned as Karli devoured her creamy center.

"Oh my God! Karli," Tya screamed.

"Mmm, Hudson," Karli moaned.

"Karli," Hudson groaned as they all three climaxed together.

Tya fell back, spent, but Karli turned to Hudson, and they kissed fervently. The lust in their eyes was still evident, and Karli wrapped her legs around Hudson's waist as he lifted her and eased himself inside her wetness again. The connection caused them to whimper in passion, and Karli held on to Hudson as he bounced her up and down on his shaft.

Tya smiled, realizing that this moment was theirs, and moved off the bed to the chair. She located her bullet in her coat pocket, turned it on, and settled for pleasuring herself as she watched Hudson and Karli make love to each other.

Hudson laid Karli on her back and lifted her legs high on his waist as he swirled and ground lovingly inside her sweet succulence. She held Hudson's face as she looked into his eyes. She knew that Hudson was making love to her, and she gave in to it. She accepted the love he was giving to her. His crystal blue eyes stared so intently and so lovingly at her, it was as if he was willing her to see past the moment into his heart, into his soul. For the first time, she saw it and truly believed it. His love.

"Hudson, baby," she whimpered, noticing his eyes mist. He knew that his feelings had been truly exposed, and the only thing in the world he wanted was Karli.

"Karli, I love you. I love you so much," he whispered huskily, staring into her hazel eyes.

He released inside her, and she climaxed with him as their eyes remained locked on each other. They shared sweet pecks as they lovingly smiled at each other, completely oblivious to Tya, who had finished up and gotten dressed.

"Hey, you two lovebirds. I think I'm going to go now and let you have your moment."

They both looked up at her and smiled.

"Thanks for a great evening," she added. "Don't worry. I'll see myself out."

"Thanks, Tya," they said together as they continued to caress each other and snuggle.

Once she left, Hudson kissed Karli and caressed her cheek. "Thank you for my Christmas gift. It was beautiful, and so are you. Inside and out. I have a gift for you."

Grinning, Karli sat up as Hudson got up and went to retrieve her gift and make sure that Tya had locked up. When he returned, Karli was sitting up with her back against the headboard, wrapped in the sheets.

"You didn't have to get me anything," she said sweetly as Hudson climbed in bed beside her.

Hudson tapped her nose. "You know you want it," he joked. "I know I didn't have to. I wanted to, just like you wanted to give me my fantasy." He gave her a velvet box. "Open it."

Smiling, Karli opened the box and gasped, then covered her mouth with her hand. It was the most stunning diamond ring she'd ever seen. "Oh my God."

Hudson bit his lip. "This," he said, taking the ring out of the box, "is a promise ring. I promise to be here for you, solely and completely." He placed the ring on the ring finger of her right hand. "I know that you have a lot to deal with and some tough decisions to get through. I realize I might not be on the winning end of this. Knowing that is hard on me, because my feelings are out there live, in color, but I accept that. I won't pressure you, but this is just to let you know that I'll wait. I'll be there for you anytime and in every way. I'm yours, Karli. I'll wait for you, even if you're never mine."

Tears sprang to Karli's eyes as she leaned in to share a sweet kiss with Hudson. In that moment, she hated her selfishness toward him, but she had a lot to sort out. Then and there, she made a promise to herself that she would figure out what she wanted just for him. He deserved more than her indecisiveness.

"I . . . I don't . . . know what to say. I wish I could promise you that I will leave my husband. I don't know how that situation will pan out, but, Hudson, I thank you for being everything to me that I have needed and all that I have wanted." She looked at him, capturing his gaze, so he could see that she meant what she was saying. "I am smitten," she whispered, then closed her eyes before continuing the poem.

"Mmm this man, this man . . . opened me up to levels of pleasures I never knew existed . . . has my mind, body, and fantasies twisted . . . Craving every inch of him, touch, smell, completely free in his presence . . . Embers of lust rage, lavish in my belly effervescent . . . What he does to me is so sinfully sweet . . . Sexually opened my aura free and complete . . . Swirled into a whirlwind of reality and matrix . . . Unbearable bliss leaves my soul beautifully naked."

She opened her eyes and met Hudson's loving gaze. She could see the faint trace of tears in his eyes.

"Hudson, that's how you make me feel." She exhaled and smiled demurely at him. "I'll figure this thing out, but regardless of what happens, I . . . I love you."

Excitedly, Hudson pulled Karli to him and nuzzled the nape of her neck. "Now, that's the best Christmas gift I've ever received."

Karli had no idea what she was going to do about her marriage, and for now, she refused to think about it. For now, she was going to enjoy her time with her man.

Chapter 21

For the past month, Karli had been trying to figure out what she wanted to do with her marriage. She and Michael weren't close at all anymore. Her daily life consisted of working, spending time with her best friend, and, most of all, being with Hudson. Every chance she had, they talked or saw one another. He consumed her thoughts and her dreams, while fulfilling her desires. Though he never pressured her, she could feel his heart break each time she left him to go home and play doting wife, and when she was at home playing doting wife, she was miserable. It was hard to believe that just six months ago, she wouldn't have traded her life with Michael for anything in the world.

Their family and friends had noticed the change too. While they gave advice, it fell on deaf ears. She'd tried everything they'd suggested, but it didn't stop the landslide that their marriage was on. It was like sand slipping through their fingers. Even though Karli felt bad about her marriage and hated that it was on a downward slope, she couldn't say that she missed it. Her heart beat for Hudson, and she knew that the moment she chose to truly give in to those feelings, divorce was imminent. What kept her there, in her marriage? Her upbringing, her unwillingness to accept failure and, most of all, the fact that she didn't want to hurt Michael. Although those were good reasons, she knew that eventually, those reasons wouldn't be enough.

Together, Karli and Michael went through the motions of marriage without acknowledging that that was all it was. The fights, the limited conversations, and the absence of an emotional connection between them loomed above, and they were just waiting for the other shoe to drop.

And now Karli was stuck taking part in a weekend that Michael had planned, and engaging in a pretense of caring, because she certainly wanted no part of it. She was too tired to deal with the fakeness.

For the fifth time, Karli glanced at her cell phone, while everyone sat around laughing, joking, listening to music, and playing card games. Michael's parents had come up for a visit, so they all had convened at Karli's parents' house for a Super Bowl party. Everyone was there, from their parents to their friends, and even some colleagues from Michael's and Karli's firms. The only person not in attendance was the one person Karli desperately wanted to see—Hudson. He'd been out of town on business for three days, and she desperately needed to hear his voice and be in his presence. He kept her grounded, and being without him left her on edge, with a bad attitude. She needed him to be able to stomach this sham of a party. She was trying to keep her best face on, but this was irritating her, and missing Hudson was only fueling her irritation.

"You're going to burn a hole into that phone," Karli's mom told Karli as she walked into the kitchen to replenish a bowl of chips.

Karli jumped. "Mama, you scared me."

She shook her head. "Whenever I said that, my grandmother used to tell me, 'Then stop doing wrong.'" She laughed, but Karli didn't find it amusing. "I was going to give you the other bowl, but it's taking you forever to come back, and now I see why. You're hovering over the phone."

Karli giggled nervously. "It's just some work stuff that I need to handle."

Her mother waved her off. "It can wait. Enjoy your family and friends, Karli. This is our time, not McCallan and Associates'."

Just then, Michael entered the kitchen, and he hugged Karli from behind. "Tell her again, Mama. For the past two months, I've been telling her the same thing. She's the hardest-working woman I know. She's always at the office, in her home office, or out on business. I love the pay, but I need someone to talk her into slowing down a bit."

"Yes, slow down, honey. My baby boy needs his wife, and eventually, we're going to need some grandchildren around here," Michael's mother joked as she and Catrina entered the kitchen.

An awkward silence immediately fell over the kitchen. No one had told Michael's mother the details about why their marriage was strained, and bringing children up again was like reopening a fresh wound. The heat radiating off Karli could be felt miles away.

Karli cleared her throat. "Mama Carol, kids will come one day, when both Michael and I are ready to have them." She paused. "Excuse me," she said rather bluntly before she grabbed her phone and exited the kitchen.

"Did I say something wrong?" Mama Carol asked.

Michael patted his mother's shoulder. "No, you didn't. Excuse me," he said, and then he went to find Karli. He found her pacing upstairs, in a guest bedroom.

"You wanna explain what the hell that was about?" he snapped. "I get it, but you didn't have to come at my mother like that."

Karli stopped pacing and flung her hands up. "What the fuck is this? Gang up on Karli day?"

Michael paused, taken aback by her level of anger and her words. "What's gotten into you?" he asked, in confusion. "This isn't you. Lately, you've been so disconnected, and when you are here, you're distant. You haven't been to church since before Thanksgiving. We haven't had sex since before Christmas, and the only real conversations we have consist of smart comments and arguments. That's why I wanted to have this family day. I was hoping that it could pull us back together again." He walked up close to her with pleading eyes. "We're sinking, Karli, and if we don't come up for air soon, our marriage will drown. How can we save us?"

Karli's phone lightly vibrated in her pants pocket, and she resisted the urge to check it. Looking up at Michael, she shook her head, with sadness etched in her eyes. "I don't even know if we can," she admitted and walked toward the door. "I'm sorry for disrespecting your mother," she threw over her shoulder.

Devastated, Michael turned to face her. "Karli," he called out, his voice laden with emotion. She didn't turn to face him, as she could feel the emotion coming from him. "Then why are we even trying?"

Faintly, she said, "I don't know," and walked out of the room.

Michael stood in the guest bedroom and began to break down. In his heart, he loved Karli, but he could virtually feel their separation happening, and he didn't know how to stop it. Silently, he wept for a marriage that he knew was no longer there. As his tears subsided, he kneeled down on one knee and put his head down in reverence.

"God, I know you're real. I know it. Please help me. Reveal to me what I need to know to help us both. Please help me save my marriage."

He stood and wiped his eyes. There was no need for a long prayer. He'd talked to God numerous times about his marital problems, but today he needed a straight-up and direct prayer, which he hoped reached heaven.

He went back downstairs, looked in the living room, and found members of his family sitting there, with concerned looks on their faces. He looked around and didn't see his wife. "Where is Karli?"

Karli's mother shrugged. "We don't know. She said she needed some fresh air and left."

"Without you guys?" he asked, looking over at Catrina and Jessica.

They nodded.

"She said she wanted to be alone," Catrina added sadly.

Michael swiped his hand down his face. The weight of the world was on his shoulders as he walked into the kitchen to get a bottle of water. His dad followed him.

"Son, we've all talked, and we want to be here for you all. Things look really bad. What's going on?"

Michael leaned on the kitchen counter, with his head down. With sorrowful eyes, he then looked up at his dad and shook his head. "I've prayed, but I don't think we're going to make it, Dad. I think Karli and I may be looking at a divorce."

Chapter 22

Karli's legs danced as she sat waiting and contemplating. She'd paced back and forth for the past thirty minutes. Finally, she got up and gazed out the window into the backyard. It was a gorgeous night, as the stars shone brightly. The view was so peaceful and serene, and the more she took it in, the more the nervous energy seemed to ooze away as she found her center.

She heard the door open and walked back into the living room. Instantly, her whole world was right, as she saw Hudson standing with his back to her, on the phone, with his luggage at his feet.

"Hey, Karli, baby. It's me. My driver just dropped me off at home. I was trying to call you back. You sounded like something was wrong. Please call me back when you get a chance. I've missed you, and I love you. Call me." He hung up and slipped his phone in his pocket. "God, I love that woman." He shook his head and picked up his luggage.

As soon as he turned around, he was met with a deep kiss as Karli wrapped her arms around his neck. Startled, he pulled back briefly, but then he quickly dropped his bags, embraced her, and kissed her back with vigor.

Moments later he stepped back and cradled her face in his hands. He could see that she was worried and upset. "Baby, what's wrong?"

Tears came to Karli's eyes, and Hudson pulled her in close to him. "It's okay, baby. I'm here now. What happened?"

Karli pulled out of his embrace and began to pace back and forth again; then she inhaled deeply. Looking over at those crystal-clear blue eyes that always centered her, she saw nothing but love, and she smiled warily but confidently. After walking up to him, she held out her hands. Her left ring finger bore her wedding rings, and her right ring finger bore her promise ring. He looked down at her hands and then up at her eyes. She took a deep breath, removed her wedding rings, and placed them in her pocket, and then she moved her promise ring over to her left hand.

"I'm ready. I'm ready to be yours, solely and completely. It hurts. It hurts to miss out on someone who is good. It hurts to fail at something that was supposed to last forever. It hurts to hurt him, but it hurts more not being with you. I don't want to hurt anymore. I want to love again. I want to be loved again. I want what we have. I want my new thing. I love my new thing. I'm filing for divorce, Hudson. I want you and only you."

Tears came to Hudson's eyes as he hugged her tight and lifted her off her feet. He was elated. He placed her back down. "Wow. Just to be sure, I'm not dreaming, right? This is for real?"

Laughing her first real laugh in a long time, she nodded and playfully tapped him. "This is real. I am real. You are real. *We* are real." She waved her hand between them. "This is us. The *us* is finally real!"

Hudson barely let her finish before he delivered a barrage of kisses all over her face and lips. Then he pulled her to him by the waist and began unfastening her clothes.

"No, no, no, baby. I can't," she protested, pulling back. "I still have to get my belongings, and I have to tell him officially that I'm leaving."

Hudson pulled her back to him. "I'll buy you a whole new wardrobe, and anything else can be retrieved later, and you can tell him in the morning. Tonight I want you. I want what's finally mine. I want you in my bed."

Giggling, Karli bit her lip. "You've been waiting a long time for this moment, and I promise you that all of that will happen. I just want to do it the right way. It's already going to be devastating enough."

Hudson exhaled and unbuttoned his suit jacket. He sat down on a sofa chair and pulled Karli between his legs. "Okay, tell him the right way, but I need you tonight. I have to have you in my bed. Please, baby."

Karli slid her phone out of her pocket and dialed her husband's cell phone. When he answered, an onslaught of questions followed. When he finally paused, Karli cleared her throat. "I need my space, Michael. I'm going to be staying at a hotel tonight, but tomorrow we'll talk." Despite his pleas, Karli continued to deny him, and he finally accepted her terms before they hung up.

Karli sat her phone on the coffee table and turned back to Hudson. "You'll have me in your bed tonight."

Without a care or concern, Hudson lifted her and carried her into the bedroom, kissing her all along the way. Once he laid her down on the bed, he stared lovingly at her. "No, tonight you'll be in *our* bed."

Chapter 23

Michael sat at his desk in a daze. He'd missed an important phone call, he was behind on his paperwork, he had to reschedule a settlement hearing, and he looked like crap. His clothing was sharp, but his face told the story of a man riddled with pain, worry, confusion, and a twinge of anger.

It'd been two weeks since Karli moved out of their home . . . their house. It hadn't been a home in months. She was living in an undisclosed hotel, and despite his efforts to woo her back, he'd gotten the paperwork he dreaded: a petition for divorce due to irreconcilable differences. His eyes watered again as he thought about the courier delivering the papers yesterday at his job, of all places.

Everyone had tried to console him, from his parents to Karli's, to their friends. None of them had been able to get in contact with her, and her colleagues and other employees at the company had been instructed to keep their mouths shut, block phone calls, and disallow visits from any of them, including Catrina. It was as if she was divorcing everyone. Karli had sent Catrina a text at the beginning of each week to let her know she was doing fine, but she wouldn't respond to any attempts Catrina made to contact her.

As he sat there, the questions began to grow in his mind. How in the hell did they move from Karli needing a little space to getting a divorce in two weeks? He knew

Karli. She was his wife. She was a planner, a thinker, and a strategist. This sudden shift from wanting to mend their differences to needing space to filing divorce papers seemed implausible to him. Though the conflict had been building, the divorce was still too sudden. They'd been married for four years, so what in the world would make her want to rush to throw it all away, without so much as a conversation about doing so? That was what hurt. Despite five years of being together as a couple and promising each other a lifetime together, he hadn't even been afforded the courtesy of a face-to-face conversation, let alone the privacy of receiving such news in the solace of his own home. He didn't know this woman. This woman wasn't his wife. He refused to believe that she could switch up like the wind on him. Something had to be amiss. He felt it in his gut.

The more he contemplated it, the more upset and depressed he became. He was fighting a battle between being devastated and wanting to wreak devastation. A raging storm swelled within his spirit. He had made a mistake, but just like her, he had tried to make amends for it and had gone above and beyond to make their marriage work. It made absolutely no sense to him that the woman who had cried and begged him to forgive her sins, who had wanted to make their marriage work, was the same one who had filed for divorce. Whether she wanted him to or not, he was going to find out what was going on with her, and they would have a conversation. She owed him that much. He wasn't going to accept this without an explanation and a fight.

After slipping out his cell phone, he dialed her number. Of course, the call went to her voice mail, as it had been doing for the past two weeks. She couldn't avoid him forever, and he was determined that she wouldn't. As he tapped his phone on his hand, an idea came to mind, and he went into the app to track her cell phone. When the phone didn't ping, he contacted the cellular provider. They explained that she had canceled their cell service for that line. He was flabbergasted. She was really making major moves without consulting him. Now he really knew something was awry.

After hanging up, he swiped his hand across his beard and then slammed his hand on the desk in frustration. "Think, Michael. Think," he said aloud. Suddenly, he snapped his fingers. He dialed another number.

"If it isn't my favorite lawyer."

"You don't have to suck up. I need your help," Michael responded.

"Is it paying help?"

"It's always paying when it comes from me, you know that."

"I'm just asking because you sound angry, and anger means it's personal. All our interactions have been on a professional level, but I'm your guy, no matter what."

"Good. I need to find out some information on someone."

"No problem, boss. Who?"

"My wife."

Why can't he just leave well enough alone? Karli thought as she sat in bed, in a huff from the conversation she was now having over the phone.

Being in marketing had its perks, and one of those perks was getting to know people in very high positions. She had learned from one such person that Michael had been snooping around, trying to find out where she was and what was going on with her.

Knowing him and his controlling ways, she was certain he'd never settle for allowing her to leave without a fuss and giving her space. Eventually, he would go on an ego trip and disregard her request to be left alone. Of course, she figured the divorce papers would be the straw that broke the camel's back when it came to Michael. She couldn't deny that for the most part, his incessant research was out of his love for her, but on the other hand, she knew he wanted to force her to go back to him, to assert what he thought was his authority over her.

After her call ended, she took a deep breath and leaned her head against the headboard, hoping Michael would let it go.

"Michael again?" Hudson asked as he eased into bed beside her.

"Yes." She nodded. "He's beginning to search for me. I don't want to hurt him with all of this. I just wish he would leave me alone."

Hudson stroked her hand with his thumb. "That's why I had my people get with you about securing your information, and I'm glad you took my advice by driving my Audi to work." He gently pulled her head to him and kissed her forehead. "Don't worry, baby. He's not going to force you to do anything you don't want to do, including having to see him and talk to him."

Cocooned in Hudson's arms, she felt safe and secure, but in the back of her mind, she had an ominous feeling that she couldn't shake.

Chapter 24

Michael sat brooding in his office. He had put his private investigator, Ross, on Karli, and every time they had a check-in, Ross had no information to share. He still hadn't located her or found out what was going on with her. This guy could find an ant in a field, but he couldn't manage to locate Michael's wife. He'd even gone as far as stalking the outside parking deck at Karli's job, and even that had yielded nothing.

Ross entered Michael's office and closed the door. Looking at Michael, Ross frowned, because Michael appeared as if he hadn't slept in days. If it weren't for the expensive clothing, he would look really unkempt, older even. The weight of the world was on his shoulders, and he appeared on the verge of completely coming undone.

Ross sat in the seat in front of Michael, who clasp his hands together. His bloodshot eyes pierced the investigator, all but begging him to deliver some news. Something. Anything. Good or bad.

"Tell me you have something," Michael bit out through grimaced lips.

Ross slid the toothpick out of his mouth and slowly shook his head. "Your wife is locked up tighter than Fort Knox. I can't get a hit on her cell, her vehicle can't be found, and I can't even spot her going in and out of work. You sure she didn't skip town on you? Either that or she's muthafuckin' Houdini."

"Shit!" Michael spat, throwing the charts off his desk. He stood and paced, rubbing his hand across his head. "She just got promoted. There's no way she's left, and she ain't Houdini. You've never *not* been able to find some- one for me. She's got to be getting help from someone."

Ross looked at him sympathetically. He felt bad for the man. Michael was usually smooth and collected, but leave it to a woman to unhinge even the most put-to- gether brother. Whatever he did to lose her must have been awful, because based on his reaction, she had to be one hell of a woman.

"Look, Michael, I'll keep searching—"

Michael turned to him and spewed, "For what? The one time I need you, you can't deliver. Get the fuck out of my office."

"Whoa! My man, I think you need to calm down—"

"I'm sick of everyone telling me what I should do or am going to do," he snarled, cutting Ross off. "If you can't find her, I will. I'm not paying you another red cent. Now, like I said before, get . . . the fuck . . . out."

Ross understood that Michael's outburst stemmed from the pain he was obviously feeling. Rather than get into a pissing contest with the man in his own office, Ross decided to do as requested and leave. Standing, he lifted his hands, and then he backed away. "As you wish. I'm sorry I couldn't be of more assistance. Call me if you need me."

Not bothering to acknowledge him, Michael yanked his leather chair away from his desk and plopped down in it. All he wanted was his wife back. That was it. Nothing in his life meant more. Nothing could go right until she was back home, in his arms, the way she was supposed to be. The way she had *vowed* to be.

After sliding open his desk drawer, he pulled out the divorce papers and ran his hands across them, then slammed them down on the desk. Holding in his tears, he bent his head down on his knuckles, hoping to find some relief from the pain. He knew he wouldn't. Relief would come only if Karli walked through that door and told him she was coming home.

A knock on his door interrupted his thoughts at that moment. "What?" he called in an aggravated tone.

The door opened slightly, and his receptionist, Stephanie, peeked inside. "Is everything all right, Attorney Sanders?" she asked, full of concern, having heard part of his outburst all the way out in her area. She stepped inside his office.

"I'm fine. Leave me," he said, more harshly than he should have.

Swallowing the lump in her throat, she nodded. "Yes, sir. If you need anything, buzz me." With that, she hurried back out and closed the door.

As soon as she left, a ding from his computer alerted him of an important email, letting him know that the universe was determined not to give him a break. He knew he'd have to push back his troubles and refocus on conducting business. Sadly, it was the only thing he had left.

"Maybe you should take some time off," Bryson said, and Michael looked up at him. He didn't even remember Bryson coming in his office or talking to him, he was so far gone.

"Can't. Work has to be done."

Bryson stood up and stopped him from signing some paperwork. "You haven't even read that," he said, lifting the file from this desk. "At least take a break and go clear your head. I'll hold down the office here for you."

Michael nodded and stood up. "Thank you, Bryson," he said, slipping on his pea coat.

Bryson walked over and patted his shoulder. "It'll be all right, man. Once things settle, it'll work out. Just watch and see."

Michael agreed, although he hardly believed him. Deep on the inside, though, he held on to the fleeting hope that he was right.

Through his misery, he decided it was going to be a bar day; he needed a few stiff drinks. He stopped at his favorite sports bar, found a seat at the bar, and tried to drown his sorrows, and as he finished his second drink, he heard a familiar voice.

"Mike? Big Mike Sanders, is that really you?"

Michael turned to his right and saw his old college buddy Hudson and laughed.

"Hudson Lewis!" He stood slowly as Hudson waved good-bye to the men he'd been with and walked over to him.

They embraced in a one-arm hug and sat down next to each other.

"Oh my fucking God! Mike! It's been, shit, what? Eight years? I haven't seen you since we all got together to go on that fellas' trip to Vegas! How the hell are you?"

Michael laughed, recalling that weekend. It had been hella eventful, and they'd all had more free and loose women than they could shake a stick at. Hudson and Michael had been college roommates for one semester, and he'd loved the fact that this white boy who looked like Brad Pitt had been as cool as any brother around. If you didn't see his lily-white skin, you'd think he was a born-and-bred black man. Michael hated clichés, but he had to admit that Hudson talked black, acted black, and had a love for black women only.

Hudson's other distinguishing trait, outside of his appearance, was his money, which was long like a muthafucka, but that was because he was a grinder like his blue-collar father. While his dad still believed in hard work, Hudson nowadays busted his ass to make sure he labored only over how to spend his money. He was a cool dude, he'd been a great friend in college, and he knew how to have a good time, which was one of the reasons why Michael had distanced himself from him. Hudson had been too wild and crazy, and Michael had had to learn how to settle down. It had worked in the end, because, business aside, he never would've gotten the opportunity with Karli if he hadn't settled down.

"Yeah, those were good times," Michael said sadly.

Hudson nodded. "I can't believe we lost contact. Why is that?"

Michael laughed. "'Cause your white ass was crazy as hell, that's why."

They laughed together.

"I would've never been able to get my business off the ground if I'd continued to fool around with you," Michael added.

Hudson shrugged and laughed. "Touché!" He playfully pushed Michael. "But times change, and people change."

Michael quickly downed the remainder of his drink. Hudson didn't know how much that statement resonated with him right now. "I'll drink another round to that."

Hudson eyed Michael closely. His old friend looked as if he was seriously going through it. Hudson could tell that he was trying to put up a façade, that something was earnestly wrong. He felt sorry for Michael. He waved over the bartender.

"Give us two shots of . . ." Hudson turned to Michael. "What are you drinking again?" he asked.

"Hennessy," Michael answered.

"Shit. It's deep." Hudson turned back to the bartender. "Two shots of Hennessy," he said, placing a comforting hand on his friend's shoulder.

They sat in silence, watching the sports channel, until the bartender returned with their drinks. They touched glasses.

"My dude," they said in unison and downed the drinks. Then they laughed at the fact they both remembered their old way of toasting.

"So what's wrong, my friend?" Hudson asked as he sat his shot glass down.

Michael shook his head. "Nothing. Just taking a much-needed break from work."

Hudson leaned back and scoffed. "You're really gonna shoot shit to me now? To me? This is Hud. The only time you ever drank anything other than beer in college was when the problem was real."

Sighing, Michael realized his old friend was right. He'd honestly forgotten how close he and Hudson used to be. Hudson still knew him like the back of his hand, and Michael smiled slightly. Maybe running into Hudson was what he'd needed to lift his spirits, because if anybody could, crazy Hud could.

"Man, forget all that. How's business?" Michael said, avoiding the question, as Hudson signaled to the bartender to pour another round.

Hudson stretched his arms out. "Straight, baby."

They both laughed as they fist bumped. Just then Michael noticed Hudson's Rolex on one wrist and the designer threads he was rocking. Yep, his boy was certified.

"And your business?" Hudson asked.

Michael stretched out his arms. "Straight, baby." They fist bumped again. "Maybe not as straight as yours, but trust, I'm good."

"Never a doubt." Hudson lifted his replenished shot glass.

"So how many women are you knocking down these days?" Michael joked as the liquor started to loosen him up a bit.

"Shit, me? You! You always pulled them! Those chicks went crazy over Mike Sanders."

Together, they laughed heartily. They loved to poke fun at each other, but they both knew they'd been equal in the "love 'em and leave 'em" game back in their day.

Hudson got serious for a moment. "Actually, my dude, I can't even lie. I'm not like that anymore. I finally found the one."

Michael turned to him, wide eyed. "For real?"

Starry eyed, Hudson thought of Karli, and a smile crossed his face. "Yeah, man. I can't explain it. She's just . . . She's *it* for me. Man, I'm in love. Soon, I plan on making her my wife."

"Damn! Congratulations! I never thought I'd see the day that Hudson Lewis settled. She's got to be one helluva woman. And I can tell you're really happy."

Hudson smiled at him. "I really am."

Michael raised his glass. "Let's toast to it." They raised their glasses again.

"My dude."

Hudson noticed the sudden sad expression on Michael's face. "You wanna tell me what's wrong now?"

Michael took a long swig of his beer. "It's just funny how life is. Here you are in love and about to go down the aisle soon . . . And I better get an invite, by the way."

"No doubt, baby!" Hudson interjected. He and Michael touched knuckles again.

"But you're going down the aisle, and I'm going out the door. I'm separated," Michael admitted.

Hudson's heart sank for his friend. "Damn, man. I see why you're on a Henny kick. I'm sorry to hear that. Anything I can do?"

Michael shook his head. "Nah, I think her mind is made up. You know what I mean? Can't do nothing but drink and pray."

Hudson tapped him. "You know what you need? You need some time with an old friend. My lady has a couple of coworkers who are single and bad. Let's kick it at my house for old time's sake, and when she gets home, I'll have her call up one of them. We'll all go out for dinner, a little dancing, and maybe you can get a little cut up." A smile appeared on his face. "Nothing beats getting over old pussy like new pussy," he joked. They both laughed, even though he was serious.

Michael shook his head. "Nah, man. I can't do that. I'm just trying to deal."

"Okay, so forget the cut up. At least come hang out with me, and let's go out later. Get your mind off it for a little while," he pleaded as Michael looked at him skeptically. "Come on. It'll be fun. Not like old times, 'cause I'm a settled man now, but good times. You need a little good in your life right now."

Michael realized he was buzzed, and decided that it might be a good idea. He did need a release from the agony. He nodded. "All right, man. But I can't drive."

"Leave your car. My driver is outside, and he'll take us. We can get your car later."

Michael nodded, and they stood up. Hudson paid their tab, and they left the sports bar, laughing and joking about old times.

Chapter 25

As they walked through the front door of Hudson's mansion, Michael knew his boy was certified. He was worth a small fortune himself, but his boy made that look like a drop in a bucket.

"Welcome to my humble abode," Hudson said as he closed the door and locked it. "Come with me."

He ushered Michael into the humongous living room, which had floor-to-ceiling windows affording a fabulous view of his immaculate backyard as well as the city.

"Sit. Let me pour you another drink," Hudson said.

Michael took his coat off and sat down on the sofa. Hudson poured them both a drink and walked back over to sit beside him. They did their famous toast, and Michael downed the amber liquid in his glass.

"Damn, dude. You're living hella good. This is nice," Michael said.

"Fruits of my labor, dude. Only the fruits of my labor. Well, mine, and the new campaign my lady put together has me raking in so much dough, and I didn't even think that was possible. She's so freaking awesome, man. Brains and beauty. I swear, I can't wait for you to meet her."

"I can't wait, either. The way she's got you blushing and bragging, she's got to be awesome. I swear, man, I've never seen you so happy. It's good to see someone enjoying being in love. It gives me a little hope again."

"And in love, I am. Never thought that would happen for me, but I must say I'm loving it. I'm loving her!" he shouted excitedly.

Suddenly, they heard the faint sound of a toilet flushing. Hudson paused and placed his glass down.

"The hell?" he asked, looking at his watch. "It's only three in the afternoon. She shouldn't be home yet, and the maid doesn't come back until tomorrow."

Michael nodded. "Go check it out. I got nine-one-one on standby, if you need it."

"You better break a bottle and help until they get here."

They laughed as Hudson got up. He went up the stairs, checked the master bedroom, and was startled to see Karli getting back in bed.

"Jesus, Hudson," she said, holding her hand to her chest.

He let out a sigh of relief. "I thought someone was in the house." He quickly noticed her sweaty, flushed face and walked over to her. "What's wrong, baby? Why are you at home in the middle of the day?" he asked, pulling her close and caressing her face.

"I wasn't feeling too well. My stomach has been upset. I have something to . . . Wait . . . what are you doing home so early?"

He kissed her forehead. "I actually ran into an old friend of mine from college. I was finished with my meeting, so we talked, and I invited him over for drinks. I was hoping that we all could go out for dinner tonight and maybe you could invite one of your colleagues. He needs a lady friend in his life to get the monkey off his back. But since you're not feeling well, I'll just finish hanging with him and reschedule it for another day."

"Oh, I'm sorry to be the party pooper," she said apologetically.

He cradled her face. "Are you kidding me? You come first. He and I can hang out anytime. If you're feeling up to it, though, come down and introduce yourself. He'd love to meet you. I've been bragging about you all afternoon."

She nodded. "Sure. Just give me a moment to freshen up. I don't want to go down there looking like death, since you've been bragging about me."

Hudson grinned. "You'll always look beautiful to me. When he leaves, I'm going to take care of you. Make you some soup and snuggle with you. How does that sound?"

"Like heaven." She kissed him softly and got up to wash her face and put on some clothes.

She changed into black leggings and an oversize sweater and stuck her feet in some black flat shoes before she headed downstairs. She heard Hudson laughing and talking to his friend as she entered the living room.

When Hudson saw her, he stood. "Mike, this is my beautiful lady—"

Michael jumped up. "Karli!" he yelled as his head began swimming.

"Michael?" Karli's eyes bucked in fear, and another wave of nausea instantly hit her. She lunged for a nearby wastebasket and spewed the contents of her stomach into it. Hudson ran over to her, gave her a napkin from the wet bar, and then turned back to Michael.

"You know her?"

"*Know her*? What the fuck is this? What kind of games are you two playing?" Michael asked in disbelief.

"Games? What are you talking about?" Hudson asked in confusion.

Karli held on to Hudson for dear life. "Hud . . . Hudson," she said nervously. "Michael is my . . . he's my—"

"I'm her fucking husband," Michael hollered. "That's my wife. You son of a—"

Before Hudson and Karli could react, Michael charged and punched Hudson clean in the face. Hudson fell on the floor. Karli jumped between them before Michael could continue the beating he was about to issue.

"Michael! Stop it. Please." She attempted to hold him back as Hudson scrambled off the floor.

He pointed at Hudson. "You knew! You sat in my face and bragged about being with my wife. We were friends. How could you do this to me?"

Hudson shook his head. "What do you mean? I didn't know anything. Karli's last name is Fitzgerald. How was I supposed to know that the Michael she was married to was really Michael Sanders?"

"Fitzgerald?" Michael asked, looking back and forth from Hudson to Karli. "So you're not even using your last name?"

Karli shook her head as the realization of what had happened set in. "No, Hudson knows me by my maiden name from a work project I did before I got married, and the only business cards I had at the time I took on the Lewis Investments account have my maiden name on them. He must've thought that Fitzgerald was my married name."

They all stood back, in shock, to learn that Hudson's Karli Fitzgerald was actually Michael's Karli Sanders. Hudson rubbed his head and plopped down on the sofa. Michael stood and looked at Karli. His heart was literally breaking. Karli trembled in fear, tears streaming down her face, at the realization that her new man and her husband knew each other and she'd been caught.

"Karli," Michael whimpered, tears streaming down his face too. "Baby, please tell me that this isn't true. Tell me that you haven't been having an affair with Hudson. Please."

Karli wailed, in pain. She'd lied to Michael and told him that she was living out of a hotel, because she couldn't bear to tell him that she was with another man. She'd figured she would wait until the divorce was final and then would make it appear as if she'd simply moved on. She had had no idea that the two men knew each other or that her chickens would soon come home to roost.

Looking up at him, with tears still running down her face, she admitted the truth by saying only, "Michael, I'm so sorry. I'm sorry."

"Karli," he said, cradling her face. "Please. Don't do this to us. Baby. This is *me*. Four years, Karli. I'm not perfect, but you know I love you. You walked down that aisle with *me*. You married *me*. We vowed to be together. *Us*. Please tell me this is not happening."

Hudson stood. "No. I love her, and you're not—"

Michael moved to rush Hudson, and Karli pushed him back. Michael pointed at him. "You shut your mouth. I'll rip your fucking head off. Going after other people's wives! She is my wife, and I will not let you take what's mine."

Hudson squared up and undid his cuff links. "Oh, you must've forgotten. I get down for mine, too, and like it or not, dude, she's not yours anymore."

They both charged each other, and Karli was stuck in between the two men she loved. She forced them apart with all the strength she could muster. In literally an instant, she'd turned longtime friends into lifetime enemies. The only reason they hadn't really gotten loose was that they were acutely aware that they might hurt Karli, and neither one of them wanted that. Their love for her outweighed their hatred of each other.

"Please! Stop this," Karli yelled. She turned to Hudson. "Please let me handle this."

Hudson stepped back, staring at Michael with malice in his eyes. He went over and sat on the sofa and drank a swig of his Henny, never taking his eyes off Michael and Karli.

"How long, Karli?" Michael asked in a teary voice. "Hmm? How long?"

Karli faced him with sorrowful eyes. "Five months."

Michael stumbled back a few steps. He wasn't prepared to hear that not only had his wife been having an affair, but she also had a full-blown relationship with his ex-friend. "Five months?" he asked, realizing that their affair must have begun not long after he disrespected her, and his eyes closed as fresh tears rushed out. "I knew something wasn't right with this shit," he muttered, shaking his head. "You were that angry with me that you would defile our bed, break our vows, and leave our marriage?"

"I was hurt," she yelled, in pain.

"And so was I!" he screamed back at her. He pointed at her. "I'm your husband, Karli. How do you think I felt finding out that you didn't even want to have my baby? Then you didn't even tell me that you were on birth control."

Karli shook her head as the dam opened and fresh, hot tears and sweat poured out uncontrollably. "I apologized for that. I tried. I begged you to forgive me. I came to you. I pleaded with you. I begged you to talk to me. I begged you to make our marriage work. I begged you to love me again. And every time, Michael—every single time—you tossed me and my feelings to the side, as if I meant nothing," she yelled as he held his head down in shame. "When you did forgive me, it was only because of what you did to me in return, so that I could forgive you. You never listened to me. Never cared about what I had to say or how I felt. And don't even pretend like you weren't here to 'hook up' with a woman. Seems to me you were pretty content to move on yourself!"

Pausing for a moment, she took a deep breath. Then she continued. "Hudson was not intentional. We found each other. I was hurting, and he helped me not hurt.

He was there for me. He loved me. Me! For who I was and what I wanted, and not some fake façade of who he wanted me to be to him."

The realization of what she was saying hit Michael like a ton of bricks. He replayed all the times she'd tried to tell him what was on her mind or to restore their marriage and he'd cut her off and dismissed her feelings. He felt horrible, realizing that in many ways he'd pushed her directly into Hudson's arms. Bryson and even his dad had tried to warn him, and he didn't heed the message. Michael glanced up at her and palmed her face between his hands.

"Karli," he said softly, staring deeply into her eyes. "I'm so sorry. I'm sorry for what I did to us, for what I did to *you*. It's clear to me now, and I'm begging you now, just like you begged me. Don't let our story end here. Not like this. I will spend every waking moment proving myself to you. Just don't end our marriage. Four years. That has to mean something. We have to mean something. He may know your body, but I know you. The Karli on the inside. The way you think. Your dreams. Your aspirations. Your fears. Your heart. I know you."

Hudson sniffed and pinched the bridge of his nose before sitting back, with his drink in his hand. He was pissed and was growing tired of witnessing Michael's efforts to woo his woman back. But out of respect for who he and Michael were to each other literally fifteen minutes ago, and for Karli, he kept his emotions at bay. However, this violin moment was going to have to end soon, before he lost it.

"Come home to me, Karli. Come home with me, please," Michael begged.

Karli was sincerely torn, for more reasons than one. She loved Michael for who he was to her, for the marriage they had once shared, for the friend he was to her, and for the love he'd given her over the years. Yet she loved Hudson. She loved him for who he was to her now, for the friendship they shared, for their business relationship, for the freedom and acceptance he gave her, and for the love they now shared. She loved them equally, but for separate reasons. And she didn't know with whom she shared a particular blessing.

She pointed to one of the chairs. "Please have a seat, Michael. I have something that, ironically, I need to share with both of you, and we're all going to need to sit down."

Begrudgingly, Michael sat in the chair opposite Hudson. Karli took a seat at the far end of the sofa that Hudson currently occupied.

"This is difficult for me. Right now, I need for all of us to be amicable and cordial. My life has assuredly been flipped upside down, and as selfish as this sounds, I need both of you," Karli told them.

"What's wrong, baby?" they both asked simultaneously, staring at her with concern.

She rubbed her forehead. "Jesus. This is a mess," she said slowly before taking a deep breath. Then she continued. "I went to the doctor today because I've been sick for the past week."

"Baby, why didn't you tell me?" Hudson asked, reaching for her hand.

"I thought it was a virus or the flu or something. I was going to go back to work, but I felt so bad, and then the news was weighing on me," she said, grabbing each man's hand. Shaking her head, she added, "I can't believe this all started, because I didn't want children, and now here we are." She gazed at each man. "I am pregnant, and I don't know who the father is. The doctor said that my due date is in September, which means that I got pregnant in December, and in December I was with both of you intimately and unprotected. So one of you is this baby's father, and I'm not sure who it is."

Immediately, Michael jumped up, in a rage. "All these years I've wanted a baby with you, and you tell me that I can't even be happy about it, because there's a possibility it could be his?" he ranted, in disbelief. "Did you stop your birth control?"

Karli shook her head. "No. It just happened."

Shaking his head in disgust, Michael scoffed. "The weather just happens, Karli. This happened because you chose to step out on our marriage."

Hudson stood up. "Calm down. This situation is stressful enough. I'm not going to let you berate her, and you're damn sure not going to put my baby's life in danger by stressing out Karli."

"*Your baby*?" Michael seethed. "You ballsy muthafucka! News flash. This baby could be mine, and if it is, you can kiss Karli good-bye, because my wife and kid are coming home with me. You will have no part in raising my child."

"Like I'd let you raise mine!" Hudson spewed. "You can't even treat the mother right!"

"At least I'm man enough to get my own woman, homeboy!"

"Enough!" Karli yelled. "I'm wrong. You're wrong. Hudson's wrong. We're all wrong. Maybe not equally, but we all had a hand in this. I haven't even had time to process the fact that I am pregnant, and you two are acting like animals! I didn't want to bring a child into this world before I was ready, and now the situation is far worse," she cried, leaning back in her seat.

Michael and Hudson eyed each other, in shock.

"So, what? What are you saying?" Michael asked. "Please don't tell me that you're thinking about not having this baby. You've already left me. Please don't take away my child."

Hudson kneeled in front of her. "Karli, I know you're scared, but the baby is here. I'm not prepared, either, but when I see you and think of the possibility of you carrying our baby, there's no greater joy."

Karli wiped her eyes. She hadn't even had time to get her own thoughts together about this pregnancy. They were all finding out together. Of course, both men would want the baby, especially now, when they both were laying claim to her. A baby wasn't enough to make her leave or stay with either man, and her main concern was whether she was ready to be a mommy. How could she bring a child into this world with such turmoil in her life? Before she could even process that information, she had to face the reality of her extramarital affair head-on.

"I don't know what I want or what I plan to do right now," she answered, looking at both men. "All I know is that this . . ." She pointed at herself and at them. "This can't be healthy for either one of us," she said as she gently rubbed her hand across her belly. The reality of her pregnancy was finally beginning to sink in.

Michael nodded. "Fine. Get your purse and your phone, because you're coming home with me."

"Over my dead body!" Hudson yelled.

"I can arrange that too," Michael growled. Karli put her hands in the air, and Michael looked at her. "What? I refuse to allow this child, who could be my seed, to grow inside you while you're living in this house. It's not happening."

"And my seed isn't living in your house," Hudson retorted.

Swallowing hard, Karli turned to Hudson. "I'm going to the hotel." When he went to protest, she shook her head. "It's not fair to either of you, and I need peace in my life. You don't want me there, and he doesn't want me here, and I need both of you, so I'm going. You'll remain in your house, and Michael will remain in his, until I make a decision." She shook her head. "I don't even know who the father is."

"Oh, we can schedule a paternity test now, and we'll know within a month, so then we can get this shit over and done with. The sooner we can sort this shit out, the sooner you and my baby can come home!" Michael yelled.

Hudson shook his head. "That should be Karli's decision." He looked over at Karli. "Baby, what do you want to do?"

"Ain't this a bitch!" Michael scoffed, in disbelief, and glared at Karli. "So he's voicing opinions on your behalf now? I can't believe this!"

Sighing, Karli shook her head. "Michael, he's right. It's my decision, and I haven't decided what I want to do. For now, I need my space. I need to think so that I can make a well-informed decision for the baby and myself."

Karli looked up at both men. Hudson readily agreed, and Michael huffed, then reluctantly nodded his agreement. He was too distraught to fight this battle.

"I'm agreeing to this only because you're not staying in his house while you're pregnant. But we still have unfinished business about our marriage. Then what about afterward? Where will you be then? Who will you choose?" Michael said.

Karli shook her head. "One battle at a time, please. I can't think."

Michael huffed and shook his head. "Fine, but you and lover boy are restricted from having relations while you're knocked up. If this child is mine, I don't want his soldiers marching on my baby's body." He went to find his keys and realized he didn't have his car. "You brought me to this damned place." He pointed at Hudson.

Karli sighed. "Use my car. I'll have the driver bring me by to get it tomorrow."

Michael smirked. "Irreconcilable differences, huh? These seven months can't fly by fast enough."

Karli and Hudson walked Michael to the garage, where he opened the door to Karli's car, jumped in, backed out, and spun away like a bat out of hell.

Hudson pulled her close. "I'm so sorry about all this, but I'm here for you and our baby."

"Thank you." She hugged him back. "I better pack up. Michael will flip if I don't keep my word."

Hudson kissed her forehead and watched as she went upstairs to pack up her belongings. He pulled out the ring box he'd had hidden in his pocket and tossed it in his hand, hoping and wondering if that proposal would actually ever happen.

Chapter 26

Karli sat in the penthouse, waiting for Catrina's call. She'd been a mess of tears for the past week. She was so distraught she had to take a week off work to be able to cope with everything that had transpired. Mostly, she wanted time to herself to think and process this crazy, twisted turn of events.

It pained her to the core to know that she'd hurt Michael so deeply. She didn't hate him. She simply loved Hudson. In fact, she still loved Michael. He'd been her knight in shining armor. He'd whisked her off her feet and made her his wife. She knew that Michael loved and cared for her, but it was his blind love that had pushed her away and into the arms of Hudson. However, the way the situation had panned out was on constant repeat in her mind. As much as she wanted to be with Hudson, she couldn't lie that the devastation she had caused was creating doubts in her mind.

Could a relationship with Hudson honestly be the right thing if it caused so much pain? Still, how could she let Hudson go? He'd been by her side through it all. He'd put his own feelings and life on pause in exchange for a sliver of her time and a morsel of her love. How much would it hurt him if she left him after all this to go back to a relationship in order to spare Michael's feelings? Didn't she owe Michael that much? Didn't she owe it to him to spare his feelings? But would she honestly be there in the moment, in the relationship with Michael, if she did go back to him?

She refused to ponder these questions anymore at the moment. Her head hurt. She needed a break, because as soon as Catrina arrived, her bestie would most definitely attempt to squeeze every ounce of information out of her, from beginning to end. Therefore, she decided to push aside her thoughts now and air them out with her bestie. She needed someone with a level head and a clear mind to guide her, because as of right now, she was lost.

The sound of her cell phone ringing brought her out of her reverie. She answered the call and gave Catrina the code she needed to access the penthouse floor. A couple of minutes later, Catrina was knocking on the door.

Karli raced to get the door, and when Catrina walked inside, her eyes bulged.

"What in the entire hell? Girl, how the hell did you get this place? Is this yours?" Catrina's eyes scanned the penthouse and then landed back on Karli. "What is really going on? This is the first time I've seen you or talked to you in a couple of weeks, since you slapped divorce papers on Michael. Why are you shutting me out? Why did you let go of your marriage?"

The barrage of questions forced Karli to rub her temples. She went into the kitchen, opened the refrigerator, and retrieved a bottled water, then offered Catrina one. When her friend declined, Karli offered her a seat on the plush sofa and sat in the chair across from her.

"This is a lot to unpack, so I'm going to start from the beginning. I hope I answer all your questions," Karli said.

Catrina sat back and spread her arms. "Well, I'm definitely all ears."

After taking a long swig of water, Karli released a deep breath and then began telling Catrina the story of her affair with Hudson and just how she had come to the point of filing for divorce from Michael. She explained how Hudson had become her client, how the affair had started, how she had tried to work it out with Michael, and how Michael's possessive ways and blind love had pushed her away. She even told Catrina about the threesome with Tya and ultimately how Michael had ended up catching her and Hudson.

Catrina sat there, flabbergasted. She hadn't even known that her best friend was having an affair, let alone a threesome, or that she was considering giving up her marriage for some random man that no one had ever met or laid eyes on. She was honestly at a loss for words, and it was evident as she sat there, gawking at Karli.

"Well, are you going to say something?" Karli asked after the air seemed to turn stale.

"I don't know what to say or where to begin." Catrina tried to wrap her mind around what her bestie had revealed. "Karli, I get the issues you were having with Michael, but you're giving up on your marriage for some random? Girl, this is your first time out in the pasture during a time you shouldn't even be grazing. How do you know this man's sweet dick ain't fucking up your head to the point you're fucking up your marriage simply for some hot sex on a platter?"

Karli rolled her eyes. "Excuse me for not being a lover of men, like some people I know—"

Catrina threw up her hand. "Oh, hell no! You don't get to judge me right now, especially not when I'm not officially committed to any of the men I deal with. Don't get mad with me because for once in your prim and proper life, you fucked up."

Instantly, tears sprung to Karli's eyes. Catrina knew that was not like her. They had always been able to keep it real with each other, and while Karli was prim and proper, she was also a sassy baddie with a slick tongue. She could dish and take whatever was given to her, so Catrina knew something more was on the horizon. She

moved to sit on the arm of Karli's chair and placed her
arm around her friend. "Girl, what's really wrong?"

Karli dabbed her eyes with a tissue. "Sorry. I'm so
emotional these days." She looked up at Catrina. "As fate
would have it, I'm pregnant."

Catrina jumped up. "Say what?" She kneeled in front
of Karli. "Are you freaking serious right now? You got off
the birth control pills?"

Karli's hands trembled as she shook her head. "No, I
never did until I found out I was pregnant, and I never
skipped. Yet here I am, in the middle of a nasty divorce,
with a new lover and pregnant."

Catrina sat on the plush rug in front of Karli, with her
legs crossed Indian-style. "I hate to ask, but do you know
whose baby it is?"

"No, I don't. I was with both men intimately. And yes,
they both know." Karli huffed, then drank more water.

Catrina smiled. "Damn. I know it's the worst timing,
but can I take a minute to bask in the fact that I'm gonna
be an auntie?"

Karli smiled for the first time in a week as she watched
Catrina beam and play with her belly. Throughout this
entire debacle, Karli had never even taken a moment
to embrace the blessing of being pregnant. It was as if
through her friend's eyes, she was beginning to warm to
the idea that being a mother entailed not losing herself
but rather the blessing of gaining more.

"Thank you for showing some excitement about the
baby. Of course, Hudson is happy. Michael is too upset
to enjoy the possibility, and me, I hadn't even decided
whether bringing a child into this world, in this situation,
is something I should consider at all."

Catrina stood and hugged her. Then she forced Karli
to look at her. "You listen to me. I may be wild and crazy,
but if you've never listened to me before, listen and trust

me on this. A baby is a gift, regardless of the situation.
No matter what, I would be excited about your baby,
and you should be too. It doesn't matter if Michael or
Hudson is happy, sad, mad, or indifferent about this
baby. This is *your* baby. Yours. You're not discussing
being a mommy anymore, as you *are* one. That means
that even through all your mess, God saw fit to bless you
with his most precious gift, a baby." She gently rubbed
Karli's belly again as a slow smile spread across Karli's
face. "This child has nothing to do with the issues you're
having. Fix your issues, and love your child."

Catrina's words hit Karli like a ton of bricks, and fresh
tears flowed from her eyes. Despite her mess, she was
a mommy. Her heart completely melted at the thought
of holding her own bundle of joy, and then and there,
she knew she could never kill an actual person living
and growing inside her, regardless of who the father
was or the drama that would follow. She could still be
the woman she aimed to be, and now she just had more
motivation to become her. In that instant, she decided
that the most important thing was delivering a healthy
baby into this world and trying her damnedest to do right
by him or her.

Karli nodded. "You're right." She giggled, rubbing her
belly. "I'm going to be a mommy." They shared a laugh.
"Oh, my goodness, Catrina. I'm going to be a mommy."

Shaking her head, Catrina ribbed her. "Duh! You're
just figuring that out? I knew you could be a little slow,
but—"

Karli threw a pillow at her as Catrina cackled at her
friend.

Catrina realized her friend was having a moment,
and so she sat back down on the arm of Karli's chair and
allowed her to be, to bask in her new normal. After a little
while, she leaned her head against Karli's, and they were

content to sit just like that until Karli's phone dinged. Karli pulled out her phone and saw she had received a text message from Hudson. He was checking to see how she was feeling.

Once Karli had finished responding, Catrina, who was now lying on the floor, with her feet on the sofa, turned to her friend, eager to continue their conversation. "This may not be the best time to pry, but I have to know the details of this thing. Who is this Hudson dude that you're so ready to give up Michael for?"

Karli smiled slightly. "Like I said, he is my client. His name is Hudson Lewis—"

Catrina's head popped up. "Wait. Wait. Hudson Lewis. You mean Lewis Investments Hudson Lewis? The sexy white guy? One of New York's most eligible bachelors? That Hudson Lewis?"

Karli looked at her sideways. "I see his reputation precedes him."

Catrina sat up and gave her the eye. "Um, yeah. I *am* a lover of men, as you stated." They giggled, and she shook her head. "Karli, are you sure about this? I mean . . . Wait a minute. Is this *his* penthouse? I know he owns this hotel."

"Yes, it is, but my goodness, you know a lot about Hudson—"

Waving her off, Catrina quipped, "Dear friend, I know a lot about *all* of New York's wealthy, sexy, and single men. Until you, Hudson was in the top five on that list."

"Consider him off it now," Karli said sternly.

Catrina shook her head and spread her arms open. "I guess that answers my question. You're sure about him. And since you're sure, I guess he is too. What about his and Michael's friendship?" Karli gave her an "Are you kidding me?" look, and Catrina waved off the question, because she knew the answer to that one too. "And what about this Tya chick?" Catrina's brow furrowed. "Are you bisexual now too?"

Karli sucked her teeth, giving her the side eye. "Hell no. It was a one-time deal. It happened. It's over."

Catrina eyed her. "Not to be a bitch, but, uh, Hudson was supposed to be a one-time deal, and we see what's happened."

Karli scoffed. "By all means, be a bitch and rub that in my face. Catrina, I'm not saying I don't deserve the shit, but you're second-guessing me like you don't even know me. I'm your freaking bestie. How do you ask me some shit like that?"

Catrina looked confused. "I'm sorry. Am I missing something? Right now, I don't know if I do know you anymore. The Karli I know was dedicated and loyal to her husband. She wasn't on no wilding-out shit, and she damn sure would never give up her marriage for a playboy like Hudson Lewis. So excuse me for trying to find out where your head is at. I'm going to love you regardless, but you have to see this from my point of view. I mean, hell, we tell each other everything, and you didn't tell me that you cheated on Michael, let alone had a full-blown affair or were getting a divorce. If it hadn't blown up in your face, I probably wouldn't have known about my niece until she was born. God forbid."

Karli held her head down in shame. Catrina was right. The recent events in her life had changed her. She'd shut everybody out to protect them from the hurt of her secret, but she'd done so also because she needed it to be kept a secret. All her family and friends loved Michael just as much as they loved her, so she knew they wouldn't understand. It was a road of loneliness that she bravely traveled for that once-in-a-lifetime love she had for Hudson.

Catrina made sense, and Karli wasn't so self-absorbed that she didn't think that she was innocent of any wrongdoing. But what could she do about that now? What had been done, had been done. Was she sorrowful? Yes. Was she ashamed? Absolutely. Was she regretful? No. How could she be? She was blessed to be the mother-to-be to a beautiful baby. The calm in all this chaos.

"I understand," Karli whispered. "I know that you feel like I'm a disappointment. I know that you feel that I have changed. And I won't lie. There's some truth to that. When you're growing and you feel stifled, it changes you. Now the cheating, that's on me. But this change is a result of my marital issues and my growth. Michael stunted my growth. I stunted our marriage." She paused briefly, swiping tears from her eyes. "I'm not proud of what I did, Catrina. I'm just telling you why I did it."

Catrina nodded her head in understanding.

Karli continued, with a smirk on her face. "And I'm assuring you that I'm not out here wilding out. I gifted Hudson the threesome with his ex, Tya, because I wanted to give him the same sexual liberation that he gave to me. He never forced that on me. All he ever wanted was me. That's the truth."

Catrina got up off the floor and sat on the sofa. Then she motioned to Karli to come over and sit next to her. Karli got up and sat beside her best friend. Catrina hugged her, and Karli felt all her emotions ooze out as she cried on her friend's shoulder. Catrina allowed her to let it all out. She knew Karli needed it. Reprimands were not needed, because this situation was going to kick Karli in the ass enough. Catrina understood that this was only the first of many meltdowns to come for her friend, and she knew it was important to simply be there to help soften the blow.

"Girl, it's going to be okay," Catrina said, consoling Karli. "I'm going to be by your side. This is now a judgment-free zone. I don't care that you had an affair, that you're getting divorced, or even that you dipped your toe in the lady pond. I might be a little jealous about the fact that you got that experience first—"

"Catrina!" Karli hollered, then laughed at her friend.

"Whatever. Somebody's gotta laugh about the irony in this shit." Catrina looked at her friend, and her expression turned serious. "On a serious note, from this point forward, you come to me if you get too stressed or bummed out. I need my niece or nephew to be healthy and happy. And I want my bestie back. We'll talk it out and work it out."

Karli hugged her again. "Thank you."

"You're welcome." Catrina sighed. With a groan, she said, "You know what we have to do next, right?"

"Face my parents."

"More like face Mama Pat," Catrina said, correcting her, and Karli grunted her frustration. "I already know. You don't have to tell me. I'm going to be there when you do, because somebody has to be the referee."

"And I'm definitely going to need one," Karli agreed as she laid her head on Catrina's shoulder once again.

Karli hoped that Hudson was strong enough to withstand the trials that were headed their way. Neither one of them had considered all these consequences, and she hoped that what they shared was solid enough to win the war. For now, she simply prayed they could get through the impending battle known as a conversation with Patricia Fitzgerald.

Chapter 27

"I can't believe you, Karli," her mother vented as she paced back and forth in her living room. "We raised you better than this. And to do this to Michael! You have lost your mind."

"If I may, Mr. and Mrs. Fitzgerald—" Hudson began.

"No, you *may* not. We don't even know you. I allowed Karli to bring your home-wrecking self into my home only because I wanted to at least see who the possible father of my grandchild is. Outside of this moment, you're not welcome in my house. Be clear, young man. I am team Michael," Karli's mother spewed.

Taken aback, Hudson sat down next to Karli on the sofa. He'd asked Karli if he could be present when she told her parents about him, but he had had no idea he would be stepping into a fiery furnace. Michael had all of Karli's friends and family wrapped around his finger. Undoubtedly, he and Karli had a long road ahead if they were to maintain a relationship.

"Mama!" Karli called out. "That was highly unnecessary and plain rude."

"Unnecessary? Rude? What's unnecessary and beyond rude is having this sorry excuse of a friend and a man, who has somehow managed to turn my daughter into a whore of woman, one who may be pregnant with another man's baby, up in my house!"

Karli felt like she was ten years old again. Tears streamed down her face, and Catrina sat down on her other side on the sofa and held her hand, while Hudson attempted to console her. Catrina, while upset, wasn't judgmental. She actually understood because she knew the full story of the troubles that had occurred between Michael and Karli. Karli's dad just sat there in an armchair, patiently watching his wife tirelessly rant.

Finally, he raised his hand. "Patricia, please calm down. I'm sure Karli has beaten herself up enough over this. She's pregnant with our grandchild. Let's cut her some slack."

Karli's mother threw her hands up. "Cut her some slack? Fine. But you *would* say something like that," she snapped and stalked off.

Karli turned to Hudson. "It may be best if you leave. It's obviously not a good time for you to be here, and I don't want to see you get hurt or be disrespected. I'm so sorry about this."

Hudson stood, pulling her up gently with him, and hugged her tight. "I don't want to leave you."

"I'll be fine. These are my parents. I can take it, but you shouldn't have to. Go get some food and rest. We'll talk tomorrow."

Hudson leaned forward and placed a supple kiss on her forehead. "I love you." He caressed her chin with his thumb. "Call me when you get to the penthouse."

She nodded, and Catrina volunteered to walk Hudson to his car. Hudson picked up his coat and placed it over his forearm. "Mr. Fitzgerald, it was a pleasure to meet you. I apologize for any disruptions that I have caused. Please give Mrs. Fitzgerald my warmest regards."

Karli's father rose from his seat and stuck out his hand, Hudson accepted it, and they shook hands. "It was a pleasure to meet you, also, although I wish it were under different circumstances. Thank you for being a gentleman in my home and for taking care of my daughter.

Right now, she and my grandchild are my only concerns. The rest will work out in time."

Hudson gave a weary smile and turned to follow Catrina to the door. Karli rubbed his back as he walked away and then turned to face her father.

"Daddy, I know you're disappointed in me. I have made such a mess of everything."

Her father hugged her close and consoled her as a new wave of tears began to fall.

"Don't cry, Karli. We all fall short. We just have to make the best of the situation when it comes."

"Mom hates me and Hudson."

Sighing, he pulled back. "No, she doesn't. It just opens up old wounds for her, and she's reacting bitterly. It has nothing to do with Hudson or you."

"Old wounds?" she questioned.

"Come with me," he ordered, and then he began walking down the long hall to his home office. Karli followed behind him, entered his office after him, and shut the door.

He poured her a glass of water and pointed to the small couch against one wall. "Sit please." He poured himself a shot of scotch and drank it down before he turned to face his daughter. "The reason your mother is so upset is that her worst fears have come true. She was worried about you having a high-powered position because you are so much like me. She was worried you'd cheat on Michael."

Karli's eyebrows furrowed, and she sipped her water. "What's that got to do with anything?"

Her father sat down beside her on the couch and patted her knee. "When I first got started with my career, I had an affair," he admitted.

Her mouth fell open as she tried to process what her father had just said. "Wh-what?"

"You were about a year old, and I was always working. I had a female colleague that I worked closely with, and before I knew it, one thing led to another and it happened. Then it kept happening, until I left your mother."

Karli had to drink more water to keep from hyperventilating. Normally, this kind of news would have devastated her and made her see her father in a new light, but given her circumstances, she could clearly understand how things could happen. "But you're back together, so what happened?"

Letting out an exasperated sigh, he looked at her. "I came back for you at first, and then I realized that I truly loved your mother and that the other lady was simply a distraction. She didn't love me, and I didn't love her."

Karli stood and walked to his window and gazed out. Her mind was swirling. She couldn't believe what she was hearing. Was she really just like her father, to the point where she was having an affair as a means of running from her issues?

Her father stood, walked over to her, and placed his hand on her shoulder. "Don't use my life as a standard for yours. I was just explaining where your mother's anger comes from."

"Do you think the same is true in my situation? Do you think Hudson and I are just going through the motions?"

He shrugged and placed his hands in his pocket. "It's different for you, Karli. You may have this man's baby. That makes your relationship different. I will say that Elaine and I knew we didn't love each other. It was just easier to be together than it was to sneak around. You, on the other hand . . . I'm not so sure. When I look at Michael, I see the love that man has for you, but when I look at Hudson, I see that same type of love. Both of them love you immensely. and ironically, you love them both."

"So what do I do? Be with the child's father? Stay with Hudson? Be with Michael? Damn them both and be single? At first, I was so sure, and now with the baby on the way, I don't know what I should do. I want to do right by my son or daughter."

"I can't answer that, but I think you need to ask yourself who you would be okay with staying with, regardless of whose baby it is. To me, that is the million-dollar question. If you're going to be with Hudson, do it right. Get the divorce before you jump in his bed again. If you're going to be with Michael, you're going to have to be prepared to cut Hudson off completely. Whoever you decide to be with, do not do it for my grandchild. Decide with your heart, for your heart."

Chapter 28

Michael sat on his bed, holding his wedding band in his hand. The television was on, but all he could focus on was the band in his hand. It didn't matter how many distractions he tried to create, nothing would help. It was moments like this that would get the better of him, if Karli chose to go through with the divorce. Moments like this that would remind him of the failure of his marriage. He wondered if Karli was feeling the same way. Did she ponder their marriage? Did she even care anymore? It hurt to think that the woman he had given his heart to and that he thought had given her heart to him could give it all up, as if the past few years of their life meant absolutely nothing. As if they had never loved each other.

He swiped his hand down his face. "I'm married, and I have no wife to celebrate our anniversary tomorrow," he said aloud.

Just then, his cell phone rang. He picked it up off the nightstand and answered.

"Hello?"

"Hey, son."

"Dad, how are you?"

His father let out a sigh. "I could ask you the same. I wanted to check on you and make sure you were doing all right."

Michael paused, and his heart filled with love. He knew his dad was calling only because of tomorrow, even if he didn't want to outright say it. It didn't matter, because right now, Michael needed that. "Thanks, Dad. I know why you're calling, and being honest, it's rough, considering what tomorrow is."

His dad took a deliberate breath. "This may not be the most opportune time, son, but I have to ask, have you all even talked since you found out? I mean, to try to sort this thing out or figure out what went wrong?"

Leaning his head back against the headboard, Michael huffed. "No, Dad. We see each other at the doctor's appointments, but when it's over, I have to leave, because *he* is there. Outside of that, I call to check in about the pregnancy and nothing more."

"Don't you think you need to talk about things?"

"Of course I do," Michael said roughly and then breathed out. "I just don't know how anymore. Hell, I don't even know if I want to know. I don't know if I'm ready to know."

After a long pause his dad said, "And that's the reason you're in this mess." When he heard Michael getting ready to protest, he cut him off. "No, son, you need to listen to me for a change. I haven't been married this long for nothing, and if you had bothered to take my advice before, you and Karli might not have ended up in this predicament."

Michael sat there stunned for a moment. His dad had always shot straight from the hip, but man to man, he had never expected him to go in on him about this situation. He had his faults, but Karli had cheated. She wanted the marriage dissolved. How could he have prevented her actions? However, he wasn't bold enough to test his dad, no matter how old he'd gotten. So he decided to shut up and listen for change. At the end of the day, what the hell did he have to lose? He was already at ground zero.

"I'm listening," he said truthfully.

"Michael, you're bullheaded. You want what you want, and that's it. The advantage to that is that it works in business. It's the reason you're the successful attorney that you are. You're a beast. You pull no punches and take no prisoners. You're powerful, in control, and dominant. A man. But, son, the disadvantage to us men is that we don't know how to change the tune. When you're dealing with your personal life, especially your wife, you have to learn how to drive the car and let her control the radio. Be the man that listens. Be the man that adjusts his attitude. Be the man who opens up and considers what your wife needs out of the relationship. Don't just focus on what you want her to bring and who you want her to be.

"That other man—he was able to step in because you checked out. The moment Karli damaged her view of herself in your eyes, you tried desperately to fit her back into your mold without understanding why the mold was broken in the first place. Neither time nor forgetfulness changes circumstances. Communication does. Listening does. Understanding does. Call your wife and have an honest talk with her, Michael, because until those papers are signed on the dotted line, she's still Mrs. Sanders."

A realization hit Michael like never before. "Let me call you back, Dad. I need to call Karli."

"Now, that's the son I raised."

"Michael?" Karli said sleepily when she answered the phone. "Is something wrong?" she asked, looking at the time. It was after ten o'clock. He never called her after eight.

"I'm sorry to wake you. I really need to talk to you."

Karli sat up straight in the bed. "Has something happened?"

Michael smiled at the fact that she thought enough to ask, and even more at the knowledge that she genuinely did care. "No, nothing has happened." He took a deep breath. "I was calling because I wanted to see if you would be open to the idea of meeting me tomorrow."

Karli rubbed her forehead. "Open to the idea?"

Michael released a nervous laugh. "I'm sorry. Forgive me, Karli. It's just that now that things are so . . . different . . . between us, I'm not sure how to talk to you anymore or what to say. I don't want to overstep my boundaries, and I don't want to offend you, either. It's hard for me because I'm in limbo in terms of where we stand."

Karli took a moment to take in what Michael was saying. It dawned on her that the changes within her had caused her to be a stranger to him. He didn't know how to approach her, and it made for awkward moments between them.

"Are you asking me if I will meet you tomorrow for our anniversary?"

Michael smiled. She said *our* anniversary, he thought. "You remembered."

Karli let out a small giggle. "How could I forget?"

Michael felt elated on the inside. It was ironic that although on this anniversary they weren't together, this moment made him feel like it would be the happiest anniversary of their lives. For one, she actually seemed to be happy about the idea of their anniversary, instead of sad or, worse, upset that he'd reminded her; and two, regardless of what was said, it might be the last time they celebrated while married.

"Well, yes, I am asking if you will go with me tomorrow to celebrate. It may be our last anniversary together, and if it is, I want to end the marriage on a good note. I want us to be able to actually talk and listen to each other. Hear each other out. Before we close our book together, let's at least end the chapter the way it should be ended. No blame game. No arguing. No hate. Simply talking and understanding. We can have lunch first and then come back to our house and talk. Will you agree to that?"

It felt like a huge boulder had been lifted off Karli's shoulders. She had wanted to do the same thing for months but had struggled to ask. She'd embedded in her mind the notion that Michael hated her and was around only to stick close to the baby growing inside her. Hearing him affirm that he wanted to have a conversation without foolishness made her heart sing. For the first time in a long time, she was happy about the prospect of seeing Michael and spending this time with him. He was right. They both needed this, especially if divorce was imminent.

"Michael, I would love that."

"Is everything all right?" Hudson asked. He had rushed into the penthouse and was now holding her close. "I rushed over when you said you needed to talk face-to-face."

After pulling back, Hudson threw his keys on the coffee table, removed his suit jacket, and loosened his tie. A look of panic and worry graced his face as he stood with one hand on his hip, nervously staring at Karli.

"Hudson, you didn't have to get excited. I have something important to tell you and simply didn't want to discuss it over the telephone. I wanted us to have a sit-down, a heart-to-heart."

Hudson rubbed the back of his neck and began pacing the floor. "Okay, see it's when you talk like that, that I get nervous. You're telling me not to get excited, but it was so important that you couldn't tell me over the phone. Face-to-faces are cause to get excited and nervous. What's going on, Karli?"

"Can you sit down with me, please?" She sat with one leg folded underneath her on the sofa and patted the seat right next to her as she gazed up at him. Reluctantly, he walked over and sat down, but he sat forward and was as stiff as a board. "Goodness. You can sit back and relax."

"Karli, seriously, I don't do surprise talks. I'm a planner. A thinker. A preparer. I don't like delving into the unknown completely blind. Face-to-face talks are that—being blindsided." When she looked downward, he placed his hand on her knee and rubbed it. "I'm sorry, baby. I'm not trying to be harsh with you, but I'd prefer that you just tell me what it is you want to tell me."

Wringing her hands, she looked up at him, unsure about telling him what was on her mind, but then she decided to go through with it, anyway. "I'm not sure how to tell you this or how you will take it, so I'm just going to come out with it. I'm meeting Michael for lunch and to talk today."

Taken aback, Hudson sat back, unable to speak for a moment. "Okay." He took in her words. "Help me understand why."

"We need it." Karli stared Hudson in the eyes. "With all that has gone on, Michael was thrust into this situation unexpectedly. Between the anger and the pregnancy, we've never actually talked about things."

"When you say *things*, what exactly does *things* mean?"

She slowly sat forward. "It means our marriage. The issues. The downfall. The divorce. The why. All he's knows is that I was unhappy, and then he found out that I was having an affair with his old college roommate and a good friend, and that I was pregnant with a baby he doesn't even know is his. I owe him the talk. He deserves that much."

"But why now?" Hudson asked. "Why not wait until the baby is born, instead of stressing you out now? You know he's going to dredge up old memories, get upset, and then upset you. And why the hell does lunch have to be involved? This shouldn't be a date type of situation."

Karli stood and began to pace. "Kind of how you're stressing me now?"

"How am I stressing you?" Hudson asked, completely taken off guard. "By worrying about your well-being? You called me over here. If you are doing this, anyway, without giving a damn about my feelings, then why call me over?"

"Because I was worried about your feelings!" Karli spat.

Hudson's jaw clenched, and he sat forward, his hands covering his mouth, as he tried to remain calm. Trying to ease the tension, Karli calmed down.

"I'm telling you because I'm not going to lie to you, Hudson. I've done that with Michael, and I don't want to do that anymore. The talk is something Michael and I failed to do before things got out of hand. The lunch . . . well, that's because it's our wedding anniversary today."

Hudson jumped up. "Are you shitting me right now? Are you telling me that he's going to take you out to celebrate your *wedding* anniversary? And you agreed to that?"

Karli put her hand up. "It's not what you think—"

"Like hell it isn't!" he screamed. "Wedding anniversaries are celebrated to remember the love of your wedding day."

"That's not what this is about, Hudson."

"Then what the hell else is it about?"

"It's about celebrating five years that have passed because we won't have a future together and figuring out why so we can both be complete enough to move on."

"Really? Move on or move *forward*?"

Karli rolled her eyes and went to explain, but Hudson didn't let her get a word out.

"Are you sure this isn't about your and Michael's future? Because last I checked, you two were still married. As long as you're still his wife, there's still a future for you two."

"I would hope that you're not suggesting that I'm trying to sneak off with Michael. You know you just said five minutes ago that you don't like unexpected surprises. Well, guess what our affair was for Michael? A surprise! You, of all people, should understand. You're focused on starting a battle, and you won the war."

With a head nod, Hudson stood, slipped his suit jacket back on, and put his keys in his pocket. "Why would I have to worry about you sneaking off when you called me over here to tell me to my face you are going back?" Hudson turned to walk away. "And just so you know, I know exactly how Michael feels. I felt that way every time you complained to me about him, then left me to go back to him, just like you're doing right now."

As Hudson went to leave, Karli speed walked over to him with tears in her eyes. He had it all wrong. Sure, everything was tossed in the air and she hadn't made a solid commitment to either man, but she didn't want him to feel as though she was running. Far from it. She was determined to face this head-on and deal with the consequences. For now, she just wanted to deliver a healthy baby. Yet she understood that as a wife, she owed Michael this moment, even if Hudson couldn't understand it.

"Hudson, wait, please."

Her teary voice caused him to stop in his steps. He swallowed the lump in his throat, because it hurt him to his core to hear Karli upset. Love was a muthafucka. He hated it and loved it at the same time.

Karli eased up to him, then placed her hands on the back of his shoulders. "Hudson, I know how this may feel to you, but this is not some slick attempt to leave you hanging in the balance. I won't be at peace until Michael and I make peace with everything that's happened. With all I've done to him, as his wife, I owe it to him to give him that peace. If you were my husband, if the shoe were on the other foot, I'd owe it to you, and I'd give it to you. I'm begging you to please not read more into this and to trust the process."

"That's difficult when I don't know where the process will end."

She turned him to face her and held his hands. "Well then, let it begin with you trusting in me. Trust that I am done with the lies, the games, and the back-and-forth. If today were about me getting back with Michael, I would tell you that. That's not what this is. I need you to trust that, even if you can't trust Michael and may be a little bit afraid to trust the process."

Closing his eyes, he tried to calm his restless spirit. As tormented as he was, he knew that Michael had to be triple that. How in the world could this one woman tear down two of the most powerful men in New York? One word. *Love*. Like he had thought before, love was a muthafucka. He wasn't convinced that this lunch carried the same meaning for Michael as it did for Karli, but what could he say or do about it? As much as he hated to admit it, Karli was right, and the fact remained that she was still his wife.

After bringing her hands to his lips, he kissed them. "I can't say that I like it or trust it, but I will be understanding. Besides, unless those papers are signed, you're still Mrs. Sanders."

They eyed each other sadly, and Hudson kissed her forehead before leaving, praying that this wouldn't be the last of them. Karli might not have felt it, but even without talking to Michael directly, Hudson knew that he would use this chance to shoot his shot. How'd he know? Because he loved Karli just like Michael did, and it was exactly what he would do himself. Why not? It was the perfect opportunity. There was nothing like strolling down memory lane and reminiscing about something as eventful as a wedding day to bring a couple back together. It was the perfect time to have this so-called "talk," which Michael could've had months ago.

But Karli had agreed to it, and she was Michael's wife, so what could he do about it? Nothing. And that was what scared him the most. He'd fight to the end of the earth for Karli, but she had to be willing to fight with him. Perhaps she would, but he realized it had to be her decision. Whatever decision she made, he would respect.

Chapter 29

It was an awkward feeling for both Michael and Karli as he held her hand to help her as she sat down. Looking around, Karli felt out of place in the house she used to call home. She hadn't been in her old house in months, and though everything was the same, she felt like a stranger.

Michael could sense Karli's apprehension as she sat down on the sofa. It was hard to believe that they were celebrating their fifth wedding anniversary as a separated couple. The house didn't feel like home to him anymore, either. He worked late nights and often traveled for business just so he could avoid this empty nest as long as he could. Without the love that he and Karli had once shared, living inside the house felt more like living in the confines of a prison.

He sat down across from her and soaked in the sight of his beautiful wife. Even at six months pregnant, she was gorgeous beyond belief, and she wore the radiance of pregnancy well. She was a breathtaking sight to behold.

The past few months had been strained, at best. Karli had kept her promise and had stayed at the penthouse, which Michael didn't care for after learning that it was actually Hudson's, but at least it wasn't Hudson's house. He'd learned to choose his battles. Both men had respected her wishes and had stayed at their respective homes and in their corners. Even the couple of times they'd ended up at her doctor's appointments together, they'd remained cordial enough to speak or keep their mouths closed. However, there was still a lot in limbo. Since the pregnancy, Karli had ceased the divorce proceedings, and Michael didn't know if it was solely because of the baby or because of her relationship with Hudson. He also didn't know where she and Hudson stood. Yet he didn't concern himself with it. Right now, he was just enjoying the rare opportunity he had received to be in her presence.

"How did you enjoy lunch?" Michael finally asked, breaking the silence of the moment.

Karli smiled at him and flipped her long locks out of her face—the pregnancy had her hair growing long and fast. "Our anniversary lunch was nice." She yawned a little. "You have to forgive me. I get a little more tired these days."

He laughed and went into the kitchen. He retrieved a bottle of water for her. She accepted it and drank a few sips to stay perky. "Thank you for the water and for lunch."

"Thank you for agreeing to have lunch with me. I know that we're not together, but it is our anniversary, and it just felt inappropriate not to share the day with you." He sat down at the other end of the sofa.

"I agree," she mustered up the courage to say. She was at a loss for words. Here was the man she'd loved for five years of her life, and it felt awkward feeling awkward around him.

"I know it feels strange," Michael said, interrupting her thoughts. "I feel the same way."

She nodded in embarrassment. "God, Michael, how did we get to this place in our lives?" she blurted.

He scooted close to her and reached out his hand, which she took. Looking into her eyes, he used his free hand to trace her delicate face.

"I'm not sure if it can be attributed to one thing. I've searched my soul, and I know that a lot of little things just added up over time. We were happy, but we masked some things, and I think by doing that, we hurt us, because when those things surfaced, we didn't know how to handle them. We didn't know how to love each other through it." He wiped a tear that was streaking down Karli's face. "It's okay. I don't want you to cry. Besides, the baby may get emotional."

They shared a laugh, and Karli caressed his hands. "Michael, I am sorry about not telling you about the birth control, and I am so sorry I cheated on you."

Clearing his throat to keep his emotions in check, he nodded. "I accept that. I know you mean that. I also apologize for not putting you first, as I promised. Somewhere along the line, I went from putting you first to putting what I wanted for you and from you first. I know that in a lot of ways that pushed you to lie about your feelings, the birth control, and Hudson."

Squeezing his hand, Karli nodded. "Thank you. I accept your apology as well."

Swallowing the lump that had formed in his throat, Michael exhaled slowly and looked deep into Karli's eyes. "Can I ask you a question?"

"Anything."

"Was Hudson your way out of our marriage? Was he your escape?"

Patting his hand, Karli shook her head. "No, Michael. Hudson began as a tryst, and then it just snowballed. He was always there, and you and I were always fighting or at odds. I hadn't planned on being with him, but somewhere along the way, we found each other. It became more for us than just a tryst. It became love."

"Ah, so you do love him," he said, more as a statement than a question, as he cast his eyes downward.

Karli nodded. "Yes, yes, I do," she admitted. "I'm sorry if that hurts you."

Michael waved it off. "It's the truth, which is all I've ever wanted. At least he means something to you. I can tell he loves you too."

Karli smiled. "Yeah, he does."

He released her hand and swiped his hand down his face. "So where does that leave us?"

She cleared her throat and eyed him closely. "Let me ask you this, Michael. Where do you stand with me? What are your feelings? Taking into account all that's happened and is still happening, how do you feel?"

Michael sat forward and rested his arms on his knees. He contemplated her questions for a few moments, then looked at her. "Honestly, I still love you. Hell, I guess I always will. If I'm real with myself, I don't know if I can trust you again. Not that I don't forgive you, but I just can't trust that if we are together, Hudson won't be a threat, even if the baby is mine. And if I'm being completely honest, my heart couldn't take being with you if the baby is his. I don't think that I could raise his child and love his child, even if you are the mother. My heart couldn't take that."

Karli reached across and rubbed his thigh. "I understand that, and I wouldn't want you to extend yourself. We all have our limits, and you're more than entitled to yours."

"Yeah, but I feel like I'd be handing you over to Hudson, though. Like I'm giving up on us."

Karli looked at him with understanding eyes and grabbed his hands reassuringly. "No, Michael, you wouldn't be doing that at all. Whether or not you decided you wanted to be with me, it still requires my decision. Even if you decided you didn't want to be with me, that doesn't mean I'd be with Hudson. It doesn't even mean that Hudson would want to be with me. The thing is, all three of us have a decision to make, and it shouldn't be based on what we think the other is going to do. We all should want the person to be there only because they wholeheartedly want to be, not out of guilt or obligation."

"True," Michael said, getting choked up. "As much as I would like to know who you decide to be with, I can't bear to hear it if it's not me. I just want to enjoy our anniversary. It may be our last one."

Smiling, Karli caressed his face. Michael peered at her with love in his eyes. After bending forward, he planted a soft kiss on her lips. Together, they touched foreheads, lingering in the moment of the kiss.

"I'll always love you, Michael."

"I'll always love you, Karli. Happy anniversary, baby."

Chapter 30

The day had finally come, and honestly, both men couldn't be more ecstatic. After fourteen hours of labor, their bundle of joy was finally about to arrive. Everything about this day was a surprise, even the sex of the baby. Karli didn't want to know a thing until the baby was born. As the time drew nearer for the baby to enter the world, both men were just as nervous as they were ecstatic. Someone would have the sad end of the stick, yet both of them had gotten attached to the life growing inside Karli.

Out of courtesy, Karli's family and friends waited in the waiting area and allowed Michael and Hudson to be in the delivery room. Though unconventional and slightly awkward, it was important to all three of them that they were all present. Neither man deserved to miss seeing his child being born. At Karli's request, the doctor was having a paternity test completed immediately after the birth so that the wait would be short for the father.

"Okay, Karli, on the count of three, we're going to push," Dr. Wiggins explained, and Karli nodded, in pain. Michael stood on the left, holding her hand, and Hudson on her right. "I need you fellas to be supportive and encouraging, okay?" Dr. Wiggins nodded directly at Hudson and Michael.

"Got it," they said in unison.

"All right, on the count of three, push. One, two, three . . . Push!" Dr. Wiggins said, and Karli pushed, squeezing the life out of both Hudson's and Michael's hands.

"Come on, baby. You've got this," Hudson said, encouraging Karli. He kissed the back of her hand.

"Yes, Mommy, you got it," Michael chimed in.

After she mustered the strength she needed, the doctor counted off again, and this time the crown of the baby's head appeared. With another break and another push, the baby was delivered, and after one small pat, the baby wailed, and tears of delight gushed down Karli's cheek.

"Congratulations, Mommy. You have a beautiful baby girl," Dr. Wiggins said, placing the baby in Karli's arms.

The moment her baby girl touched her arms, she knew she'd made the right decision to be her mother. She was perfect. Karli felt she wasn't worthy of this perfect bundle of joy, but she would dedicate her life to raising, teaching, and loving this little one, while proving she could be the type of woman to lead her daughter by example. "Oh, my God! You're so gorgeous. I love you so much, baby girl," Karli cooed and cried.

"She looks just like you, Karli," Michael said, and Hudson nodded at the newborn's striking resemblance to Karli.

"Yeah, she does." Hudson smiled. "So beautiful."

The nurse took the baby to clean her up as the doctor finished with Karli. Each man congratulated Karli and told her how wonderful she'd done as they waited for the baby to be cleaned, wrapped, and given back to Karli.

"Thank you both. Thank you for being there for us." Karli kissed the back of each of their hands.

"She's gorgeous, and she has the most beautiful blue eyes I've ever seen," the nurse said, handing the baby back to Karli.

A hush fell over the room, and suddenly Hudson broke down in tears. "Oh my . . . oh my God . . . she's my baby.

She's my baby girl. We have a baby girl!" he wailed as Karli smiled and handed him the baby. He bent down and kissed Karli's forehead as they both cried tears of joy. "Thank you, baby. Thank you for my baby."

As Hudson cooed over the baby, Michael bent down and whispered in Karli's ear, "Congratulations, Mommy. You and Hudson will make great parents. I love you." He kissed her cheek, and Karli briefly held his hand in sadness before he let go and left the room.

"Mike! Mike!" Hudson called out to him after Michael ran out of the delivery room.

Michael came back in the delivery room and faced Hudson with tears in his eyes. "Yeah?"

Hudson slowly approached him. "For what it's worth, I am sorry. I'm sorry about how this turned out, and I'm sorry for hurting and betraying you." Hudson held his hand out for a peaceful handshake.

Michael squared up and shook his hand. "I appreciate that. Listen, just do me a favor and take care of her, please. Love her the way she deserves to be loved."

Hudson nodded and patted his shoulder.

Without another word, Michael left the hospital. He didn't need to see the results of the paternity test to know that the baby was Hudson's. He didn't even need the evidence of the baby's blue eyes. He'd known all along that he wasn't the father. He had found out the month after Karli announced the pregnancy that he was sterile. He'd hoped that by some miracle the results of his own test were wrong or that Karli would choose him over Hudson, but she'd chosen Hudson. She'd proved that the day she left their home on their anniversary without telling him whom she'd chosen. Love was many things, but it was never unsure. While he knew that Karli would always have love for him, she was in love with Hudson. The baby's blue eyes were proof positive of that.

Chapter 31

"No, no, baby. Don't touch that," Karli stopped her baby from grabbing a thorny rose and bumped into someone.

"I'm so sorry, sir," she said, apologizing, as she turned around. "Michael?"

He smiled, excitement dancing in his eyes. "Karli." He looked over and saw that Hudson was also there. "Hudson."

"Hello, Mike," Hudson said uneasily.

Michael cleared his throat and looked at the beautiful one-year-old baby girl. "And what is your name?" He played with her hand.

"We named her Heather Marie," Karli answered. "Heather Marie Lewis."

Michael smiled. "After Hudson's mom and your mom's middle name. That's a beautiful tribute."

"How have you been?" Karli asked, genuinely concerned.

"Business is booming, and I've been straight. I can't complain." He smiled at them and tried not to stare at their wedding bands. "Congratulations on your nuptials. I saw the announcement in the paper a few months back."

"Thank you," they said in unison.

"Listen, I'm going to take Heather over there so we can look for some nice flowers for Grandma," Hudson said, taking the baby out of Karli's arms. "It is good to see you, Mike. Take care of yourself."

"Likewise."

Flipping her hair back, Karli smiled. "It is good to see you."

Michael smiled and drank in her mesmerizing features. "You as well. How's married life treating you?"

"It's good. I've learned to do things differently this time around, and Hudson is amazing."

Michael smiled. "That's great. I really am happy for you two."

"Thank you, Michael." She smiled at him again. "So no lucky lady in your life?"

"No. I date, but nothing serious."

"I'm sure the right one will come along," she said, looking over and noticing that Heather was getting fussy. "I better go before she really starts whining," she joked, then grew serious again. "Take care of yourself, and tell your parents I said hello."

"You too," he said before she walked off and met up with Hudson.

Hudson kissed Karli's forehead and handed the baby to her, then wrapped his arm around his girls.

As Michael stared at Karli in the distance, he couldn't help but reflect. "The right one already came along, Karli. I'll wait a lifetime for you," he whispered to himself.

"I found the flowers. Are you ready to go?" a voice called behind Michael.

He turned slowly and nodded. "Sure."

"Is everything all right, honey?" the woman asked.

Michael smiled demurely before taking a deep breath and wrapping his arm around her shoulders. "With you here, it will be. Let's go."

Chapter 32

"We have to take another trip soon," Hudson suggested between kisses as they entered their hotel room.

After taking the hour-long ferry ride, getting to their hotel, and checking in, they were literally on fire and could barely contain themselves when they finally got to their room.

"Whenever you want, Mr. Lewis. Your wish is my command." She kissed him deeply. Hudson moaned as he began removing her panties. She pulled back. "I have to use the bathroom, but I'm going to be ready for you."

Hudson threw his head back in agony. "Okay. Please hurry, baby." Karli batted her eyes and seductively strolled into the bathroom. Hudson followed her every step with his eyes. He swore his wife got finer and finer every day.

He heaved a sigh as she shut the bathroom door. He had to make this time special for her. He wasn't oblivious to the fact that his schedule was affecting their marriage. Karli had sacrificed and lost so much in the process of leaving her ex-husband that he wanted to make sure she never regretted her decision. Even her relationship with her mother had only recently been getting back on track.

He couldn't believe that they'd been married a for year already, and while he loved being with her, time seemed to escape him. He couldn't think of one real moment they'd had together, besides when Heather was an infant and, well, when they enjoyed their sexual moments. But the intimacy they had shared when he was her man on the side had been lost.

It didn't help that they no longer worked together. At first, when Karli's boss, Jack, found out about their relationship, he had been excited. To him, it meant that he and the partners at McCallan were more secure in the contract they had with Lewis Investments. Some associates expressed their disdain, however, arguing that the relationship could be a hindrance to Karli's focus, but Jack could see only the dollar signs. More people became disgruntled when they found out about her impending pregnancy, but Jack ignored this.

However, once Hudson and Karli were married, even Jack had to take action. Even though he felt that the marriage assured that Lewis Investments would never take their business elsewhere, the associates and even some partners at McCallan felt the marriage gave Karli an unfair advantage. Although Hudson had faith that Karli and her team would never allow their work to falter, business was still business. As a businessman, Hudson would never do business with a company that wasn't meeting expectations, wife or no wife. Karli knew that and understood it.

While they both talked until they were blue in the face, their words fell on deaf ears, because no one would ever believe that a husband would leave a company his wife worked for. Therefore, at the end of her one-year contingency, Karli was removed and another associate was placed on the contract, and Karli wasn't even allowed to be a part of the team. Therefore, when Hudson said that she'd sacrificed and lost a lot, he meant it. And he was making it his personal mission to bring back their intimacy and closeness.

After popping the cork in the champagne bottle, Hudson poured two glasses of champagne and began removing his clothes. He was just about to sit on the bed when Karli called out to him.

"Hudson," she sang.

Smiling, he walked into the bathroom and saw his wife standing behind the glass door to the shower. He placed one glass of champagne on the bathroom counter and held on to the other. Then he pulled the shower door open and stepped inside.

For a moment, he simply stood there, mesmerized by the beauty of his wife. Her light caramel skin, her stunning almond-shaped hazel eyes, her curvy figure, and her rotund derriere were just as breathtaking as the day he met her. Then his mind drifted to the love she possessed for him, the sacrifices she'd made for him, and the child she'd borne for him, and he was overwhelmed with love.

After he pulled her to him by the waist, he could only hold her and leaned his forehead against hers. Tears welled in his eyes.

"Hudson?" Karli said, instantly filled with concern.

He captured her lips and kissed her so tenderly and sweetly that she swooned, becoming weak in the knees. He had to grip her to keep her from falling.

"I love you so much, Karli," he shared. "Please forgive me. It seems as if the moment you blessed me by coming into my life, I began to forget what made you come to me in the first place. I've been negligent of your feelings and time, and that changes today . . . this moment."

Speechless, Karli lovingly wiped the tears from his eyes and her own.

"Happy one-year anniversary, and here's to making the next years the best years of your life." He placed the glass of champagne to her lips. When she parted them, he poured a little champagne in her mouth, and then he took a sip.

Karli melted into him. "I love you so much, Hudson. That was everything that I needed."

Hudson savored the moment for a bit, then pulled back, with a sinful glint in his eyes. "I have something else you need."

She winked lustfully at him, and Hudson lightly pushed her back under the showerhead, allowing the hot, steamy water to flow down her body. Easing close to her, he poured the rest of the champagne down her neck and let it run down her breasts. After kneeling to catch the dripping liquid, Hudson captured her left breast and suckled the mixture of champagne and water from her nipple while massaging her right breast. Karli moaned deeply, gripping a handful of his blond hair. Once he'd devoured the left breast, he moved to the right, making Karli pant in anticipation.

Placing the glass on the shelf behind him, he turned back to her and stared at her with the same fire she'd grown to love. As those intense crystal blue orbs sexily drank her in, Hudson lifted Karli up on his waist and slipped his stiff manhood inside her honey pot. Her wetness indicated she was ready for him, and she accepted him with ease. She gasped at their connection as they lovingly stared into each other's eyes. Bracing her against the shower wall, Hudson delivered slow thrusts in and out of her succulence. He wanted to savor every inch of her.

"Ooh, Hudson," she moaned loudly as the water continued to flow over them.

He was taking her to a place of euphoria with each powerful stroke. As she gripped his shoulders for the insatiable ride, she lovingly stared into his eyes, and it was if their souls reconnected . . . their passion was rekindled. Yes. This indeed was the man she'd fallen in love with. The purity and extreme pleasure of the moment brought tears to her eyes, and that served as confirmation to Hudson that all was forgiven and they were back at that place they used to be.

Gripping her waist, he moved her away from the wall and thrust completely inside her, bouncing her in quick fluid motions up and down on his shaft. Her moans became trapped in her throat as he delivered that feel-good pleasure that teetered on the edge of pain but was so good that all she could feel was pleasure.

"Ahh . . . baby! Ah . . . I'm about to cum!" Karli bit out as her face contorted and her legs began to quiver.

"Cum for me, baby," Hudson whispered as he continued delivering his tantalizing pleasure.

"Hudson!" Karli released a powerful climax as she trembled against him.

Her love faces were sending him over the edge as he braced her against the wall again and began to thrust faster, making her yell out in pleasure.

"I'm cumming, baby," Hudson yelled as he pressed against her. "Argh!"

Karli eased off him and slowly kneeled down. She slipped Hudson's member into her watery mouth and softly licked and suckled him, drawing the remaining juices from him.

He rubbed the top of her head, with his head tilted back in pleasure. "Mmm, Karli. Yes!" He gripped the wall to keep from falling to his knees as he released another load down the back of her throat.

She licked until she'd taken every drop, and swallowed his thick syrup with delight. Hudson looked at her with lustful eyes, satisfied to his core. He picked her up and pushed the shower door open with his free hand and laid her on the bathroom counter. Spreading her legs, he licked his lips, then kneeled down and thrust his tongue into her creamy essence. Swirling his tongue in and out and around her throbbing bud drove Karli to the point of delirium. Her soft, deep grunts urged Hudson on as she tried to grab ahold of something to alleviate the intense ecstasy she was feeling.

"Hud . . . Hud . . . Hudson!" she barely managed to say as she grabbed handfuls of his hair with both of her hands. "Oh my God," she screamed as she tried to back away from his mouth work.

He held her in place as she came in his mouth, and he continued licking, determined to suck every orgasm out of her. Karli was damn near seeing stars, she was so far gone from their passionate lovemaking. Karli's legs quivered uncontrollably as her head thrashed from side to side.

"Hudson!" she hollered, and then she went limp, too exhausted to battle him.

Hudson stood slowly, with a satisfied grin on his face, and gently pulled Karli to him. She was so sensitive that she recoiled from his touch, but he lovingly held her in his arms and softly caressed her back. Once she'd calmed down, he picked her up and carried her like a baby into the bedroom. He sat her in the chair briefly and wrapped a towel around her wet hair and then placed her in the king-size bed. She lazily lay there, in euphoria, with her eyes half closed, as Hudson went to put the DO NOT DISTURB sign on the door. When he climbed in bed beside her, she was out like a light.

He smiled to himself, admiring her beautiful, peaceful face. He leaned over to turn off the lamp, and the hotel phone rang.

"Hello?" he said when he answered.

"Mr. Lewis?" said a young woman. "This is the front desk."

"Yes, this is he."

"I really hate to bother you on your anniversary weekend, and I know your suite is rather large. However, we, unfortunately, received a complaint of loud . . . um . . . noise coming from your room. Would you and Mrs. Lewis be able to reduce the noise, please?" she said, obviously embarrassed and nervous.

He chuckled softly. "Of course. Please accept our deepest apologies. Is there anything else?"

"No, sir, not at all. Thank you. I apologize for having to call you all and interrupt your evening. Thank you again, Mr. Lewis, and we'll have another bottle of our very best champagne delivered to your room in the morning, on the house. How does that sound?"

"Perfect. Thank you. And please send one to the neighbors whom we disturbed and place it on my tab."

"Yes, sir. Thank you, Mr. Lewis, sir."

"Is there anything else?"

"No, sir. That's it. You have a very good night, Mr. Lewis."

"Good night to you," he said and hung up the phone.

Hudson settled next to his sleeping wife and pulled her against him. "Bet the neighbors know my name," he joked to himself. He closed his eyes and drifted off.

Chapter 33

"Mmm, Michael."

The moaning sounds instantly transported Michael back in time. As he dipped in and out of her succulence, his mind drifted to Karli. A sly smile spread across his face as old memories invaded his mind. Her softness, the touch of her fingertips gripping his back. Her scent. Her gushy buttercream center. Her moans.

"Michael!" The moans grew deeper.

Gripping her mounds, Michael skillfully arched and dipped in and out of the sweet honey pot. Long stroking with his massive member, he felt his muscles begin to tense up and saw that his veins showed as she slicked him with her wetness.

"Fuck! It feels good," Michael moaned, with his eyes closed. Karli's old words danced in his mind. *Ooh, Michael. Baby, I love you,* he thought.

Gripping her waist, he pulled her toward him, and he thrust harder and deeper inside her center. Her moans were so low and sexy that they kicked him into overdrive, forcing her to take all he had to give.

"Shit! I'm cumming!" she moaned loudly. "Ahh! Oh God! Yes! Yes!" she let out as her body went limp and shook ferociously.

Michael continued pumping inside her as sweat beaded his back. His relentlessness made her yelp in satisfaction, and the tingling sensation forced her to beg for mercy.

"Please stop. I can't . . . I can't take . . . ," she panted as her body tingled and twitched.

"Who's pussy is this?" Michael roared. *Yours, Daddy,* he thought.

"Yours! Oh shit! Yours, Michael!" she screamed as another orgasmic wave hit her, causing him to come to a climax.

After pulling out, Michael ripped off the condom, gripped his member in his hand, and guided himself inside her mouth.

His head fell back as her warm mouth pulled another climax out of him. "Shit! Suck that shit. Oh yeah," he moaned when his thick syrup exploded in her mouth as he slowly slid in and out.

Ooh, Michael. You like that, baby? he thought.

"This dick is so tasty."

The voice violently shook him out of his reverie. It was not something that Karli would've said, and it instantly brought him to his reality. Moving to the side and falling back on the bed, Michael kept his eyes closed tightly and exhaled, trying to bring back the memory of Karli.

"Are you all right?" she asked, rubbing her hand across his chest.

Michael blew out a breath, slightly irritated. The moment was gone, and the voice speaking to him was not Karli's. He swallowed back the hurt and anger he was experiencing. Hurt, because it'd been two years since Karli left, and anger, because the only time he could still feel her presence was when he was dick deep inside some pussy, and now this voice was reminding him that she wasn't Karli.

Finally, he opened his eyes and looked over and smiled. The sweetest set of brown eyes stared back at him. He slid his fingers down the side of her face as she brushed her sweat-drenched bangs behind her ear.

"Yes, Catrina, I'm fine."

She bit her lip. "Are you sure?"

He swallowed hard. "Yes, I'm sure. Why?"

She shrugged. "I don't know. Sometimes, you have this far-off look in your eyes. Like you're here but not here."

Smiling demurely, Michael traced her lips with his thumb. "Don't worry. I'm here."

She lay back. "How long are we going to keep this up?"

"What do you mean? We're good."

"We're meeting in these hotels because I can't come to your house and you're not comfortable in mine. We haven't told our parents, and I still haven't told Karli . . ."

Instantly, Michael sat on the edge of the bed and rubbed his hand down his face. "Here you go—"

Cutting him off, Catrina huffed, "Yes, here I go again!" She sat up and pressed her back against the headboard. "Michael, we've been together for a little over a year, and I feel horrible lying to my best friend about the fact that I'm in a relationship and sleeping with her ex-husband!"

"Did she ask you if we were together?"

"No, but—"

"Then, you're not lying to her. You just haven't told her. There's a difference."

Catrina slid her hand through her hair. It was messed up. She already knew it. She and Michael had got together by happenstance. She had been comforting him throughout his depression, caused by his failed marriage to her best friend. One day, one thing had led to another and they'd christened his desk in his office.

"Hey, you," Catrina greeted after walking into Michael's office with a brown paper bag in her hand.

Michael stood gazing out his office window. He looked dapper on the outside, but he'd learned to put on a façade over the past year. His Ralph Lauren button-down caressed his muscles perfectly, and the gold Cartier wristwatch and the Cartier gold-encrusted, diamond cuff links shone brightly against his cinnamon-colored skin. His Ralph Lauren dress slacks hung nicely, showing off his masculine thighs and tight derriere.

Though he stood there, looking like the Adonis that he was, on the inside he was troubled. He was a broken man. He lived every day by going through the motions. He'd resigned from his position as deacon at church, and now he rarely even showed up. He had even begun drinking on a regular basis and cursing again. The only thing he managed to do right was lawyering. He poured himself into his work. If nothing else, this divorce had made him dive so hard into his work that the firm had moved from a spot in the top twenty to a spot in the top three in the ranking of sports entertainment law firms across the country. Yet, it was moments like this that reminded him that no matter how powerful a man he'd become, there was always one person who could break him like he was nothing. Her name was Karli.

"What are you doing here?" he asked blandly.

Ignoring his dry greeting, Catrina sat the bag down on his desk and leaned against it. Crossing her arms, she cleared her throat to swallow her hurt feelings. "Well, that is a way to greet a person. I stopped by only to bring you something to eat. I'm sure you haven't eaten, and I thought maybe you could also use some company."

"I'd rather be alone, if you don't mind," he scoffed, never breaking his gaze out the window.

Confused, Catrina stood up straight. "Michael, why are you treating me this way? Did I do something to you?"

Putting his head down, he let out a deep breath. "It's not you. It's just you were with her this weekend . . .

celebrating . . . and I don't need any reminders of her or
what happened this weekend."

The realization hit Catrina like a ton of bricks. She'd
been Karli's maid of honor for her nuptials to Hudson
this past Saturday. Michael knew about the wedding,
and her presence now was reminding him of the fact
that Karli had married another man. She hadn't told
him, but every paper and style magazine in New York
had followed the story of one of New York's most eligible
bachelors tying the knot, so it was not as if he could avoid
it. Michael was crazy to think that Catrina wouldn't be
a part of it. She was Karli's best friend, after all. The
ironic part was that she'd come by his office because she
had figured he'd be a little down about his ex-wife's new
marriage and she'd wanted to ease his burden, not add
to it. She had been feeling horrible and wanted to assure
him that he still had people who cared about him. He
still had people who were in his corner.

"I'm so sorry. I didn't realize. I only wanted to cheer
you up and take your mind off it. I figured it would be
on your mind."

Finally, Michael turned to face her. "I'm sorry,
Catrina." He walked over to the desk. "I didn't mean to
treat you badly. I'm just in a bad-ass mood." He let out
a harsh chuckle. "You'd think after all this time I would
be over it. It's just hard, you know?" He swiped his hand
down his face.

"No apologies necessary." She grabbed his hands. "I
understand it's difficult. No one expects you to 'just get
over it' because it's been a year. You've spent years
loving Karli. It's going to take time, and anybody who
honestly cares about you knows that."

A slight smile graced Michael's face, and he leaned in
and hugged Catrina tightly. "Thank you. You've always
been there for me, despite the fact that you're her best

friend. I can't thank you enough for bearing with me. You have kept me sane, when I know I would've lost it. I don't tell you enough, but I swear on life, I'm indebted to you."

Pulling back and still gripping his arms, Catrina whispered, *"Friends don't hold debts, nor do they count favors. You owe me nothing."*

As they gazed into each other's eyes, Michael slowly licked his thick lips. That single motion made Catrina squirm, as if electricity had bolted through her. The look in Michael's eyes turned from hurt to something that Catrina couldn't decipher.

"Catrina," he breathed.

"Um . . . I guess you're wondering what I brought you to eat," she said hurriedly, breaking their gaze and easing out of his arms. After turning her back to him, she opened the brown bag. *"I have your favorites, turkey and ham club sandwiches, and I got those cupcakes she used to buy for you from Brooklyn Cupcake. Oh, and Voss water."*

"How did you know these are my favorites?" he asked, staring at her, as he devoured one of the chocolate cheesecake cupcakes.

She shrugged nervously. *"Good memory, I guess. Karli always talked about the things you like, so I guess it stuck."*

"It stuck, huh?" He licked the remaining icing off his thumb.

"Yeah, uh-huh." She handed him a napkin, and when he reached for it, he grabbed her hand and brought her close to him. Their breathing was erratic. *"What . . . what are we doing, Michael?"*

"What do you want to do?"

She wrapped her arms around his neck, and they dove into a deep and sensual kiss that damn near *made Catrina delirious. Michael unzipped her skirt and dropped it like a pro as Catrina brought her shaky hands up to unbutton his shirt. Once his shirt was off, Michael pressed a button to make sure his blinds were all closed and to automatically lock the door. He lifted Catrina's blouse above her head and let it fall to the floor. Roughly, he spun her around and lifted her onto his desk, then removed his tank. After reaching for his suit jacket, which lay on the chair behind them, he retrieved a condom and unbuckled his pants. Once they dropped to the floor, he gripped Catrina's lace thong and slid it down over her petite ass to her ankles.*

Biting her lip, Catrina gazed sexily back at Michael. She instantly lusted for this fine specimen of a man. Every muscle was tight and cut, and the meat hanging between his legs made her mouth water.

Michael's eyes twinkled when he noticed Catrina lusting over him. The boy still had the power to make the ladies swoon. He winked at her as the Magnum snapped into place. "See something you like?"

When Catrina nodded, he smacked her ass and rubbed her cheeks, then tested the water by nudging his thumb inside. She was slick and wet, ready for him. After sliding himself inside her wetness, he thrust hard and deep.

"I said, See something you like?"

She moaned and her head fell forward as she bit out, "Yes. God, yes."

Michael grinned devilishly as he had his way with Catrina. He pounded her from the back, lifted her up, and pounded her from the front, and ended up with her sitting in his lap backward. After a thirty-minute round, they were both spent, and Catrina stood and leaned her naked body against the desk, facing him, as he sat in his plush office chair.

"Oh my God, Michael. What have we done?"

"Had sex . . . good sex." He winked at her.

"But Karli—"

"Is divorced and remarried to Hudson," he spewed as he stood up. "Don't bring her up."

Catrina shrugged. "Okay. But what about me? She's my best friend."

"And Hudson was my friend, so?"

Her brow furrowed. "So did you just use me for a revenge fuck? Is that all this was to you?" she asked angrily.

Michael laughed. "Actually, that would've been a great idea if I was still married to your cheating best friend."

Catrina huffed and turned around to dress. Michael walked over to her and pulled her close.

"It wasn't, Catrina. I'm sorry." When she side eyed him, he said, "I'm serious. Look, it was a moment between you and me. No one else has to know about this. And for a moment, my mind was off . . . her."

He and Catrina shared a quiet laugh.

"So, do you want to come to my restroom and clean up, then help me do a little office cleanup before my employees and my cleaning staff have a field day at our expense?" he asked her.

Catrina nodded.

Michael turned and headed in the direction of the restroom.

"Michael," she called softly, and he turned to face her. She walked up to him. "Was it only just a moment?"

A contemplative expression crossed his face as he eased Catrina into her arms. "Well, Ms. Catrina, to be honest, that ball is in your court. No pressure. You have to deal with her. I don't. Still, she's my ex, and as much as I hate it, I have this fucked-up need to protect her feel-

*ings. But if you want to know if I'm okay with this . . .
Nothing about any of this is okay, but what's done has
already been done, by all three of us. So it is what it is."
Winking at her, he said, "And something tells me you feel
the same way." With that, he grabbed her hand and took
her to the restroom, where they had another quick round
of sex before cleaning up themselves and the office.*

Ever since then, they had been dating and hiding
it from everyone. Their families had suffered a great hurt
from the end of Michael and Karli's marriage, so they
didn't want to add to it by telling everyone about their
relationship. But after a year something had to give.

She got up and walked around to the other side of the
bed and sat beside him, then pulled his hand into hers.
"You don't have to spare her feelings, Michael. She damn
sure didn't spare yours."

Snatching his hand away, he seethed, "Again, you
don't have to throw Hudson up in my face, as if I don't
know what she did to me."

Sucking her teeth, she scoffed, "As if Hudson is the
only thing she did to you."

"And the birth control thing. You don't have to destroy
your friend over shit I know to put yourself on a pedestal."

Jumping up, she snapped, "So I guess you *knew* about
Tya too!"

"Tya? Who the hell is Tya?"

Hitting her forehead, Catrina wished she could suck
the words back in, but she'd put it out into the atmo-
sphere. She couldn't take it back. "Listen—"

"No! Who the fuck is Tya, and what does she have to do
with Karli and me?" Michael said angrily, cutting her off.

Catrina shook her head before crossing her arms.
"Tya . . . she . . . um . . . well . . . she's Hudson's ex, and
Karli had a threesome with her and Hudson."

Michael stood up, completely flabbergasted. "That's not true. Karli would never. I know her. She would never."

"She would never with you, but with Hudson, she did."

Bile settled in Michael's throat, and he had to swallow fast to keep from blowing chunks. He couldn't believe the amount of treachery that Karli had committed, with the urging of Hudson. Sleeping with Hudson was one thing, but having a lesbian experience with some random chick she didn't know was downright disrespectful and hurtful. Despite himself, tears of hurt and anger welled in his eyes, and he hurriedly wiped them to keep them from falling.

Catrina felt horrible for revealing that part of the story to Michael, but he needed to know. If he understood the lengths Karli had gone to, to be free of her marriage, perhaps he could learn to let go. "See? You don't owe Karli a thing."

He looked at her sideways. "But you do. My failed marriage wasn't permission for us to get together. I know Karli did her thing first, and regardless of whatever else she has done, we both have long since moved on. Still, that part, that's *our* shit to worry about. That had absolutely nothing to do with your relationship with Karli, and while the opportunity is there, I don't want to destroy your friendship with her, either."

He had told a half-truth. Surely, things wouldn't be the same if Karli found out about Catrina and him, but the real reason he didn't want Karli to know was that he held out hope that one day that damn Hudson would screw up and Karli would come back to him. He would be lying if he said that this latest information that Catrina had spilled, to try to throw him for a loop, didn't give him a better understanding of Karli's deception. Yet, that didn't matter, as cheating was nothing but cheating. Besides, Karli didn't leave him for Tya. She left him for Hudson.

Despite all of that, he'd welcome Karli back with open arms, and this time, he'd do whatever she needed and wanted in order for him to keep her. She could work wherever, she would not have to worry about kids, and they could have sex in front of freeway traffic to satisfy her sexual desires if that was what she wanted. Anything to make her Karli Sanders again. But that day would never come if she ever found out that he was sleeping with her best friend.

Catrina shook her head, half ashamed. She didn't want to hurt Karli, but she did want her shot at something real with Michael. She'd never been the settling-down type, but being with Michael had opened her up to a world she'd never considered. She understood on every possible level why Karli had married Michael. She just couldn't fathom why she had let him go. Hudson was a good guy and all, but Michael was the best. At least in her eyes he was, and since her best friend didn't want him, she did. Was that so wrong?

Catrina turned to face him. "I'd be willing to give up my friendship with her, if it came down to it, for you. I want us to have something real." She palmed his face. "You deserve something real."

It hurt him deeply to hear the lengths that Catrina would go just to be with him, because deep down, he knew it could never work. Even if he wanted it to. He cared for Catrina . . . loved her even, but not the way that she wanted. She was looking for him to be the man that he was to Karli, and honestly, those feelings and actions were reserved only for Karli. He couldn't see himself giving in to anyone else like that. Not even Catrina. The problem was Catrina assumed he wanted something real with another woman. Not so. He had had the real deal, and the only woman he ever wanted that type of relationship with was Karli. But he couldn't bring himself to tell her that. It would surely devastate her.

He kissed the inside of her palm. "Thank you for thinking of me, Catrina, but you don't want to give up on your friendship with Karli. Trust me. In the end, you'll regret it. I refuse to be the cause of that." He began making his way to the bathroom.

"Is it really because of our friendship, or is it because you hope that you'll one day be back with her?" Catrina sneered, causing him to stop in his tracks.

"Say what?" Michael asked, turning slowly to face her.

"Admit it, Michael. You refuse to move on because you haven't moved on!" Catrina said angrily. "Every time I talk about moving forward and telling Karli about us, you have a different damn excuse! Just admit it! You're hung up on your ex-wife, while she's wifed up to your ex-friend!"

Michael glared at her, instantly becoming enraged. The words she had spoken cut deep. "Again, I'm fully aware of what my ex-wife did, and I don't need you to tell me what happened! I was there! I lived it! But damn! Excuse me for having a shred of fucking human goddamned decency!" he shouted, shaking his head. "Fucking unbelievable!"

Filled with emotion, Catrina ran over to him, turned him around to face her, and hugged him tightly. "I'm so sorry, Michael. I am. I shouldn't have said that. I was wrong. You've worked so hard to get over what happened. You're a good person, and I guess I just . . . I need that in my life."

Compassion took over Michael, and he hugged her back. At the end of the day, he was wrong too. She was dead on point with her assessment, and ultimately, he was stringing her along because she was familiar. She was the last remnant of Karli that he could hold on to, and she had the added perk of having good punanny.

"It's okay." He lifted her face to look into her eyes. "I apologize. I shouldn't use that language and tone with you. You're the best thing in my life right now."

Smiling, she blushed. "I am?"

"Of course you are." He hugged her again and then looked back down at her. "You've been there for me during a time when I didn't think I would make it. I will always love and appreciate you for that. We've been friends forever, and now we have more. I don't want to lose that. Can't we just have what we have?"

Catrina's heart sang as she nodded her head. "Sure. You know you have me wrapped around your finger." She giggled, then kissed his lips. "Whenever the time comes, I know you'll reveal it, but until then, yes, we can have what we have, because, baby, what we have is so good."

They shared a laugh as they both went into the bathroom together. Michael took a leak and flushed his condom just as Catrina stepped in the shower.

"Care to join?" she asked seductively.

Michael smiled devilishly. "You have an early morning meeting, and I have a midday flight. Jumping in that shower will make us both late in the morning."

She laughed. "True. I'll be out in a minute."

He walked out of the bathroom and sat on the bed. Just as he did, his cell phone rang. He looked at it and rolled his eyes before answering. "What's up?"

"Hey, you. Is it cool to come over?"

Michael sucked his teeth. "Let me take a rain check on that."

The lady on the other end huffed. "You're loss," she said, pouting.

"If you think you're a loss for me, then you're sorely mistaken," he scoffed and then press the END button on his phone.

He'd planned to meet up with this little hot chick he'd met named Angelica, but Catrina had a way of thwarting his plans. Even if she left his hotel room in time, she'd severely killed his vibe. Though he missed Karli, he still had needs.

And he would exchange vows with only one person, and *she* was now married to another man and was apparently giving it to women. He shook his head at the foolishness Hudson had his wife, his *ex-wife*, involved in, and it infuriated him. How could she have let him pawn her body and her morals off like that? That was no way to treat his Karli. Hudson didn't deserve her, because he didn't know her value. Karli needed only to be reminded that she was worthy, and Michael was the only one who could do that. Then and there, he made the decision that he was going to get his wife back by any means necessary. From now on, that would be his focus.

Epilogue

Michael sat in his office, waiting on his next appointment with a prospective client. Staring out the window, he leaned back in his plush leather chair, with his legs crossed, squeezing his stress ball. He had two points of pain running through his mind. The first one was the same as it had been for the past two years, Hudson. He'd caught wind of the fact that he and Karli had decided to go off and celebrate their one-year wedding anniversary. To say Michael was jealous was an understatement. She should have been celebrating their seventh year of marriage to him, but instead she was sharing the moment with that damn Hudson. A new year. A new start. A new marriage. He squeezed the ball tighter as his mind roamed over all the things she and Hudson were probably doing to celebrate their moment. If it was anything like their one-year anniversary, she'd probably end up pregnant again. Hell, since Hudson was able to bring the freak out of Karli, it was probably better. He squeezed the ball again just from that thought alone.

His second point of pain was that damn Catrina. She was beginning to double down on her insane attempts to lock him down, and it was becoming a problem. He didn't know how much longer he could come up with excuses to avoid her persistent requests. More than that, he didn't know how much longer he could tolerate her aggravation. The pussy wasn't that good for him to keep stopping himself from hurting her feelings. Besides, it wasn't like she was the only booty he was tapping, so he didn't have to give that much of a damn, anyway. He tried to avoid a confrontation for no other reason than she'd always been his friend, and he appreciated her sticking by him through the divorce. But this extra rah-rah attitude was killing their vibe, and he wished she'd turn back into the fun-loving, fly-by-the-seat-of-her-pants," quick-fuck friend that he knew and loved.

He turned back to his desk, put down the stress ball, and shook his laptop awake. He had exactly five minutes left before his prospective client showed up, so he decided to pull the file and review the preliminary facts and his paperwork, in case the client decided she wanted to place him on retainer. He wanted to have everything prepared for his secretary, Stephanie, and the staff so that there wouldn't be no holdup in the event that he was able to close the deal. As he opened the file and began to lay out all the details, his desk phone buzzed.

"Yes, Stephanie?" he called over the speaker.

"Your ten o'clock appointment is here," she said.

"Sure. Bring her back, if you will. With the welcome packet, please."

"Absolutely," Stephanie confirmed.

Soon his office door opened, and Stephanie allowed the woman to enter before her. Michael stood and met them by the door, and then Stephanie handed him the welcome packet folder. "Ms. Willowbrook, this is Attorney Sanders. Attorney Sanders, this is Ms. Willowbrook."

The woman gave Michael her hand, and he delicately took it in his and shook it properly, with one hand over the top of hers.

"Pleased to meet you, Ms. Willowbrook. Won't you please come in and have a seat?"

"Thank you, Attorney Sanders," she greeted as they both walked over and took their respective seats and Stephanie made her exit from his office. "I want to personally thank you again for taking this meeting with me on such short notice."

Michael waved off the comment. "I assure you, Ms. Willowbrook, it's not a problem. I would do anything for Scott," he assured her, referring to the sports agent Scott Nicholson, who was not only his longtime friend but also a business associate who'd recommended some of his top clients. Scott kept him fed with the big fish, so whenever Scott phoned him for a favor, he gladly answered the call.

Michael went on. "Now, before we begin, I wanted to go over a few items in the welcome packet. I know that nothing is set in stone at this moment, but whether we enter into an agreement or not, it is my practice to allow my potential clients to have a better understanding of Sanders, Craig, and Associates, who we are and our track record. Sometimes, it answers questions that you may already have, but mostly, it answers questions that you may not have realized that you needed to ask."

For the next five minutes, Michael covered the preliminary information as he stared at the beautiful woman in front of him. He couldn't help but think that young women these days were far more developed than the women he knew back in his twenties. Good grief. These young women looked like they were being manufactured on a supermodel assembly line. The young woman before him was no exception. Her thick, long black hair lay perfectly over her shoulders. Her smoldering light brown eyes, with flecks of green, and her pouty lips indicated that she obviously had African American genes but had also inherited those of another minority. Perhaps Middle Eastern. Her olive skin tone gave her body a natural glow, and her perfect figure-eight curves looked so good on her, he couldn't tell if they were natural or were from years of gym training, waist-slimming concoctions, and green tea detox drinks.

The formfitting dress left nothing to chance. She was a fine specimen of a woman, and if he weren't on the nearer side of forty, he might've tried to shoot his shot. Well, that and the fact that she was already involved in a relationship. He may have been that man who slept around, but he wasn't trying to be with anyone who had someone. He'd been hurt that way, and he would not bring that pain to another human being, with the only exception being Hudson. He didn't owe him a damn thing, but a "Fuck you!" and swift kick up the ass.

"You're right, Attorney Sanders. This has answered a lot of questions that we had not thought about," Ms. Willowbrook said, bringing him out of his reverie. "It is all very impressive."

"I'm glad about it. We make it a habit to narrow down the things we believe our potential clients will need to make informed decisions. It's why we are the best not only in New York but also in the rest of the country. Nobody cares that they say we're only number three."

They shared a hearty laugh.

"Well, based on my first impressions and my personal opinion, I must agree with you. Sanders, Craig, and Associates is at the very top of the pyramid," she replied.

He pointed at her as they shared another laugh. "I knew you all were Sanders, Craig, and Associates kind of clients!" After they settled down, Michael added, "Now, let me know any questions you already have at this time. I'm going to jot them down and consider them. I might not answer some of them right away. I simply want to get an idea of your immediate needs and concerns."

As she asked questions, he jotted down them and labeled which he could answer now and which he would address once he received more information from her.

Once she finished, he pulled up a file on his laptop and read over some things.

"Okay, Ms. Willowbrook, let me try to gather as much information as I can. Since your girlfriend, Ximena, is overseas, playing basketball in Spain, we'll have to set up a time for her to Skype and join us in this conversation," Michael commented, wondering how a woman so fine could actually be a lesbian. "We won't be much longer, but if you don't mind, I do need to get something to drink." He stood to his feet and stretched. "Would you like a bottled water, Ms. Willowbrook?"

"Yes," she answered as Michael turned to walk over to his mini-refrigerator. "And please call me Tya."

Michael paused as he opened the refrigerator. "I'm sorry. Did you say Tya?"

"Yes, sir."

Immediately, Michael began recalling the information that Catrina had revealed to him about Hudson and Karli's threesome rendezvous. She'd told him that the woman, who had once been Hudson's ex-girlfriend, was a lesbian. It couldn't be. It absolutely could not be.

After handing Tya a bottled water, Michael sat in his seat and searched through his questions for just the one he was looking for. "Okay, Tya, you said that Ximena was interested in making some investments. We would have to look into reputable firms. In fact, New York has a choice of several that have local bases. Chance, Equity . . . and one of the top ones is Lewis Investments."

She held her hand up. "No, anywhere but Lewis Investments," she said so fast that it caused Michael to look at her in wonderment. "Let's just say I didn't have a good experience with the firm. I'd rather hear what Chance or Equity has to offer." She smiled.

Michael nodded. "Indeed. We'll get to that in just one moment."

Bingo. Michael smiled on the inside. *When friends call in a favor, always take the call*, he thought.

Hudson was on his way to getting overthrown, and the key to the kingdom had just walked into his office building. That key was named Tya Willowbrook.

The End

Karli's Poetry

Written by Tammie T. Bell Davis and Untamed

The View

Penthouse horizon view, city lights twinkling in my
eyes, mesmerized
The pleasurable cries of lovemaking sounds echoing
desire as you ravage me from behind
My hands plastered on the steamed glass
Your hands gripping and claiming my ass
The way your breath whispers through my hair softly
as you kiss on my neck
My body doesn't stand a chance
Mmm, this view is amazing, your view from behind is
even better
Your aggressive touch turns me on, hotter, sticky, wetter
Oh, the Peeping Toms are getting a show of my sinister
look across the skyline as I move my hand below
Touching the wetness you've aroused in me while I let
out a sexy oh!
Foreplay driving me crazy, teasing me without penetra-
tion
Stimulating my senses, making me beg, losing control,
I can't escape it
Flip me over, skin to skin, legs held, pulled close to you
Slide into kitty as she purrs for your coming and we
both enjoy the view.

T.T.B.D.

1.17.16

In Between

Fahrenheit on high, steamy vapors cause a sexy scene
Your eyes look up, down, and all around, but my cottony
thighs want you in between
Candlelight foreplay shadows picturesque on the walls
You grab my neck and cover my mouth so our sex
sounds don't reach down the hall
Mmm, Daddy, your touch has kitty purring, ready for
the beast of your lion's roar
Up against the wall, legs around your waist, sexing our
way to the floor
Pulsating rhythmic vibrations in harmony with our
lust entwined
Deeper the penetration each thrust inside
I'm cumming, Daddy, cumming, Daddy, you're about
to feel my warm juices flow
Don't hold back, cum with me, let the fireworks explode
Damn, what a sexy ride, pleasure like you wouldn't
believe
You sexed me up, down, and all around, but my cottony
thighs claimed you in between.

T.T.B.D.

1.27.16

Smitten

Mmm, this man, this man
Opened me up to levels of pleasures I never knew existed
Has my mind, body, and fantasies twisted
Craving every inch of him, touch, smell, completely free in his presence
Embers of lust rage lavish in my belly effervescent
What he does to me is so sinfully sweet
Sexually opened my aura free and complete
Swirled into a whirlwind of reality and matrix
Unbearable bliss leaves my soul beautifully naked
Damn, he has me opened, animalistic stimulation
Ms. Kitty vibrates out of control, awaiting his aggressive penetration
Claiming my aroused nipples with soft lips of pure sexiness
His hand slid down to feel the silkiness he erupted under my dress
Parted my lips with his fingers, playing with the bud of my rose
I'm losing it and begging for more, yet he remains in control
He regulates my heartbeat, my breath has lost air
My eyes roll back in ecstasy as he drains my body bare.

T.T.B.D.

1.29.16

Betrayal

Secret kisses shared under the dark skies
Lust-filled thoughts seeping through the eyes
Loyalty is great, but temptation is greater
Love is good, but lust is better
When the mirror reflects reality
New revelations bring out clarity
Nothing done in the dark ever escapes unscathed
Silent prayers go unanswered for the unsaved
In your pity, you will wallow
Your regrets you swallow
Your apologies, why bother
When it's fantasies that were coddled
Empathy turns to anger, sympathy to hate
Can't run from what was created in this way
Dark skies open up, a dawn of a new day
Split in half, left open to the perils of the betrayed

Untamed.

2.10.16